Dedication

To all those afraid to be the real you, don't be. Someone somewhere loves you for exactly who you are.

Chapter One

ASHLEY

EVER WISH YOU could have a do-over? The last six months of my life has been hit after hit, and this shitty morning is the icing on the fucking cake. Why can't I seem to catch a break? What did I do in my previous lives to warrant such a terrible string of bad luck? I'm just your normal, run-of-the-mill girl who wants to follow her dreams. That seems reasonable enough, no?

Of all mornings for me to be running behind schedule and stuck in traffic, it had to be this one. Ugh, fuck me! Sitting in the car, sweating my ass off because the air conditioning in my 1999 Honda Civic has decided that this is the summer it will stop working, is not helping my mood what so ever. Of course, this also happens to be the same summer that New Jersey is having a never-ending heat wave. It's already over ninety degrees, and it's not even ten o'clock in the morning.

My face is starting to grease up as the sun bakes it. Having the windows down doesn't help if the car isn't moving fast enough to create a breeze. With melting makeup and my hair sticking to the sides of my face, I'm going to look fantastic when I finally get to the interview.

I overslept an hour this morning thanks to being up all night prepping for today—for this interview with Tanner Garrison—quarterback for the Jets. Supposedly this is going to be their big year, thanks to the luck of the draft. After trading up for a higher draft pick, the Jets were able to get some up-and-coming hotshot wide receiver who's supposed to help fix their offense's lack of good ball handlers, like I have any clue what the hell any of that means. Which is why I didn't want to do this interview at first.

James Carter is the paper's usual sportswriter, but his wife went into labor three days ago and had their first baby, so I was picked to take his place. I know nothing about sports, but our editor, Dominick Cranmer, had said that I was the best choice on such short notice. Yes, I'm a good writer—but not a sports writer.

"Ashley, you're the most qualified of the available choices," Dom told me yesterday after he dropped the bomb. "This is a big interview, and Garrison's agent finally agreed to it but said tomorrow is the only time slot they can offer. They aren't granting any other interviews to discuss the upcoming season. This is basically an exclusive. Besides, you're always complaining about not getting your chance to write a big piece, so here's your chance." He seemed to sense my reluctance. My face must have said everything that was running through my mind.

"But, Dom, I'm not a sports writer. I don't know anything about football. I write lifestyle pieces—hot clubs, great restaurants, newest trends, concerts, plays, anything hot at the moment—not sports! Sure, I know of him and where he likes to hang out, but I know crap about his professional life. Can't James do a phone interview? He won't have to leave home for that," I offered up as a reasonable alternative.

"No, Ashley. He can't. His wife's being discharged from the hospital tomorrow. There's no way to predict a timeframe for it," Dom stated matter-of-factly. "I'll give you the rest of the day off. Go home. Do some googling on Garrison and the Jets. I'll have someone email you James' notes and outline for the interview. Afterward, you and James can sit down together and put together a good article—make sure everything fits for a sports piece since you aren't used to them."

I know he was trying to be generous with the timeline, and it would've been an adequate amount of time to prepare for an interview, if it were in my given area of expertise.

Knowing this is a great opportunity, I should've been ecstatic. The excitement around the Jets potential this year has been buzzing for months. I have ninety-six dollars in my bank account, and if this pans out well, it could mean a great paycheck. It's a freaking exclusive.

I sighed internally knowing I couldn't turn this assignment down, and nodded in agreement with Dom. I was standing to leave when he gave me a few words of encouragement.

"Ash," he said, "you're going to be fine with this assignment. You're qualified for this. If you can handle the snobby, up-and-coming wannabes who come to party in the clubs, you can certainly handle Tanner Garrison. If I didn't think you could do this, I wouldn't have assigned it to you."

I've worked at *The City Press* for three years now. I write for the Lifestyle section of the paper; which club was packed this week, which new celebs were partying it up in NYC, which restaurant has a month-long waiting list or what is currently trending—those are the topics that I mostly cover. Nothing big, but decent enough. I'm doing what I love, what I've always wanted to do, despite my mother's disapproval.

My mother insists that, while there's nothing wrong with writing articles for *The Press*, I should go into something more stable and steady. "Why not be a teacher?" My mom said once. "You'd make a great teacher, Ashley." But I've never wanted to be a teacher. I wanted to be a writer.

I interned at *The Press* during college and worked hard enough that afterward, I was chosen as the only intern to be hired full-time. Dom has always liked me, right from the very beginning, which is why I feel he's giving me this chance. It isn't that I'm ungrateful for the opportunity, I just hate being outside of my comfort zone. I feel as though I haven't been in my comfort zone for the last six months, and a long six months it's been.

My bad luck seemed to start then when I discovered my boyfriend, Jason, was cheating on me. I suppose if you ask my mother, though, she'll say my bad luck started two and half years ago, when I started dating Jason. My parents never liked him.

"He just rubs me the wrong way, Ashley," my mother had always said. "He's not the guy for you." She claimed it wasn't one thing in particular but just something about Jason as a whole didn't sit right with her. Either way, she was right. I guess mother's intuition really is accurate—even if I'd never admit it to her. She still doesn't know the real reasons we broke up or how much debt he put me in before I ended it. Let's just say I don't want to see the look on her face if she found out the truth. She'd say that since she'd been right about my choice in him, maybe I should consider another career before it turned out she was right about that as well.

Jason and I had shared an apartment in Jersey City. That is, until I'd found him having an afternoon romp in our sheets with someone who certainly wasn't me one Thursday when he should've been working, and I kicked him out.

I came home early that day to grab a few outfit choices to bring with me to my best friend, Quinn's. We were heading to the city that night so I could check out a club for the weekend edition of the paper. I knew something was off the minute I walked through the door. A pair of women's shoes were laying on the living room floor. And they weren't mine—I didn't own electric blue stilettoes.

Then I heard them.

"Yes! Yes, Jason! Harder!" The unknown woman somewhere in my apartment yelled. Her moans, pants, and screams of pleasure filled the empty space, echoing around me.

"Yeah, you like that? You like it, don't you?" Jason responded.

My feet started walking toward the bedroom. I'm still not sure why. It was obvious what I'd find in there, but I guess my eyes wanted to see it for themselves.

The door wasn't closed, just slightly ajar, as though it had been totally forgotten in the rush to get down to business. Clearly, the two hadn't been expecting me to pop in during the middle of their afternoon rendezvous. And, sure enough, when my head peaked around the door, there they were! Jason had her bent over our bed, fucking her from behind. One of his hands gripped her hip hard—so hard that red fingerprints covered her hip and Jason's knuckles had gone white. His other hand was wrapped up in her bottled-blonde hair, using it as leverage. He had it pulled taut as he slammed into her. Her blood-red nails were dug into the sheets. My sheets! The ones Jason and I had picked out together when we moved in the year before.

The laugh I thought had been forming in my mind must have actually been forming in my throat because it slipped out before I had a chance to stop it. It was a laugh of pure irony—the irony being I would've loved for Jason to be fucking me the way he was fucking this slut, but I never had the balls to ask for it out loud. Sure, I asked in my head thousands of times during sex, but I never managed to get the words "Fuck me!" or "Own me!" to actually make their way out of my mouth. And now, he was finally fucking the way I wanted to be fucked, but it wasn't me on the receiving end.

Hearing my escaped laugh, Jason stopped moving. As he turned his head, his eyes widened. He pulled out of his afternoon delight and turned his whole body toward me as he started to mutter his excuses.

"Ash, baby, this isn't what it looks like. It isn't what you think," he said pathetically.

Wow, that's all he's got?

My brain to mouth filter, which was always painfully present and making it impossible to vocalize the things I wanted to say, must have taken a vacation at that moment because the thought slipped right passed my lips.

"No, really babe. I swear I can explain." He was still completely naked, and so was the blonde, who didn't seem at all bothered by me being there. Taking them both in, I noticed the motherfucker wasn't even wearing a condom. The reality of the situation hit me with full force in that moment. Un-fucking-believable! How long had this been going on and how many times had he slept with someone else and not even thought about using a condom?

Oh my God! What if he'd given me something and I didn't even know it? I was disgusted and nauseated all at once.

"Get out!" I yelled at the blonde, who was still not even trying to cover up her fake double-D's— or any of the rest of her body for that matter. When she didn't move fast enough for my liking, I yelled again. "GET THE FUCK OUT! NOW!" Finally, she moved more like the dirty little whore who had been caught fucking someone else's man she was.

Jason started moving toward me, his dirty dick still hard, taunting me with his betrayal, and I snapped.

"You, too!" I barked at him. "GO! Follow your whore!" I pointed toward the door, in case he'd forgotten where it was.

"Ashley, please baby, let me explain. She's nothing. I swear!" Jason pleaded, still heading toward me, a little slower now, as though I were a caged animal he was unsure of.

He was right to be unsure of me because, at that moment, I was unsure of myself. I couldn't decide which emotion was going to win the battle to the top, betrayal or disgust. The two vied inside my head, both fighting to get out. I couldn't stand the sight of him, and apparently neither could my stomach. Nausea rolled in to join the betrayal and disgust.

"Jason, come any closer to me right now, and I will rip off your cheating dick and shove it down your throat. Get the fuck out!" I screamed at him, more quietly this time. I don't know if it could've even been considered a scream. My adrenaline wasn't pumping as fast anymore, and my anger was slowly fading to hurt and embarrassment. I just wanted him out before I lost it and started crying. So many emotions tumbling around inside one woman at one time isn't a good thing. I was a volcano about to erupt.

"Fine, Ash! You know what? Fuck this," he said, turning and grabbing his pants off the floor. "This is all your fault anyway," he added as he pulled them on.

"My fault?" I scoffed. "How is it my fault that you were just fucking some slut in our bed in the middle of the afternoon?" I asked, truly baffled.

"If you weren't such a stuck-up prude, I wouldn't have been bored or needed to bang someone else to feel satisfied." Jason spat the words out viciously, as though he'd been inside my head and already knew my unspoken problem.

Oh, hell no. I wasn't about to let him turn his betrayal around on me—no fucking way.

"Get the fuck out right now! Get the fuck away from me! I really can't be held accountable for my actions right now, Jason. I'm leaving in an hour to go back to work. I suggest you come back then to get your shit. If you don't, I swear I'll burn whatever's left, you disgusting bastard!" I screamed so loud I felt the veins bulging in my neck, anger winning out in the battle of emotions.

How dare this motherfucker try to tell me it was my fault he couldn't keep his dick to himself? He couldn't find the balls to ask his girlfriend for rougher sex or whatever it was that he wanted but wasn't getting? I knew it was the pot calling the kettle black and all, but he hadn't just found me getting nailed by some other guy. He didn't seem to have a problem asking that bitch for what he wanted. I'd needed that anger, otherwise I knew I would've crumple to the floor. He hit the nail on the head with his prude comment, as if he knew exactly where to aim to inflict the most damage.

"Yeah, whatever Ashley. Truth hurts, doesn't it?" He threw out as he walked out the bedroom door.

I sank down the wall as he slammed the door behind him. I sat there, hoping to calm the chaos in my head, trying to wrap my mind around the reality of everything that had just happened.

If he wanted something more, why didn't he ever ask? Did I missed the signs? Did I come off as too much of a goody-goody to be willing to try new things? I racked my brain for answers I wasn't sure I wanted. Maybe it was my fault. I searched my memory for cues from Jason that I may have missed. Nothing stood out to me.

After a few minutes of sulking, I snapped back to reality. I knew I needed to get the hell out of that room. I moved as fast as I could, grabbing what I hoped was everything I would need for the night. I needed to get to Quinn. I needed my best friend. She would know where to go from here.

Chapter Two

ASHLEY

THOUGHTS OF THAT awful afternoon swirl through my mind while I sit in this damned traffic. The traffic from Hoboken, where I now live with Quinn, to Morristown, where the Jets' practice facility is located, is at a maddening standstill, and isn't helping me keep my mind on the present.

My disastrous relationship hadn't just ended with finding Jason in bed with the blonde or the extremely sore spot he pushed on his way out the door. Soon after that, I came to find out that he also maxed out my emergency credit cards—the ones I kept for unexpected mishaps of life, like my breakup with Jason. I never carried them around with me, I kept them at home in the drawer in the kitchen along with my extra checks, current bills, and take out menus.

Jason has a decent job working on computer software and makes good money. I never thought he would use them, so I didn't think twice about leaving them there. Jason never seemed like that kind of guy to me.

When the statements came in the mail about a week or so after Jason moved out, I was shocked. He'd put nearly two grand on one card and over four on the other. In ONE month! Hotels, bars, high-end restaurants, and lingerie stores. He must not have really cared about getting caught with his pants down because he had to have known I'd find out as soon as the statements came in. Or he planned to keep hiding them from me? Maybe that's what he wanted all along—me to find out. He'd probably been hoping I'd find out so he could take the coward's way out instead of breaking up with me himself.

What the hell had I ever done to him? Okay, he was bored, so he went to someone else for what I wasn't giving him. But why did he have to be so cruel? So vindictive and over the top. As if the cheating weren't enough, he had to hurt me in the worst possible way—with my money and in my bed. Why not just break up with me? Or at least ask me to spice up our sex life? I would've if he asked. Hell, I'd wanted the same thing. I just didn't know how to go about asking for it. It was like something taboo. What kind of woman asks to be treated dirty? What kind of girl asks to be manhandled in the bedroom without seeming like a freak or a slut?

"You're not a freak, Ash! Everyone is into the down and dirty, sweets!" Quinn says every time we talk about this subject. She's the only one I'll talk about my secret desires with.

"You're just trying to make me feel better," I said back to her last time we had this conversation.

"When the fuck have I ever lied just to make anyone feel better? Have you forgotten my uncouth way of being too blatantly honest? You bitch about it all the time."

I'm suddenly reminded of the poor sales clerk at Neiman Marcus who Quinn nearly made cry. The poor girl hadn't done anything wrong except catch Quinn on a bad day.

"Yes, you're right. You're never nice for anyone's benefit other than your own. I'm sure the girl from Neiman Marcus remembers that fact about you too," I sassed.

"Oh, come on! I snap at one poorly dressed sales girl one time, and now I'm never nice? I was having a bad day and about to start my period. Cut me some slack. Bad days and PMS never mix well for anyone." Quinn defended herself before turning back to our original conversation. "Seriously, though, if you want some spice in the bedroom, ask for it. You

know how that saying goes. 'Lady in the streets, but a freak in the sheets," she reminded. I had no choice but to giggle.

I smile thinking back to that conversation and Quinn's advice.

We'd been unpacking some boxes that day, about a week after I moved in with her. After Jason had maxed me out, Quinn offered up her extra bedroom to me. I grudgingly agreed, only after we argued about it at first. I'd been in a bad place at the time, so I couldn't see how awesome Quinn was being.

I was stressed out about money, which was something new for me. I'm not a rich girl like Quinn, but I'm also not used to being a paycheck-to-paycheck girl. After opening the statements from the credit cards Jason used, I knew the road ahead would be bumpy. There's no way in hell I'd be seeing that money from Jason, and those cards needed to be paid off. I couldn't let him destroy my credit along with everything else he already destroyed—like my trust and confidence.

There was four months left on our lease when we broke up. Thank God, we hadn't sent in the renewal yet because the lease was only in my name. So I was the only one legally responsible for making sure it got paid. My savings had only been enough to cover the remaining rent, which was two thousand a month for that now-awful apartment. I didn't want to live there anymore, let alone pay two grand a month for it.

It wasn't bad when I was splitting everything with Jason. But shouldering the full rent, utilities, regular bills, student loans and now these huge credit card bills, I was wiped out! Yup, Jason had fucked me good! And not in the sense that either of us apparently wanted. Quinn had pushed me to go after Jason for the money, but it wasn't worth it to me. I didn't want to have to see him again and relive the memories of him banging that chick.

When Quinn had offered me the spare bedroom in her apartment, I'd agreed immediately. Until she told me not to worry about paying rent. Then I freaked out on her.

"I am not a fucking charity case, Quinn Taylor!" I told her.

"I never said you were, sweets!" She stared me down, daring me to argue. "But I don't need the money and right now you do." Quinn has always had money to burn and didn't see what the problem was. Her

father is some hot shot investment something-or-other in the city. She works for him, has a great job, but he pays her rent.

"Then I'm not moving in. If you don't let me pay half the rent, then I'm not moving in here with you. I'll find somewhere else to live."

"Ugh, fine! How much do you want to pay then?" She huffed, clearly annoyed at my stubbornness.

"Half," was my answer.

Quinn picked her head up and looked at me seriously this time. "Ashley, don't take this the wrong way, but I can't let you pay half."

"Why not?"

"Because you can't afford to pay half right now. So tell me how much will make you happy, and you can pay that. How about what you were paying with Jason? Will that make you happy?" she asked me, still not telling me how much the rent was.

"Well, is the rent here two thousand?" I asked, knowing it most likely wasn't.

"No, it's not. I pay five grand a month here, and I know that you can't afford twenty-five hundred a month. I really don't want you to pay anything at all. My father pays for this place, not me. Trust me, he can afford it."

"But I'm not that person, and you know it. I'm not mooching off my friend's rich parents," I answered, meaning every word.

"Fine, tell me how much to get you to shut the hell up and move the fuck in here with me."

"Umm, how about fifteen hundred?" I knew it was more than I could afford, but at least I would feel like I was paying my way, not taking advantage.

"Fine! Whatever! But not a dollar more, and utilities are included. Subject closed!" Quinn said, amending my offer and effectively ending the conversation.

I moved in with Quinn about two months ago.

I'm slowly climbing from the red into the black. My security deposit from the apartment in Jersey City covered one credit card Jason ran up and a little bit of the other. My savings helped me cover the other half of the rent I'm still stretched slightly beyond my limit, but I'm making do.

Knowing I'm not the kind of girl to ask for it, Quinn tries to hide her help from me. She doesn't think I notice the extra twenties she sticks in my wallet from time to time or the meals she makes sure are there waiting for me when I get home so I don't need to pay for dinner. Since Quinn goes through the trouble to try to help me discreetly, I let it go, even though it bothers me. I suppose that's what best friends are for.

Quinn and I had met our freshman year of college and have been inseparable ever since. Seven years running, and I couldn't be more thankful for the randomness of college roommate assignments. Quinn's the only one I feel comfortable talking about my "issues" with. I don't think there's many people out there more open-minded than she is.

We've talked about Jason for hours upon hours finally discovering that it wasn't losing Jason I was upset over, but the way it had ended and what he'd said to me had hit a nerve. At the time, I believed I loved him, but now I'm pretty sure I didn't. Thinking back, I probably stayed so long because I felt secure with him.

His claim that if I weren't such a prude, he would've been sexually satisfied still bothers me after all these months. Still brings out my insecurities, making me wonder if anyone I've ever been with was fully satisfied. I'm not shy per se, but I guess I'm kind of reserved. Usually followed Jason's lead when we were intimate—missionary, on top, rarely taken from behind, and always in a bed. I've racked my brain for any hints he might've made about wanting more, but he never did, which was why his little stunt caught me completely by surprise.

I'd wanted more too, still do. I want someone to push me up against a wall, pin my hands over my head. Total Christian Grey elevator-style! Someone to tell me how much they want me and how hard I make them. Someone who'll push me to my knees and give me no choice but to keep my mouth open as he shoves his cock in it without even asking, and tell me how good it feels to fuck me without remorse. I want all that and then some, but how the hell does one ask someone for that without coming off like a complete whore? Again.

Pulling into the practice facility of the Jets for what could be the interview of my career while thinking about being on my knees with a mouth full of dick, isn't how I wanted this morning to go. I glance at the clock on my dashboard, and notice I'm ten minutes late

Great!

I'm late, sweaty, probably smell like a farm animal, and as if all that wasn't enough, I'm also turned on by my previous thoughts. Checking my rearview mirror, I'm pleased to see my makeup isn't too bad. I fix my hair quickly and rush from the parking lot to go interview the playboy quarterback, Tanner Garrison.

After doing my research yesterday, I'm even more hesitant about this interview. Pictures of the hot quarterback are all over the Internet. He's a local boy who grew up on Staten Island, so he's definitely a big deal around here. The fact that he's downright delicious, with bright green eyes and a messy crop of brown hair, doesn't hurt either. You can tell he knows it, too. He's always photographed with one particular bombshell—stunning, super skinny, great boobs, perfectly dressed in the latest fashions, and never a hair out of place.

This Melissa Finnegan girl is in a lot of photos with him. Most articles say she's his girlfriend, but there's just as many with pictures of him with other women, and the captions always claim he's stepping out on Melissa again. Seems like he's a typical player—on and off the field. It's disgusting, and makes me feel awful for Melissa if she is his girlfriend. I know how she feels. At least the whole world didn't get a front row seat to witness my embarrassment.

This should be a fun interview. I don't know the first fucking thing about football, and now after thinking about Jason, getting myself all worked up again, I don't know how I'll put up with this guy. I can't stand that I have to interview someone who is nothing more than your everyday jock with a padded bank account and a sense of entitlement that makes him believe he can do whatever the hell he wants.

Here goes nothing.

Chapter Three

TANNER

I **STILL CAN'T** believe I let my agent talk me into doing this interview. He knows how much I hate them. How much I hate the spotlight. But Davis also knows how to manipulate me.

"Oh, come on, Tanner. It's for *The City Press*. You know how much New York loves their quarterback. You can do no wrong here. It'll be good for your image and help the team. *The Press* has been asking for this interview for months now. It's the only one I'm asking you to do pre-season," Davis had said, knowing he'd get exactly what he wanted with that line of reasoning.

I'm a sucker for giving back to the local fans. Having grown up here, these were my stomping grounds. I love New York, and now I get to play football here. Davis also knows I'll do almost anything to make me look like the real me instead of the asshole everyone thinks I am. Where the stupid, spoiled, rich playboy rep I have comes from, I have no clue, but that's *not* me. I'm not some womanizing asshole who hops from one chick to the next while being in a relationship with someone. Geez, Ma would smack the shit out of me if that were true. She made sure she raised a boy who respects women, and I do.

Don't get me wrong, I enjoy the company of a fine woman looking for a good time, but I don't have casual sex. Not anymore, anyway. I hang out with my friends, but I don't get close to many women anymore. Just Melissa. She's the only woman I really trust. She's stood by me through thick and thin and been a fantastic friend. I haven't found any other woman I feel truly likes me for me and not just what she thinks she can get from me.

That's the trouble with having money and fame. People always want something from you. I don't mind the fans who want autographs or pictures. That part I actually like. The fans are a big part of the game. Without them, there'd be no football. It's mooches who I can't stand. People who don't give two shits about you, just what you can do for them. People who seep out of the woodwork once you've made it to the top. And right now, I'm pretty high up.

Since we were able to pick up Darren Starks, our new wide receiver, everyone is predicting this to be our year. We had a great run last season, but I had no one to throw the ball to or anyone who could seem to hold onto it for more than five yards at a time. We made it to the first round of the playoffs, but lost to San Diego. This year, I'm hoping we make it much further.

This interview better be all about football. The minute it becomes about anything else, I'm done. There's nothing I hate more than when these things take a turn toward wanting some juicy piece of personal information. Guys are always looking for details about my latest "conquest", wishing they were able to grab a girl like the ones I'm seen with in public. The women I choose to spend time with are beautiful, and most are genuinely great people too. I don't know why the press and gossip rags jump right to thinking that I'm sleeping with them. All of these women are casual acquaintances of mine or business associates. We both benefit from being seen together, but it's never sexual.

I usually pair up with them to promote some cause —mostly charity work. They get me to help with whatever they're trying to raise money for, and I like to think that I get positive press from these things, but usually it just spurs a new cheating scandal. I've tried explaining that

Melissa and I aren't an item, but no one wants to hear it. They only want a good story, which usually means it's full of shit.

I stopped trying to change everyone's assumptions a while ago after realizing my efforts didn't matter. People will think what they want, no matter what. At the end of the day, all that matters is what was accomplished for a greater cause, so I try to ignore the stupid shit they print.

Truth is, ever since that bitch, Carrie, I haven't had a casual hook up. It's not worth it for me. She singlehandedly cemented the fact that all anyone wants is to see what they can gain from me. Sure, I had fun in college, slept with my share of girls, and never gave it a second thought. That all came crashing down with Carrie. She showed up right after the draft, where I was a first round pick, and claimed she was pregnant with my kid. The oldest trick in the book. I'd only slept with her once, a week before. As if I was stupid enough not to notice that the timing was off.

After I told her I knew there was no way the baby could be mine, I never heard from her again. Nonetheless, the whole experience killed casual sex for me, and I stopped sleeping around, no matter how much fun it had been. Trusting anyone went out the window, with the exception of Melissa. Fortune hunters were everywhere, and I didn't need some girl pretending to like me so she could get knocked up and essentially tie me to her for the rest of my life. No, thank you.

Trying to wind down my internal tirade, I glance at the clock and see that it's ten past ten. This interview was supposed to start at ten on the dot. She's late. I don't like late. Lateness shows a lack of respect for other people's time. How hard is it to be on time? I get a five-yard penalty if I'm late. Sometimes that shit can throw off the whole game.

The scowl on my face must be worse than I'd thought because the moment the door to the conference room opens and the breathtaking brunette walking through it looks up, a horrified expression takes over her face, and she mutters a string of apologies.

"I'm so sorry, Mr. Garrison," she rushes to say while smoothing down her skirt. "I didn't factor in traffic when I left this morning. I'm not too familiar with this area and didn't anticipate the amount I ran into. I hope it wasn't a terrible inconvenience for you, standing here waiting. I know how busy you are, especially this time of the season," she rambles, not bothering to stop and take a breath, as I stand here, scowling at her, not muttering a single word.

Wow, snap out of it, asshole.

My brain yells at me, telling me to say something, but not sending any words to my mouth for me to speak. I take a few steps toward her, and thankfully my mouth and brain finally start working together as I stick out my hand to take hers and say, "No, no inconvenience at all. Miss...?"

"Mitchell. Ashley Mitchell. Thank you so much for doing this interview with us," she replies, putting her hand in mine.

The second our fingers touch, my whole body sparks, like I've just touched a live wire. The molecules in the air around us seem to crack and fizzle. It's as though she has a superpower that renders me immobile. I'm not even sure I'm breathing. No one's ever thrown me this off-kilter in under thirty seconds.

What the hell is wrong with me?

Being around beautiful women is nothing new to me, so what's the deal with this one? Why does she have me feeling something I can't quite put my finger on?

I'm mesmerized by her face. She has the most beautiful skin. Her light tan makes her blue eyes shine in a shade I haven't seen before. Her chestnut hair hangs, slightly damp, framing her face. Her eyebrows furrow and I realize I'm doing it again—staring at her silently.

Snapping out of the beauty-induced stupor, I remember my manners and say, "It's no problem, Miss Mitchell."

Placing my hand on the small of her back, I direct her toward the table in the middle of the room. The same tingling sensation hits me as soon as I touch her.

Does she feel it too?

"Please, have a seat. Can I have anything brought in for you to drink? Water? Coffee? I know it must be pretty hot out there already," I say lamely. *Talking about the weather. Yeah, great line, genius.* I must sound like a total loser.

"No, thank you, Mr. Garrison," she replies, still looking a little flushed.

Pulling out the chair, I take the seat across from her. "Please, call me Tanner."

"Okay, Tanner. Well, since I was late, I don't want to keep you any longer than necessary, so would you like to start?" she asks, reaching into her bag, pulling out a small recorder. "Is it okay if I record our conversation?"

"Sure, let's get started then."

Might as well get this over with so I can go back to being unaffected by this woman. Something about her makes me feel off, and I don't like it. It feels as though someone has tilted my world off its axis.

She presses the record button and begins. "Okay, so let's start with last season. If you could change one thing about it, what would it be?"

At first glance, she seems unaffected, but when I look into her eyes, I wonder if she's as flustered as I am.

Based on her body language, she seems entirely at ease, but her eyes tell a different story. Their color has gone from a bright ocean blue to a darker, dimmer gray-blue, leaving me wondering the reason for the change but no time to actually think about it. I should probably answer her questions instead of wondering whether or not it's because I affect her the way she does me.

"Well, I would change the playoff loss," I answer with a laugh. "I would've loved to have gone to the Super Bowl. But I guess that's what anyone would say."

She looks reflective for a minute and then says, "No, not everyone would say that. Most people would say something selfish like higher completion percentage or higher quarterback rating. Most people would say something that makes them look better, but not you, huh?" Her voice has taken on a tone somewhere between amazement and annoyance, and the expression on her face gives a similar impression. Interesting.

Suddenly feeling the need to defend myself I tell her, "Well, it's not all about me, is it? Football is a team sport. It's about us as a team, not me as an individual."

"Speaking of the team, what do you do as team captain to keep up morale throughout the season?" Ashley asks checking her notes not even looking at me while she waits for a response.

"Hmm... That's a tough one because I don't feel that's true. It's not just me who keeps the morale up. Again, that's something we do as a team. We really are like a band of brothers. If someone has a bad game, we work through the problem together. I'm not perfect, and I don't expect everyone else to be. Negativity never helps anything, and I do my best to offer my help instead of criticize." I answer honestly. I really hate negativity. It's one of the main reasons I really don't like the spotlight. There's always so much adverse energy surrounding it.

"That's a really good philosophy, Tanner." Ashley smiles at me. I love the way my name sounds coming out of her mouth. Almost sensual. I wonder what it would sound like if she were screaming it out in pleasure.

Where the fuck did that thought come from?

Thinking about this woman in my bedroom screaming in ecstasy is not a good thing. What the hell is going on with me? My dick has decided to hijack my train of thought and the last thing I need right now is a fucking a hard on. The way she keeps crossing and uncrossing her legs, giving me a glimpse of what's hiding under her skirt, isn't helping. I'm seriously fucked if I can't get a hold of myself before I say or do something dumb.

"So," Ashley continues, looking down to check her notes. She bites her lip, drawing my attention to her mouth. Her lips are plump and coated in some kind of shiny gloss. I'm sure they would look really good wrapped around my cock.

Fuck, her lips wrapped around my cock, really?

So much for getting a handle on things. "What are your thoughts about your passing game this year? How do you think your new wide receiver is going to help?"

Football, Tanner. Think about football. Nothing sexual about football.

"Darren is definitely a great asset. We work together very well. I'm sure we're going to put up some great numbers. I'm definitely considering him for my fantasy team," I answer with a smirk. "But, honestly there's really no way to know what will happen this year. We're just going to keep a positive outlook."

"That's good to know. I'll make sure I pass that little bit of info along to anyone I know with a fantasy team. How do you feel about the win against Cincinnati?" she smiles a smile that I can only imagine she uses when she has a secret.

"I feel really good about it. We all do. I think it's a sign of good things to come. All the pieces came together, and we were rewarded for all our hard work with a win." I smile back. Talking about winning always makes me happy.

"What are you doing to prepare for this week's game against Philly?" She dives into the question with no witty remarks or changes in her position. Nothing to distract my thoughts. *Thank fucking God.*

"The same as we always do. We treat every team with the same respect and never expect to win. When you go in expecting a win, that's when you lose. So we're watching game films, pushing ourselves a little harder at each practice, making the necessary adjustments, and practicing plays until we feel that we've gotten them right," I explain.

"Well, I wish you and the team nothing but luck going forward," she says in a tone I hope is sincere, but I can't be sure. I feel as though there's more to come. And then she opens her perfect little mouth and says, "But before we wrap this up, I do have to ask one question for the ladies... Are you single?"

Oh shit. Is she asking for the interview or for her own personal knowledge? Hoping it's the latter, I decide to answer honestly. Honesty is always the best policy, right?

"Yes, I'm single," I say, hoping that'll be the end of this line of questioning.

"So, no girlfriend, huh? What about the latest gossip going around about you?" There's a weird gleam in her eye now that I don't like.

My temper is beginning to flare. She could be referring to any number of things since so much different crap is always being written about me. "Which gossip would that be?"

"Oh, come on. You know what I'm talking about. The rumor that you don't do committed relationships and are just stringing poor Melissa along." Her eyes sparkle as though this kind of questioning is her favorite pastime.

"Well, that's certainly news to me. I guess I should keep up with the magazines to find out about my own personal life." I'm beyond furious, but at least I'm no longer thinking about fucking her, instead preferring to strangle her now. She's conned me, had me thinking she's a sweet little reporter wanting to get the inside scoop for the city, but nope. She's just another mooch trying to see what she can get out of me. In her case, it's a story about where I'm currently putting my dick.

"Oh please, you have to know about your rep, especially since you make no attempt to hide anything or set the record straight." Ashley practically snorts out the sentence, accusing me of being a liar and womanizer. Okay, game over. I'm done.

"I should inform you that you aren't the first person to try to get the inside scoop on my personal life. Most of those people no longer have jobs." I smirk, trying to contain the anger that's burning just under the surface.

"Nice deflection. I'm not surprised that I'm not the first to ask. But you still haven't answered the question." When the fuck did this become an interrogation? How did we wind up here? Five minutes ago, I was picturing her naked, and right now, I'm picturing my hands around her throat. And not in a way that would prolong her pleasure…

"Since it seems you've already got your mind made up, I guess my answer doesn't matter. I think our time here is up." I don't wait to hear what she has to say before storming out of the conference room. Grabbing my phone from my pocket, I pull up Davis' number and make my way to the locker room.

He picks up quickly. "How did it go?" Davis asks innocently.

"Get the editor of *The Press* on the phone! I want the interview pulled. That reporter didn't give two shits about football or the team. It was a fucking fishing expedition for information about my dating life and how I'm apparently a piece of shit with no regard for the girlfriend I don't have. You know how I feel about this shit, Davis! GET IT PULLED! I agreed to an interview about the upcoming season, not where I put my dick. I'm done!"

Davis knows it's not my style—having my personal shit out there like that, especially when it makes me look like an asshole. If I didn't love football and my team as much as I do, I'd be out! I don’t understand how anyone can deal with this shit all the time. At least I get a break in the off-season, but from July to January, everyone seems to be more interested in what play my cock is getting than what’s happening on the field.

Chapter Four

ASHLEY

WHAT THE FUCK was I thinking? I have no idea why I did that, especially since I could lose my job for this sort of slip-up. Maybe I can claim temporary insanity. It's obvious my sanity is questionable today. My intentions were not to take the interview in that direction, I was merely curious about his love life. Tanner had been sitting there all altruistic, talking about doing everything as a team, not taking any of the spotlight for himself. It had really thrown me for a loop. He'd seemed the complete opposite of everything I had read about him last night.

The fact that he's so hot it's distracting hadn't helped. God, pictures don't do that man any justice. His hair had been a hot mess, in a good way—as though he cared enough to make sure he wasn't rocking bedhead but not enough to put any effort into an actual style. It looked so silky, and I'd wondered more than once during the interview if it's as soft as it seems. And good Lord, those eyes. They're the most unique green I have ever seen, a dark grass green with sparkling gold flecks in them. The man obviously isn't afraid to dress brightly, considering the lime green shirt and tie he wore with his dark gray suit pants which looked as though they were tailored just to fit his perfect body. A body I'm sure looks truly magnificent naked.

From the moment we'd shaken hands, everything had taken a weird turn. I kept catching him staring at me, almost in a daze. There was a bizarre electricity in the air that seemed to be passing all around us, clouding my judgment. Suddenly, my inner curiosity had taken control of my mouth and decided to try to prove the man was all an act. I mean, he had to have been acting. No way can someone run through that many women, have that hotness level, and still be the nice guy he appeared to be.

My phone rings, its shrill tone in the quiet conference room waking me from my pity party. Dom's name flashes across the screen. *Oh man, this can't be good.*

"Hello?" I answer timidly, afraid of the lecture that's surely waiting at the other end of the line.

"What the hell did you do, Ashley? What the hell were you thinking? I give you the chance for a huge break, and you throw it away? Why? I just got a very unpleasant phone call from Garrison's agent telling me I'd better pull the interview. Do you know how hard James and I worked for this? It was an exclusive, Ashley. Exclusive. I don't know if I can fix this. I'm disappointed in you. Maybe you were right when you said you couldn't handle this interview. I have to go and see how much damage control I can do." The line goes dead without me getting a single word in. Disappointed. Great, another person in my life who's disappointed in me. I hadn't come in here with any intention other than getting a great story.

Shit. The tears well in my eyes as I make the trek back to my car. This is the longest walk of shame in history. Not only did I fuck this up for me, but for the paper as well. Just another thing in my life that hasn't gone as planned. I must have been a serial killer in my previous life. That's the only explanation I can think of for the atrocious luck that has taken over my life lately. What kind of person has this many bad things happen in such a short amount of time? This time, I can't fully blame that bitch Karma, just my stupid mouth and my need to prove that Tanner

Garrison was full of shit. At least I can't think of anything more that could go wrong now.

I just had to jinx myself, right? All I want to do is go home, drink a bottle of wine, and eat a gallon of ice cream. But my piece-of-shit car has other plans. I turn the key again and again, but the damn car won't start. The engine keeps trying to turn, but nothing happens. My battery must be dead.

Seriously, fuck my life.

Here come the tears. I know there's no stopping them now. I'm crying, sweating, and racking my brain trying to figure out what the hell to do. I can't afford a tow truck, and don't want to call Quinn right now. The second she picks up the phone, she'll know something is wrong and rehashing everything that just happened isn't high up on the list of the things I want to do at the moment.

Getting out of the car, I pop the hood, hoping maybe fiddling with the battery or something will help. *Please, God, just cut me a break for a minute!* Funny how this was supposed to be the day everything turned around and instead I've had the morning from hell.

One would think that after so many crappy things happening in one morning, perhaps the universe would take pity on me. Not if your name is Ashley Mitchell. Instead, the universe seems hell-bent on piling on as much misery as possible. I'm pretty sure my breaking point isn't far off.

"Everything okay?" I hear the last person I want to see ask from the truck that's pulled up beside me. Why does he have to be the one to witness the rest of my morning meltdown? Not wanting him to see me this upset, I muster up all the composure left in me, wipe my tears discreetly, stand tall, and take what I hope will be a calming breath.

"Yes. Everything's fine. Thanks, though," I answer as politely as I can without turning around.

"You sure? It doesn't seem like it. Just wanted to make sure you're good before I leave." God damn his good guy act.

The truck door makes a small squeak as it opens. *No, please, no! Don't come over here.* Why can't he just be the asshole I want him to be?

"No, really, it's okay, Mr. Garrison. I'm fine. You can go," My voice sounds pretty convincing until I hiccup—well, more like a sob-hiccup blend, but I'm sure he hears it.

To make matters worse, my phone rings, Dom's name flashing on the screen again. If I pick it up, Tanner will definitely notice my crying, but there is no way that I can ignore it because Dom is already furious with me.

"Hello?" I answer, forcing every bit of self-control I have left into my voice.

"I don't know what you did or said, and I don't really care, but you better find a way to apologize to Garrison. His agent said he would talk to him to see if he'll let us run the article as long as he gets to approve it first. So you better write the article of your life, and whatever you did to piss him off better be left out. I'm not kidding. You better fix this mess. I thought you were better than this."

Damn, he knows exactly how to make me feel like shit... I have nothing to say but, "Okay, I will Dominick. I will. I'm sorry." All of my remaining calm goes out the window as the call ends, and I can't keep the tears in anymore.

Tanner clears his throat behind me, alerting me that he's still here while I have a mental breakdown in the middle of the parking lot. There's nothing left of myself to pull together—It's at least a hundred degrees, I'm crying, pretty sure that my job is on the line—but I try anyway. I need to try to smooth things over with the man witnessing my meltdown.

Shutting the hood of the car, I turn toward him. "I'm sorry, Mr. Garrison. I didn't mean to upset you earlier. That wasn't my intention, honestly. It wasn't anything personal. I'll be fine here. I don't want to waste any more of your time today. Again, I apologize. Nothing about your personal life will be written if you're still willing to give me the chance to print the article. You have my word." Finishing my little speech, I round my car, get in, and close the door, desperately wanting him to leave so I can get myself together and call for help. Maybe my dad would be willing to come get me. But I need Tanner to leave first.

Chapter Five

TANNER

SOMETIMES I WISH I could be the asshole everyone thinks I am. Ashley must really believe all the shit written about me if she thinks I'm going to leave her alone, crying in her car that won't start on a one-hundred-degree day. Her arrogant, know-it-all attitude during the interview pissed me the fuck off, but I can't seem to hold on to that anger after seeing her so broken down. She must've thought I'd left when she took that call because after she hung up, she hung her head in her hands and started crying.

Ten minutes ago, I wanted her fired, wanted nothing more than to see her the way she is now—upset and remorseful. But now seeing her so torn up doesn't make me feel as good as I thought it would, and I just want to fix it. She still hasn't looked at me. Each time she speaks, she keeps her head down, hiding her face, and it seems I've gone back to being Mr. Garrison.

If I let her print the article...? The meaning of her words dawns on me. Damn, Davis moves fast. I almost feel bad for her, but she has brought this on herself.

I stand, watching her sit in her hot box of a car trying to decide what to do here. She'll probably pass out if she stays in there much longer, so

I walk up to her window and knock. "Ashley, I don't have any jumper cables, but let me give you a ride somewhere, and we can deal with your car later."

"No, thank you. I'll be fine, Mr. Garrison." She shakes her head.

"If you stay in there any longer, I'm going to be calling you an ambulance instead of just driving you home. And stop calling me Mr. Garrison. I told you, it's Tanner." I semi-yell at her through the closed car window.

"No, thank you. I'll be fine, I swear. Please just carry on with your day. I really appreciate the offer, though," she declines again, as though I'm giving her a choice.

Jesus, she has to be dying in there. Enough of this. I open the door and feel the heat immediately. "No, Ashley. You're coming with me. You may very well think I'm a womanizing asshole, but I won't leave you sitting here in a one-hundred-fifty-degree car. No way in hell. So please just get out of the car so I can take you where you need to go." I rant, reaching into the car to pull her out. She has to be nuts if she thinks I'm going to leave her here in this heat. She tries to resist, so I grip her hand a little tighter and try to get her to step out of the car.

"You must've misunderstood me. I'm not leaving you here. Let's get a move on, please," I clarify, hoping she'll actually make a move to get into my truck.

She finally picks her head up and looks at me, giving me the first glimpse of her face since I stormed out of the interview. Her face is red and blotchy. Her eyes are a little swollen and her nose is running. She looks like she's been through the ringer. It's times like this I'm thankful my mother raised me well. Stopping to help this woman was the last thing I wanted to do, but I knew my conscience would've eaten me alive if I didn't. The urge to make sure Ashley's okay is compellingly strong, and I never let people affect me this way. It's how you get yourself into trouble.

"Come on. I'll take you home, and we'll settle your car later. Everything will be all right," I say sincerely despite all the weirdness I'm feeling toward this woman. My emotions are all over the place and I'm typically not an emotional guy. First, I'd wanted to fuck her, then I'd wanted to wring her neck, and now all I want to do is put a smile on her face.

Ashley must've finally reached her breaking point because she grabs her purse, gets out, and locks the door before she closes it. Quickly, I guide her to the passenger side of my truck before she can change her mind and fight me about this ride again.

Opening the door, I wait while she climbs in and puts her seat belt on, grateful for the lack of argument. I close her door and walk to my side of the car, trying to figure out what the hell I'm doing and how I'm going to play this ride home. I don't want her to feel uncomfortable, and I'd really like for her to get out of the depressed state she's in, but she seems to want absolutely nothing to do with me.

As I climb into the car, Ashley's still avoiding eye contact, staring out the window. I place my hand on top of hers to get her attention and the same current of electricity from the beginning of the interview courses through me. "Please don't sit there and think you have to hide from me. You've had a bad day, it happens, but I'm not trying to make it any worse. Want to talk about it?"

Even as the words leave my mouth, I know it's a stupid question. I'm part of her bad day, but it wasn't entirely my fault. She pushed the wrong button, and I reacted brashly. She obviously didn't know how much of a touchy subject my personal life is for me, but she should've been told to steer clear of anything remotely close to it.

She makes me feel so out of sorts and it only made it worse. I feel this sudden, unexplainable connection, and then she tries to get me to admit to all the shitty things written about me. If she had been asking for personal reasons, if I knew she feels this connection too, maybe it would have made things a little different.

"This morning just hasn't gone the way I was hoping," she surprises me, answering so softly I almost don't hear her.

"Well, how were you hoping it would go?" I ask, trying to keep her talking.

"This interview was supposed to open some doors for me, so I was hoping it'd go well. I didn't really want to do this interview, no offense. I do lifestyle pieces, not sports, but it dropped into my lap, and it seemed like a really great opportunity to expand my writing horizons." Ashley sighs as though a ten-pound weight has been lifted from her chest. She still hasn't pulled her hand away from mine, and that makes me glad. But I don't know why. I have no idea what the hell is happening or why I have no control over it.

"Who was that on the phone before?"

"Dominick, my editor." She looks away again and hastily pulls her hand from mine as if she's touching the enemy.

"What did he want?" I know I shouldn't push, especially since she's retreating back again, but the need to know how much my temper has cost her is overwhelming. I'm not sure why I even care. If she had just stuck to football none of this would've even happened.

"I'd prefer not to talk about it if you don't mind. Please let me know where you're heading so I can have someone pick me up," she says, pulling out her phone.

Wow, okay, so I'd been an ass earlier, but what is it with this woman? She thinks I'm going to just drop her off in a random place on my way home for someone to pick her up? "I'm taking you home. Tell me which way that is, and we can get going."

"You don't need to do that. Just drop me off somewhere on your way, and I'll be fine."

"Christ, Ashley. I'm not dropping you off somewhere on the side of the road like a piece a trash. Give me some fucking credit, will you? Just tell me which way to head, and I'll drop you off. Case closed." It's the first time I've cursed in front of her, and my mother would slap the shit out of me if she could hear me, but this woman seems hell-bent on pushing every single button I have.

"Hoboken," she answers. "I live in Hoboken."

"Well, I'm kind of heading that way anyway, if that makes you feel more comfortable." I tell her, hoping she'll feel better knowing I'm not going completely out of my way.

"Oh, okay," she responds very softly, a slight hitch in her voice, as she continues to stare out the window, wiping her eyes occasionally. If I didn't have two sisters, I might not have been able to tell the light touching of her face was really an attempt to wipe away any escaping tears. God, I hate when women cry.

"I have no problem with you running the article as long as you leave my personal life out of it. And for what it's worth, I'm sorry you're having such a bad morning." I figure it's worth putting her out of her misery. I'm still not sure why my gut keeps telling me to comfort her and make her feel better, but I guess I'm going with it since it seems I have no say in the matter. Hopefully, she'll relax now.

Chapter Six

ASHLEY

"*I* ***HAVE NO*** *problem with you running the article..."*

Oh my God! No way, he's got to be messing with me. I really hope not.

"I'm sorry, but did you just say you'll let the article run?" I ask needing to make sure I heard him correctly.

He nods, "I have no problem with the article as long as it doesn't turn out to be about my dating life."

"The article will only feature your professional feats and the team as a whole. Nothing else. You have my word. I'll even email it to you personally so you can approve it." I rush out quickly, wanting him to know I take my job seriously and what happen in the interview was just a fluke lapse in judgement. I'll write the best, most agreeable, non-gossip piece about him ever. If I can smooth things over with Tanner and have this article print on time, it will fix things with Dom and, with any luck, save my job.

"The article's set to run on Sunday. I'll make sure I have it done by Thursday so you can look it over and I can still have it in by the deadline for print. Does that sound alright, Mr. Garrison?" I'm sure I must sound as giddy as a kid on Christmas morning, and I hope this new development means my terrible day is turning around.

"If it means you'll be this upbeat for the rest of the ride, then yes that works just fine for me. And for the last damn time, my name is Tanner," he answers, practically growling the last part at me, and causing my cheeks to burn at his comment about me being upbeat.

"So how about we find some more to add to our interview? Why don't you tell me some things that you feel comfortable sharing? I'll make this the best piece that has ever been written about you." I smile at him. I'm not sure why, but I suddenly do want it to be the best article ever written about him. I went into the interview thinking he was just some hotshot playboy, and during the interview I thought he was a bullshit artist trying to make himself look better, but now I'm starting to think that he really is the good guy he claims to be.

The jury is still out on the dating part of his life, but that isn't really any of my business. Still, some part of me truly hopes the gossip isn't true, and for some reason that bothers me. I have a feeling that it has something to do with the crazy current that pulses between us.

Tanner didn't have to stop and help me, and most people in this area wouldn't have. Let's face it, people from New York and Jersey aren't always the nicest. That's why people think we're assholes. It's really luck of the draw, though. There are as many nice people here as there are assholes. There are assholes like me who turn down the help of gorgeous men because they're a hot mess, and there are nice guys like Tanner who are assumed to be assholes. The fact he stayed and waited me out proves I'd been wrong in my original assumptions of him.

Despite being wrapped up in my total mortification, I found something about his authoritative nature a turn on. The way he'd put his foot down and wouldn't take no for an answer had been like a direct hit to my core.

"Well, let's see," Tanner says. *Oh shit.* I forgot I'd asked him a question before I got lost in my thoughts. "I love playing in New York. I couldn't have been luckier when I was drafted here. My family was super happy too. My mom never missed a game during my pee wee and high school days. When I went to Ohio State, she was upset because she wouldn't be able to be at all my games anymore. It was too much travel for her. She wanted me to stay home and play for Rutgers so she could at least make it to my home games. But I couldn't pass up an opportunity to be a Buckeye. Not even for Ma."

"I'm guessing you're close with your family." I smile at him before I realize what I've just said. Shit. "Oh, I'm so sorry, does that count as a part of your personal life you'd prefer not to talk about?" Oh no, I hope I didn't just blow it again.

"No, it's fine. I am really close with my family. My parents and sisters are amazing. They're all still on Staten Island where I grew up. We still have Sunday dinner when I can pull it off, which isn't too often during the season. My last Sunday dinner with them for the year will probably be next week. My schedule's about to get really crazy. Unfortunately, that means I also won't have much time for community work with the city kids again until after the season." He's growing more talkative now, and it's great. With all the added insight into his life, I can make the article much better.

"Do you do a lot with the kids of the community? Is that something you enjoy?"

"That might be one of my favorite parts. I really love to give back to the community, and there's nothing better than watching the way the kids light up. It's like I am their biggest hero. That's part of the reason I hate having my dating life out there the way reporters like to spin it. If kids read that I'm out doing this or that with numerous different women, even though I'm not, it gives the kids the wrong impression. I like to consider myself a good influence on today's youth. There are just some messages that I don't want to send." Well, that explains a lot about his disdain toward the members of the press who like to drag his rep through the mud. Even more reason for me to make the article the best it can be.

"I can totally understand where you were coming from earlier now. I promise we'll give the right message in this article," I say with conviction. Even though I'm a journalist, writing about people's personal lives has never been my thing. I hardly ever write about people unless they're out on the town, and even then it's usually just where they were spotted in the city or where they're going to be, little pieces of information here and there. But I don't write things just for the sake of a story.

"So why don't you tell me something about you? How is it that you're here doing this interview if you aren't a sports writer?" he asks. Why he wants to know anything about me is baffling, but I don't want to piss him off again.

"Well, James is our usual sports writer. His wife had a baby three days ago. She should be released from the hospital today. Apparently, the hospital wouldn't give them a window for release. Dom, my editor, decided I was the best choice possible given the short notice. So, here I am. Again, no offense, but I even suggested that James try to do a phone interview, but that got vetoed." I explain the whole story honestly, feeling that he isn't the kind of person who'll be insulted by the truth.

"I'll try not to cry myself to sleep tonight after hearing that," he smirks at me. "Here, we're almost at the Hoboken exit. Put your address in so I know where I'm going." He says, pointing to the built-in GPS in the dashboard.

"Listen, I feel like I owe you an apology. I came into today with an opinion which wasn't based on any facts whatsoever. All the articles and tabloids painted you a certain way. Based on my own recent life experiences, I judged you before I should have, and I was wrong. So I'm sorry." I lower my head and busy myself with the GPS, not wanting to look at him at the moment. That apology was really hard for me to say. I think the way things played out with Jason might have clouded my judgment, making me think every man is a cheating scumbag.

Tanner slides his hand back into mine and squeezes. "Thank you. I know that wasn't easy to do. Most people don't have the courage to admit when they're wrong. But you did. That tells me something about you." He squeezes my hand again but doesn't let go.

His praise stirs something in me. I find myself smiling, enjoying his touch. What the hell is going on with me? I let him keep my hand, and we sit in comfortable silence for the rest of the ride.

"Do you live here alone?" Tanner asks as we pull up to the building I live in.

"No, I live with my best friend, Quinn," I reply, glad to be home so I can start putting this awful morning behind me and start working on the article. "I really appreciate you driving me home. You didn't have to. And thank you for giving me a second chance to write the article. I promise you won't be disappointed. If you give me your email address, I'll forward it to you as soon as I finish it."

"Can I see your phone?"

"Umm, sure." I dig in my bag for my phone, a little puzzled by what he wants it for, but find it and hand it over.

He takes the phone and enters some information before handing it back to me. "I programmed my number for you. Give me a call when you finish, and we can set something up," he says with a big smile on his face.

"Okay, yes. Sure," Holy shit! I can't believe that Tanner Garrison has just given me his number. I know it's for professional reasons, but I'm still a girl, and he's still super-hot.

"I hope the rest of your day goes better, Ashley."

I feel the blush creep into my cheeks at his words, and I get out of the truck. Why couldn't someone else have witnessed my morning from hell? I turn and wave after I've walked to the entrance of my building, still reeling from the craziness of the day thus far.

Pulling out my phone, I call Dom to let him know I've got everything worked out with Tanner, but it goes right to voicemail, so I leave a message explaining everything and let him know I'll touch base with him later. Time to start working.

I head to my room and change into some comfy clothes before making my way to the kitchen to grab a giant cup of coffee and something to eat so I can get to work. I start the coffee maker and try to think about what to write. By the time I'm adding cream and sugar to my coffee, the ideas are flowing, and I set up my station in the living room. Despite wanting to get the article done quickly, I can't seem to focus on writing. Instead, I can't stop thinking about his amazing smile, and the way my hands are still tingling from his touch. Why does he have such an effect on me? I'm in man-hating mode right now, so how'd he get through my armor?

"What's with the lovesick puppy look on your face, sweets?" Quinn says, appearing out of thin air, scaring the shit out of me and making me spill coffee on myself.

"Seriously, Quinn? What the fuck? Trying to give me a heart attack?" I snap giving her the dirtiest look possible.

"Well, I wasn't exactly quiet when I came in. Not my fault you were so lost in thought that you didn't hear me," She says plopping down next to me on the couch. "But really, what's with the look on your face right now? And how'd your interview go this morning?"

"Oh my God, Quinn, it was the morning from hell. Seriously, anything that could have gone wrong did, plus some," I tell her, laying my head in her lap. "I made such an ass out of myself."

"What did you do, dumbass? Did you trip and fall into the room and make a graceful grand entrance?" She laughs.

"Are you re-reading Fifty Shades again?" I ask, knowing how much she loves that book.

"No, but since you mentioned it, maybe I should," she smirks. "So tell me all about your horrible interview."

I tell her all about my morning, going all the way back to waking up late and hitting traffic. I don't leave out any details. This is Quinn, and I really need her to help figure out what the hell is going on with me.

Based on her facial expressions, one would think that she'd been the one to live through all the events of this morning. It's funny watching her reactions go from shock to horror.

I end my story with Tanner giving me his number and dropping me off. "So what do you think?"

"I think that all that stuff could only happen to you. And all in one morning, no less. You poor thing. You need a spa day to recover. The rest of this conversation involves a drink, the alcoholic kind." She smiles at me with pity in her eyes before heading to the kitchen to get some drinks, even though it's only one in the afternoon.

After returning with two glasses of wine, she says, "I'm not really sure what I think just yet. Now knowing all this information, it's obvious you were fantasizing about him when I walked in. The far-off look in your eyes, the light shade of pink on your cheeks, and I think there might have even been a little drool dripping from the corner of your mouth." She laughs. The bitch actually laughs as though it's the funniest thing she has heard all year.

"What? I wasn't fantasizing about him, just thinking about how hot he is," I reply, slapping my hand against the couch indignantly. I hadn't gotten to the fantasizing yet.

"Honestly, I think what you really need is to get laid. You haven't had any in a while, and I think it's messing with your mind. You know, experts say that a woman should have at least one orgasm daily. You aren't following the rules, so your mind isn't working at its highest potential. Want to go out and buy a new, really big vibrator? That will help, and maybe you can even write a better article," she says, completely straight-faced. I know her well enough to know that she isn't kidding. She's serious.

I smack her with a pillow, laughing. "You read too much Cosmo and way too many smut books."

Chapter Seven

TANNER

I FEEL LIKE I have a new asshole after today's meeting with Coach. I haven't been yelled at like that since I was a teenager and got caught breaking curfew. But that boy at practice had waited patiently for his chance to hand me his football, until a grown man had come barreling through the crowd, nearly stampeding over him trying to get in front of him. I don't understand why Coach is so pissed. The guy had it coming. Who cares if there is a video of me flipping out over it on YouTube? I certainly don't. Some fans need to be put in their place, and that asshole was one of them. What kind of grown man pushes a kid trying to get an autograph out of the way as though he doesn't matter because he's a kid? That shit really gets me pissed. Fuck him! For Christ's sake, the kid couldn't have been more than nine.

When that dickhead had knocked him over, the poor kid got stepped on by at least four people. His mom hadn't been able to get through the crowd to help him, and no one had seemed to care that they were about to trample a child. I'd lost it. I'd yelled for those idiots to get the hell back and pushed those who didn't listen out of the way as I tried to get to the boy. He'd had tears in his eyes, and I could tell he was trying not to cry. I called an end to the autograph session, telling everyone they could thank the asshole who thought he could manhandle kids for the early ending. Then I'd taken the kid, Jesse, and his mom back to the locker room where everyone from practice signed his football. I even gave him my practice jersey and made sure he got tickets to a game—front row seats behind the team bench. He's going to get the royal treatment at the game too. If that makes me an asshole, then I'll gladly be an asshole.

Practice had been great up until then. I love open practices, especially the Kid's Day ones. The kids all get front spots along a section of the field where the players can come up and sign autographs for them. We sign some before the beginning of practice and then again at the end. It's usually a blast. But today had been a different story. Coach said the incident made me look like a straight-up asshole, yelling and pushing fans. Oh well! I'd do it again gladly. The whole ordeal has my mood completely soured, and I'm angry.

I text Melissa, hoping she's around because I need to work out some of this aggression. She's usually always around for a hard fuck when I need her.

Me: *I'm in a bad mood. Awful incident after practice. Need to work out some aggression. You around?*

Melissa: *Always around for you! What happened?*

Me: *Tell you later. Heading home now. Can you meet me there?*

Melissa: *Of course! See you in 30!*

Thank God! The best way for me to get out of this nasty mood is to fuck it out. I'd learned years ago that the only thing that helps me get out of this kind of mood is sex. It was Melissa who helped me figure it out back in college. I'd tried running, workouts, and drinking, but none of that had alleviated my frustration. And the drinking just made me more of an ass. One day, when I'd been in a foul mood, she'd simply undressed and told me to take control back, to fuck her. We'd had sex a few times before that, but nothing crazy. She was the only repeat girl in my college days.

Most girls I'd been with had gotten clingy and needy after we'd had sex. Like most guys, I'd wanted to enjoy college and have fun, not get into any serious relationships. Besides, no one ever struck my interest enough for me to ever consider settling down. Melissa, though, she was the most down to Earth chick I had ever met. Maybe that's why she is the only close friend I have besides Alex. She's more like one of the guys. She's always been down for whatever, from sitting around playing cards to crazy adventures. Drama-free. Just how I like my women.

The fact her sexual appetite matches mine has always been a plus. I might not sleep around, but I do have my preferences. I love to dominate, call the shots, and I love to talk dirty. Nothing is hotter than dirty words in the bedroom. And Melissa loves when we get down and dirty, getting off on it just as much as me, and she's okay with anything when it comes to sex.

My dick's getting hard just thinking about how much better I'll feel after I've fucked the hell out of her. I haven't found a single thing that woman says no to. We even had a few threesomes back in the day. She's the only woman I know who openly admits to loving anal. Such a rare find. The way she owns her sexuality is so hot, and we never have that awkward after-sex period either. We can have downright nasty sex and immediately bounce back to the friend zone. There are no romantic feelings, but we do care about each other as a person. I hope that she's up for a couple rounds today because I'm pretty sure it'll take me some time to get this shit worked out. I haven't been this wound up in a long time.

After spending most of the ride thinking about all the ways I'm going to ride her over and over again, my cock is rock hard by the time I turn onto my street. When I pull into my driveway, Melissa is already there waiting for me. She stands, leaning against her car in a red trench coat and black fuck-me pumps that I can't wait to feel digging into my ass. My mood's lightening already just from thinking about it. This woman always knows exactly what I need.

Pushing the garage door opener, I pull in, get out and wait for Melissa to follow. She heads right for the alarm keypad, punches in the code, and heads inside. I let her get as far as the kitchen island before grabbing her by the hair and pulling her back to me.

Grinding my cock against her ass, I bring my mouth to her ear and inform her of my plans for the evening. "I hope you don't have plans for the rest of the day because I'm going to need to fuck you over and over before this mood gets any better. I'm probably going to need to be inside you everywhere today. Let's start by you wrapping that mouth of yours around my cock."

She whimpers at the mention of my cock in her mouth like I knew she would.

"Do you like the sound of that? Having my cock in your mouth? I bet if I stick my hand under this coat, I'll find your bare pussy already wet, won't I? And I know your pussy's bare under there because you're just naughty enough to leave the house wearing only a coat and those sexy shoes. Aren't you, Melissa?" I ask, knowing my words are foreplay to her.

"Yes," she says, her voice breathy. I know what she likes just as much as she knows what I like, and I know she's turned on. I push her forward toward the counter and press her upper body down against it. I leave my left hand tangled in her hair, pulling slightly, just enough to cause a sting. I don't get off on hurting her, but I enjoy letting her know who's in charge here. With my free hand, I trail a finger from her knee up her thigh and push her legs apart, allowing me access to the apex of her thighs.

"Just as I thought, Mel, soaked. You've been thinking about this since I texted, haven't you?" I ask, sliding my finger back and forth through her wetness, causing her to whimper again.

"Yes, I couldn't wait. It's been a while since you've been in a mood, and you know I love it when you fuck me hard and raw."

My dick twitches at her words. Man, does she love it dirty…

"Don't worry. You're going to get it just how you like it. After I fuck your mouth, we're going to work on this wet pussy next. After that, I think I'll need to visit your ass. It's been a while since we stretched you out everywhere." I drag my wet fingers back toward her ass, relishing her gasp as I rim her, massaging her own wetness into the tight hole.

She rocks back into my hand, initiating more contact. God, I'd almost forgotten how much she loves it when I play with her ass. Using more wetness from her pussy, I coat my fingers again before inserting them back into the place she wants it most right now.

"Mmm..." She sighs, rocking herself back to take my fingers in further.

"Your ass is so warm and tight. You love the idea of my cock slamming into it over and over again, don't you, Mel?" Each time I call her Mel, she seems to slip more into the zone. That's always what I call her during these hard fucking sessions. I've never felt right calling her baby or anything that sounds intimate. We aren't a couple, no matter what the housewives read in the magazines in line at the supermarket. So I started calling her Mel, and it's become a sort of alter ego for her, bringing out her inner vixen, and I love it.

"God, yes!" she screams, writhing in pleasure as I finger her a little harder, dragging my fingers nearly all the way out before pushing back in.

"Well, then I suggest you turn around and get those luscious lips of yours around my cock," I order, slightly tugging on her hair so she knows I mean business. We don't have oral sex often, so I need to let her know I really want to fuck her mouth.

She pushes off the counter and turns, dropping to her knees in one swift movement, faster than a dog to a bone. Her hands go straight to the waistband of my sweatpants, pulling both my pants and boxers down together. My cock stands proudly, happy to be freed from the confines of my briefs, and I think Melissa actually drools a little as her eyes land on my raging hard-on.

"Coat off. I want to be able to watch your tits bounce up and down while I fuck your mouth."

She quickly sheds her coat and tosses it to the side before wrapping her hand around my shaft and stroking up and down a few times.

"Stop playing and suck my dick!" I'm not in the mood for games any longer. She licks a circle around the head of my dick. The heat from her mouth feels good, but I want the suction. Deciding I don't want to wait any longer, I slide one hand down to her nipple and the other into her hair at the crown of her head. I squeeze her nipple with enough force to make her gasp and use the other hand to push her head onto my cock as her mouth opens. I grunt as I thrust my whole length into her mouth, hitting the back of her throat. I pull back and thrust again and again.

Like a good girl, Melissa keeps a good suction going until I'm close enough to coming that I pull completely out of her mouth. She keeps sucking until the last second, so when my cock falls from her mouth, it makes a light popping sound.

Pulling her up from her knees, I lift her onto the counter and give her a little nudge to get her to lay back. I pull her all the way to the edge of the counter while pulling my sweats and boxers off the rest of the way and ditching my shirt. Then I lower my head and give her pussy a few long licks up and down.

"Oh, yes!" She purrs.

On my trip back up, I circle my tongue around her clit once, twice, before gently sucking it into my mouth. I pull her nub between my teeth and bite down lightly until I hear her moan again.

"Stop fucking around, Tag! Make me come!" she demands. Guess I'm not the only one who is done with games.

I circle her clit a few more times and then slide my fingers into her pussy, hooking them up to reach her G-spot. Melissa lets out a long, throaty groan, letting me know that I'm right where I need to be. Wrapping my lips around her clit, I add some suction, and that's all it takes to send her over the edge.

"Ahh! Yes, yes… More, Tag, more!"

I add a little pressure as her pussy starts to clench around my fingers, a gush of fluids coating them as her orgasm hits its peak. Melissa writhes in pleasure, not even noticing the unforgiving granite countertop beneath her. I lean over to grab the condom from my discarded sweats and roll it on quickly. Before she fully comes down from her high, I slam my cock into her, making her scream out in surprise and bliss. I use the thumb of one hand to rub her clit lightly and the other to massage her other entrance.

"Ah, God, that feels amazing, Tag. I love when you take me everywhere," she says, panting. "Your huge cock hits every goddamn spot possible. Fuck, yes!"

"Oh yeah? How much do you love this huge cock?" I grunt, slamming into her hard. I stop rubbing her clit, needing to use that hand to make sure that I don't fuck her right off the island. I know she's enjoying my thumb in her ass much more anyway.

"So much, Tag! So fucking much!" she screams, on the verge of coming again. A few more thrusts, and I'm sure she'll fall over the edge. It's hard to keep myself from coming, but I have one more stop on this ride before I let go.

"Come, Mel! Come now so I can slide my cock into your ass!" I command, and just as I'd expected, my words push her to her climax.

She comes with a scream of "Oh My God." Thank God she's a squirter. She's lubed me up enough to slide into her final entrance without a problem. I wouldn't use this little lube with someone not accustomed to being fucked in the ass, but with Melissa, I know it's enough.

I pull out of her pussy and nudge her back entrance in warning before I push in an inch or two. I place my thumb back on her clit to prolong her pleasure while I slide into her ass. I look to her for cues of discomfort, but Melissa seems to be in pure ecstasy. Using a bit of force, I slide all the way home.

"Oh God!" I cry out just as Melissa lets out a "Mmm…"

"Does that feel good, dirty girl? I know you love it when I fuck this ass." I thrust harder, giving her ass a nice smack, loving the way the sound of the slap reverberate through the room.

"Of course it does, Tag! Everything that you do with that incredible cock of yours feels fantastic," she coos.

I continue thrusting until I feel my balls start to tighten, and I know the release that I need is just moments away. I use my thumb on Mel's clit again, knowing the stimulation and a few more dirty words should seal the deal for her and, in turn, seal the deal for me.

"You need to come now! I want this glorious ass of yours milking me," I say, continuing to apply the perfect amount of pressure to her clit.

"Jesus, Tag! I don't know if I can come again."

"Don't give me that shit. I know you can. And you'd better do it now," I tell her through gritted teeth. If I ride her any harder right now, I'm afraid I might break her in two.

"Holy shit!" Melissa screams as her third orgasm takes her fully by surprise.

"Fuck yeah!" I roar as I come harder than I have in a long while. I feel as though I've been coming for hours when my release finally ends, and I slump forward onto Melissa, using her stomach as a pillow.

"Christ, you really were wound up, huh? We haven't hit it like that in a while, Tanner. I love it when you lick my pussy." Melissa says as she runs her fingers through my hair. I hate when she does that. Playing with my hair, telling me how much she loves when I eat her pussy. I don't really like doing it. Or having her suck my dick. It's too intimate for me. I'm good with it once in a blue moon or in situations like today, but not on a regular basis. I know Melissa loves to suck dick, but I don't know what or who she does with her mouth most of the time, just like I don't know who else she lets between her legs. She says it's just me, but we're not a couple, so who knows? She could very well be getting taken care of elsewhere when I haven't called for sex in a few weeks. I'm on the road a lot. I wouldn't blame her. I get it.

"It was a bad day at practice. Just google it. I'm sure you'll see the video. Some dickheads practically trampled some kid trying to get an autograph, and I lost it. Coach ripped me a new one. What for, I'm not really sure. I don't get what he's so worked up about. If I hadn't freaked, that poor kid would have gotten really hurt. But yet again, I'm the asshole. Surprise, right?" I explain, trying not to get worked up again, but I can feel the anger coming back.

My phone rings from the pocket of my sweatpants, so I sit up, pulling away from Melissa and reach down for it. The call is from a number not programmed into my phone. I've learned from experience to never answer numbers I don't know. It's always someone wanting something. It really amazes me how these people get my number. But there's something telling me I really need to answer this call.

"Hello?"

"Hi, Mr. Garrison. I mean Tanner. This is Ashley Mitchell from *The City Press*. I wanted to talk to you about the article. Do you have a minute?"

That explains the need to answer. The same spark from the interview ignites at the sound of her voice. *Hmm, the connection we have works through the phone too.* I've honestly tried to forget about Ashley. Since

I'm not normally one to meet new people and hang out like old friends, I chalked up our encounter to just a weird day. But feeling the energy between us again, over the phone no less, is hard to ignore.

"Sure, Ashley. What's up?" I ask sliding the condom off and tossing it in the trash. I pull my pants back on, and walk to the refrigerator to grab a bottle of water for Melissa, then toss it to her.

"Well, I saw the video from your practice today, and between that and our conversation in the car the other day, I think I could spin a really great human interest piece on you instead of just writing about football," she says.

"What does that mean? I told you how I feel about my personal life being in the papers. That's one of the conditions of the article," I remind her.

"I know it is. I thought we could focus more on the passionate side of you that doesn't get seen on the field. The guy in the video today saving that boy. You're going to get a crap-load of bad press from this, and it'll make you look exactly like the asshole you aren't. But if we spin the article to talk about how much you love the fans and the kids and how seeing that kid in danger made you do what was necessary to make sure he didn't get hurt, yada yada. . . I promise I'll make you look fantastic. Just tell me about it from your perspective, and I'll write about you as a person instead of your stats that people can get on ESPN.com. What do you think?" she asks, sounding excited.

"Hmm, that's not a half-bad idea. I like it. I still get final approval, right?" I still want to see the piece before it gets published to make sure I like it.

"Of course. Everything stays the same except the main focus of the article."

"Okay, go for it." Maybe this new angle will get Coach off my back and help get everyone to stop thinking I'm a complete asshole.

"Okay, tell me what I need to know that isn't in the videos online, and I'll get to work," she says. I hear a steely determination in her voice, and I feel as though I can trust her to make the article something different. I may have no control over my mind when it comes to this girl, but my gut tells me to trust her.

"All right, today was a special practice focused on kids. We do them sometimes during pre-season open practices. There's a link on our website about it where you can get more details. After practice, I went over to sign some autographs for the kids, and this asshole pushed a little boy named Jesse, who was patiently waiting his turn out of the way, and no one tried to help him up. These were grown men stepping on and over him like garbage. His mom couldn't get through to help him. So I told everyone to get the hell out of the way and pushed the ones who wouldn't move so I could get to the kid. He was crying when I got to him, probably scared out of his mind and most likely hurt. I saw quite a few people step on him and kick him trying to rush forward. It was like watching a Black Friday crowd trying to get into Walmart. So I ended the autograph session and told everyone to blame the asshole for pushing kids." My hands start to shake again as I think about little Jesse.

"Good Lord. Seriously? Let's take out a kid for an autograph," Ashley says sarcastically. "What jerks! Okay, Tanner. I've got this. I'll make sure everyone knows who the real assholes are in this situation. Anything else I can put in it?"

"I took the kid back to the locker room. All the team players signed his football, and I gave him my practice jersey. I also told him he'd get tickets to a home game. First row behind the team bench. That kid is going to have the time of his life that day. I really hope that it makes up for what happened to him today. It should've never happened." I sigh. I truly hope this doesn't turn him off from going to events in the future because that would be awful.

"That's amazing. I'm sure he'll remember everything you've done for him more than the events that led to it. Think about being little again. What would you remember more: a locker room full of pro football players signing autographs for you and giving you all types of cool things or some jerk who pushed you down in the blur of a few scary minutes? You did something great for that boy, even if nobody else has seen it yet. But they will! They will! I think I might be able to get this on the front page. Are you going to be giving a statement to anyone else? If you are, would you mind waiting until I run my story? It would still give me the exclusive, and that would do wonders for me."

"No problem. Will you still run it on Sunday? I don't know how long I'll be allowed to go without making a statement. Management and my agent are going to push for one," I tell her honestly. I feel surprisingly lighter after just a few minutes talking to Ashley, even more than I had after fucking the hell out of Melissa. *Interesting.* I'm starting to think that no matter how much I deny this connection to Ashley, there's something more than attraction to it.

"I'll start writing now. Give me a day or two tops. I'll call you as soon as I finish my rough draft. What do you think?"

"Sounds good. Call me, and we can get together to go over everything," I'm now convinced it would be in my best interest to see her again, and the article is a good excuse.

"Okay, sounds perfect. I'm going to get to work."

"Okay… And Ashley? Thank you," I say sincerely before hanging up. I have the feeling she'll do wonders for me with this piece. I hope.

"What was all that about?" Melissa asks, still sitting naked on the counter, when I come back into the kitchen.

Why do I have no desire to fuck her again?

"That was the reporter I met with the other day. She wanted permission to spin the article a different way, tell everyone my side of today. Hopefully, it'll work the way she says," I say with a smile, feeling very optimistic. The press loves to make an ass of me, but I have faith in Ashley, knowing how desperately she wants this article to be amazing.

"Oh, that's great. I hope it all works out. That poor kid." Melissa slips off the counter and saunters towards me, placing her hand on my chest before sliding it lower. I realize she's trying to go for round two when she reaches my waistband, but I don't seem to have any more aggression to work out.

"Nah, I'm good. Want to grab some dinner? I'm starving." I walk toward the stairs, ready to shower and get dressed. I try not to let the pouty face Melissa gives me affect me. Three orgasms must have been plenty. She's always been drama free, so I'm sure she'll be over it in two seconds. "Don't give me that face. You got off three times. Go shower. I think you'll find some clothes lying around in the guest room. And move it. I'm really hungry."

"Ugh, fine! But you're buying, and I'm in the mood for filet mignon," she says, following me up the stairs.

"I'll buy you lobster and filet if you're ready in fifteen minutes."

Chapter Eight

ASHLEY

WHEN I SENT Tanner a copy of the article this morning, he said it was perfect and he couldn't wait to see the final draft. We've made plans to meet up tonight to go over it. After talking to Tanner yesterday, I called Dom and told him about my idea for the article. He loved it, but didn't think I'd be able to get approval from Tanner or his agent. When I told him I'd already spoken to Tanner personally and gotten the approval, he couldn't believe it.

I spent all of last evening working on the piece, and I'm excited to bring it to light. When Tanner told me what had really happened at the open practice, I was beyond pissed off. The way the video has been spun online doesn't show the truth at all. All the grainy cell phone video shows is an irate Tanner yelling and pushing people. It's not all that clear, so it's easy to think Tanner's just being an asshole. I can't wait to show everyone the real Tanner Garrison.

We decided to meet for dinner at Dina and Harrison's in Hoboken. I'm ten minutes early, but that's a good thing. It's just around the corner from my house, but since I was late for our last meeting, I thought it might be a good idea to be a little early for this one.

As the waiter seats me at our table, he asks if I'd like something to drink while I wait. I decide a glass of wine might help quell my nerves.

The restaurant has a generic city feel to it. Dark and discreet, nothing bright or flashy. Simple and casual. The deep red carpet pairs well with the dark paneled walls. The tables are all old-fashioned and round. No booths. Each has a linen tablecloth set with a single candle in the middle. I find the atmosphere to be very comfortable, until there's a change in the air.

The hairs on the back of my neck stand up, and goosebumps spread across my skin, as if a cool breeze has blown through. Looking toward the door, I see Tanner heading my way, the unusual sensation getting stronger the closer he gets.

He looks downright delicious in black dress pants and a gray button-down shirt that clings to the broadness of his lean, muscular shoulders. The splash of gold in his tie makes the flecks in his eyes shine. His square jaw and chiseled cheekbones make a deadly combination for my panties. Jesus, it should be illegal for someone to look that damn good. It's as though someone carved him out of stone in tribute to an ancient Greek god.

I'm jolted out of my perusal of him by a little chuckle, and I look up to see a devilish smirk on his face which only makes his features more striking.

"Well, hello, Ashley. It's nice to see you again," he says, leaning down to kiss my cheek.

I blush. I'm probably as red as a tomato between getting caught checking him out and the kiss he's just given me.

Pull your shit together, Ashley. You don't want to make an ass out of yourself in front of him... again.

"Good evening, Tanner. Thank you for meeting me, and thank you for having my car brought to the shop the other day as well. You didn't need to do that."

I couldn't have been more shocked to find my car in my parking spot the morning after the interview with a note on the dash saying it was fixed. Never in a million years would I have thought Tanner would do something like that. Who knew the asshole, playboy quarterback was actually a nice guy? Me, that's who, and now it's my mission to make sure other people see the person he really is.

"Don't even think twice about it. It was nothing." His stern voice warns me that he means business, and I shouldn't bring it up again.

"I hope you haven't been waiting long. I apologize I'm late." He says grabbing his menu.

"You aren't late. I was just early. I only ordered a glass of wine. I wasn't sure what you would want." I don't tell him that I needed some alcohol to prep for this meeting.

"That's fine. Do you want to order before we get to business?"

"Sure."

After we place our orders with the waiter, we stare at each other for a few moments before I snap out of my daze and reach into my bag to grab the finished article for him.

"This really is amazing. I can't thank you enough. Coach was so pissed at me over everything, but I didn't really care. This will help me on two fronts, calming down management and keeping me from looking like an ass. But honestly, if this makes me an asshole, I'd rather be an asshole," he says, looking over the pages.

"I'd rather be the asshole who helps a kid than be the asshole who doesn't, too," I say, agreeing with his stance.

"Now that that's out of the way, how about you tell me more about you?" He steeples his fingers in front of him as though he's waiting to hear the secrets of life come out of my mouth.

"I'm just your everyday girl. There isn't much to know about me"

"Yes, there is. I'm trying to understand this uncanny connection we have. I think the only way to do that is to get to know each other. You know, I wasn't going to answer the phone when you first called. I hardly ever answer numbers I don't know. But I had this strong feeling that I needed to answer. And when I got off the phone with you, my horrible mood had disappeared like magic. I think you and I need to get to know each other better. Don't you? I know you feel it as well. This goes far beyond attraction," he says, sounding very sure of himself.

"What is it that you want to know?" I ask, wondering where he's trying to take this conversation.

"As much as I can. Give me some basics. You know much more about me than I do about you."

"I'm pretty boring. I'm from New Jersey originally. Went to Ramapo and studied journalism. I've wanted to be a journalist for as long as I can remember. I lucked out with an internship at *The Press*. My best friend, Quinn, and I met in college. She was my roommate freshman year. We just moved in together again about two months ago." I hope that's enough to keep him happy. I take a sip of wine, waiting for him to steer the conversation somewhere else.

"Where did you live before?"

"Jersey City." I glance around the restaurant, hoping to find some kind of inspiration to use so I can change the subject. He's getting dangerously close to things I don't want to talk about.

"Why'd you move?"

"It was time for a change." That's all I'm willing to give him on that one.

Thankfully, our salads arrive, providing a distraction.

"I'll let that slide for now."

I look up from my salad and stare at him. He responds with a wink. A fucking wink. It does nothing to curb my desire to see the man naked. In fact, the urge intensifies.

We chit-chat idly about neutral topics for the rest of dinner but turn back to business once more before we call it a night.

"So the article looks good to you? I want to make sure you're happy with it before it hits the front page Sunday."

"The front page?" He looks surprised.

"Yes. I can't thank you enough for giving me this chance. It's going to be as huge for me as it will be for you, I'm sure. I want this to give people a glimpse of the person I see when I look at you. Honestly, I'd thought you were an ass before meeting you too, but it didn't take much to change my mind. Hopefully, everyone else will be as easy as me to convince." I don't realize the double-meaning in my words until he smiles deviously at me.

"So you're telling me you're easy?" he asks with a smirk still resting on his lips as he rises from his seat.

"I guess when it comes to you, yes." *Why the hell did I just say that?* My filter is nowhere to be found.

"We'll see. We'll definitely see," he informs me on our way to the door. I don't even remember him paying the check.

"When did you get the bill? Let me get it. It's on the paper. You did a great thing for them and me by letting us print the article. It's the least that we can do."

"Nonsense. I have a running tab here. This happens to be one of my favorite places for dinner, very serene."

"That's very thoughtful. Thank you for dinner, and thank you again for giving me this opportunity. I hope that things go well for you when the paper hits the stands," I tell him. Sunday is bound to be a big day in my career, and I hope that it is in his as well.

"Anytime, Ashley. Anytime." He smiles. "Until next time."

BY THE TIME I make it to the office Monday morning, my cell has rung at least fifty times. The article is a huge hit. Everyone wants a piece of Tanner. I couldn't be happier for him—or myself. Dom is thrilled as well. Apparently the article has made both the morning news and the local sports talk shows. *The Associated Press* has also picked it up, splashing it all over the internet. Boomer and Carton, a big local sports radio show, spent half an hour discussing it. I don't think anything short of a catastrophe could wipe the smile off my face. My luck finally seems to be turning around.

A knock on my door takes my attention away from my musings, and I look over to see a delivery man holding a huge bouquet of pink and white lilies, standing in the doorway.

"Are you Miss Mitchell?" he asks.

"Yes."

"Can you please sign here? These are for you," he says, holding out a clipboard with his free hand.

"Who would send me flowers?" I ask to no one in particular as I sign for the delivery and take the flowers. *I love lilies.*

"Check the card. Have a good day," he says on his way out the door.

I place the vase on my desk and pull the card out of its envelope, anxious to see who they're from.

Congratulations on a great article!
Looks like you did a great job for both of us!
-Tanner

Chapter Nine

ASHLEY

THE NEXT FEW weeks are total mayhem. After the article about Tanner blew up, I'd gotten the opportunity to write for the paper much more often. Now everyone wants me to visit their establishments, see their new play openings, and cover book signings. I guess if I was able to sell Tanner Garrison as America's newest sweetheart, I can convince people to visit any club, event, or restaurant in the city. I'm writing about three or four pieces a week now. Quinn and I haven't had a single chance to celebrate all the new, exciting things happening in my life, so we've decided to fix that tonight by dancing our asses off while I check out a hot new club for work.

I haven't heard from Tanner since the flowers were delivered. I assume he's been consumed with improving his image. Plus, the season has just started, so he's now getting into his full swing. I'm happy for him. I've caught a few interviews he's done since and had made sure to watch the season home opener last weekend. Because it was the game little Jesse got tickets for, there was a lot of coverage. It's brought even more light to the true Tanner.

Quinn walks into the living room in a micro dress, snapping me out of my thoughts of Tanner. "Damn. How much more of your ass are you going to let hang out tonight?"

She looks hot as hell, and I'm totally jealous. Her red halter dress has pushed her boobs so high up I think she could eat off of them if she wanted to. It has a slit that goes almost up to her hip on the left side, showing off her killer legs. Her shoes are equally fantastic, but I'm not sure how she plans to walk in them. They have to be almost six inches tall, and they're completely covered in crystals. If the lighting in the club isn't dim enough, Quinn's shoes could definitely blind someone.

"I'm planning on getting laid tonight, so the more ass the better. Wait until you see the outfit I picked out for you, chica. You need to get laid tonight too, and I have the perfect dress to accomplish that mission." She has a devious smile on her face, which means I'm utterly screwed. When Quinn is in a mood like this, she's a force to be reckoned with.

"Have you forgotten that I'm not like you, my dear? I can't go out dressed like that and be comfortable," I remind her. Sometimes I'd swear she doesn't hear a word I say.

"Tough shit. I'm pretty sure your vag has grown cobwebs, and you're practically a born again virgin. We need to open that baby up before you die of celibacy."

I roll my eyes at her before walking to her bedroom to check out the crazy dress she has planned for me. "Seriously? You're so dramatic! My vagina is fine, and I'm nowhere near being a born again virgin yet. I think it has to have been five years before you can consider yourself born again."

Quinn has officially lost it. She has to be out of her fucking mind. The dress she's picked out for me makes her look as conservative as an Amish woman in hers. "Quinn! Have you been smoking crack today? You cannot think that I'm leaving the house wearing that. Did you rob a hooker for that dress?"

"Now who's being dramatic? Honestly, you need to live a little, Ash. And for the record, six months is more than enough of a dry spell, and I'm sure little dick Jason had no idea what he was doing, so it's been almost three years since you've had a decent lay. So shut the fuck up and put it on. I want to go get drunk and laid. Move it, bitch."

Knowing she's not going to give it up, I put on the dress she's laid out for me. It's iridescent, backless, and has what resembles dental floss for straps. I'm practically naked in it, and if the hem rises even a half inch, the whole club will see my va-jay-jay. At least I got a wax this week.

The dress has a semi-cowl neck and hangs low on my chest, showing off plenty of cleavage. My boobs may not be as nice as Quinn's, but I have to admit I look pretty hot. She's paired the dress with nude stilettos, which thankfully aren't as high as hers. Once my hair and makeup are done, I take a look in Quinn's full-length mirror. *I look damn fuckable.*

"Damn, bitch. I think you look better than me. You'd better put that hotness to use tonight, or I swear I'll disown you as my best friend. What's the name of this club again?" Standing next to each other all done up, Quinn and I look like the who's who of New York City.

"Levitate. It's a penthouse level club in Soho. It has floor to ceiling windows so you feel suspended in the sky. I can't wait to see the view. The bar specializes in martinis, so I hope you're planning on getting really drunk because I can't wait to try all the different flavors."

"Well, let's not keep you waiting any longer, bitch. The car's here." Quinn hands me my clutch, and we make our way downstairs.

When we pull up to the club and I see the queue, I'm grateful that my name's on the list. I wouldn't want to wait in that crazy line to get in. My press badge ensures that we get the VIP treatment—an awesome perk of my job. People want a great review when they find out I'm coming. The club's only been open a few weeks, but it's already creating a lot of buzz, which has turned it into a hotspot. I don't actually meet with the owner or any employees, though. I don't want the staff inside to know who I am. I want the same experience anyone else would get.

This view is a fantastic start. We ride the private elevator just for club patrons, and once I step off, the first thing I notice is the three-hundred-sixty-degree view of New York City. It's breathtaking. The club has an open floor plan. Smart idea. I feel as though I'm hanging out in the middle of the sky.

There are several bars. One in each corner and two on longer parallel sides of the club that I guess you'd consider the main ones. The DJ is set up between them. There's something oddly familiar about him, but I can't place the guy. There are two staircases on opposite ends of the room leading up to the second floor VIP area.

The second floor seems to have the same open vibe as downstairs does, except its balconies overlook the entire first floor. We find two more bars up here, but since the VIP area is nearly empty at the moment Quinn and I head downstairs to check out some of the featured martinis.

"This place is seriously amazing," Quinn shouts over the music.

"I know," I yell back. We take our drinks and head to the dance floor. It's time to have some fun. Just another part of the job that's fantastic. I love that part of my work is to go out and have a good time and then write about it for the rest of the city to read. I get a night with my best friend, preferential treatment, and a whipped cream martini. Life is pretty good.

"Come on Ash. You can do better than that," Quinn says, obviously unimpressed with my dancing. When she pulls my arm, I wind up in front of her, and she starts grinding up against me. I do love that my bestie has no shame and couldn't care less what anyone thinks. I wish some of that attitude would rub off on me.

As I start shaking my ass, I let the world fall away. Over the din, I hear someone speaking to Quinn but can't make out the words. After a moment, I feel her pull away and a much larger person takes her place. As she sneaks away, she flashes me a thumbs up and grabs a guy to dance with a few feet away. I decide to go with it. It can't hurt to let loose for one night. The songs all blend together, one after the other, and I'm actually relaxed and having a good time.

Maybe Quinn's been right and I just need to let loose a little more. My body sways with the mystery man's in perfect time to the music. The warmth from his hands on my hips radiates through my body, setting it ablaze. He has a soft but firm touch. Innocent but deliberate. The way my body has been mesmerized by the combination of his touch and the beat of the music is unreal but masterful. I feel at home, which is slightly unsettling, but I don't want to put a stop to this moment.

"Maybe we should have had the interview in a club. You seem much more relaxed and in your element," a husky voice I recognize whispers in my ear. My body freezes mid-movement and I glance toward Quinn with wide eyes only to see a shit-eating grin on her face. That bitch. She could have told me who it was. In a split-second, my body's reactions over the last half hour all make sense. Picking the beat back up, our bodies move in unison again, this time to Chris Porter's *The Water Dance*.

"Mr. Garrison, so great to see you again. To what do I owe the pleasure?" I ask, still facing forward, my ass still pressed against him. I love this song and know the lyrics well, so my moves correlate perfectly to the lyrics. *First she dips down low, then she dips down deeper.* Dropping down low, I make sure my ass hits all the right spots as I drag it up his legs on my way back up.

"Damn, Ashley. And please call me Tanner. You owe this pleasure to being the hottest girl here tonight. I noticed you from upstairs, and felt the need to come down and find out who the beauty dancing her ass off was. Finding out it was you was more than a pleasant surprise. What do you say to grabbing another drink with me?"

Holy shit. So many thoughts swirl through my head. Did he really just say that I'm the hottest woman here? Why does the thought of spending the night with him make my panties wet? *Don't go there, Ash. He only asked you to get a drink, not get in his bed.* Plus, this is the wrong time to be getting all hot and bothered by the same man who's been making appearances in my late night fantasies. I'm supposed to be checking out the club, not thinking about leaving it early to get bent over by a hot quarterback.

"Stop thinking so hard, Ashley. How about I grab us another round and meet you upstairs. What are you drinking, baby?" he asks as his hands continue to caress my hips while we move to the rhythm. His fingers apply the perfect amount of pressure to my hips, making them undulate to the tempo the way he wants. I'm lost in the sensation of his hands on me, his lips on my ear as he whispers into it and the fact he just called me baby. I'm complete putty in his hands, his to mold as he pleases.

"I'm sampling the martini menu. Surprise me. I've already had the whipped cream one." I say, finding a little sass and grinding my ass against his cock one more time before turning around and whispering, "See you upstairs."

I saunter off toward the staircase, feeling extremely pleased with myself and my exit when I walk smack into my past.

"Sorry, I wasn't paying attention," I apologize before looking up to see Jason with a scowl on his face. "Oh, Jason." I thought I'd recognized the DJ earlier, but I hadn't been able to place him. Seeing Jason's face makes it click. He's one of his friends. Jason and I had gone to a few clubs where he DJ'ed at over the last two years.

"Well, hello, Ashley. Looking pretty slut-tastic this evening. How many free drinks have you gotten tonight with that ass-grinding move you just pulled on the tool headed to the bar?" he asks, giving Tanner's back the evil eye. Why he's pissed off, I haven't got a clue. He cheated on me.

"Fuck you, Jason. Where's your Bimbo Barbie? Shouldn't you be dick-deep in the STD pool by this time of night?" I spit back, angry that his mere presence has ruined my great mood.

"Nice one. Still doesn't change the fact that you're out tonight flaunting that body at every poor schmuck in here. Maybe I should go tell the guy getting you a drink the pretty wrapping won't mean anything once he has you flat on your back. I should save him the awkwardness of fucking you because I'm sure he can find someone else worth the money he's going to spend keeping you drunk."

What the fuck is Jason's problem? Hasn't he already hurt me enough? I'm over his shit. I've had enough to last a lifetime. I don't think I could have stopped my hand from tossing the rest of my drink in his direction if I'd wanted too. I've definitely had enough of this conversation, so now that my martini is dripping from his face, he's going to get a piece of my mind.

"Go fuck yourself! You act like I wronged you. You racked up my credit cards with your whores and then fucked one of them in our bed. If anyone should be throwing insults around, it's me, you piece of shit. And for the record, if you were a real man and a decent lay maybe I would have actually been able to get into fucking you. Not my fault you couldn't do it for me." I'm so livid that I barely notice Tanner has returned, looking pretty pissed himself.

"You're nothing but a cunt, Ash," Jason yells, wiping the drink from his face.

"Everything alright here, Ashley?" Tanner asks, handing me my new drink. "Try not to throw this one on anyone, baby."

He lays a hand possessively behind my neck, but I'm too rattled to enjoy his touch. I wonder how long he's been standing there and just how much he's heard.

"Any particular reason you're standing here insulting my girl?" Tanner asks, looking murderous. The last thing I want is him anywhere near Jason, so I need to find a way to defuse this situation fast.

"Holy shit! You're Tanner Garrison," Jason says in awe, seeming to forget he's dripping vodka everywhere.

"Yes, he is, and you're a good-for-nothing douchebag who was just leaving. Have a nice life, Jason, and stay the fuck away from me." I turn to face Tanner. "Don't bother giving him the time of day, Tanner. Just a few minutes ago, he said you were a tool who was wasting his time on me." I smile as I rat out Jason's previous insults to Tanner.

Tanner smiles at Jason before dropping a kiss on the top of my head. "You could never be a waste of time, Ashley. Don't worry about that. But even if you were, I'd rather be the tool wasting his time on you than the loser covered in vodka who let you get away."

Grabbing his hand, I head toward the stairs, and hope like hell he doesn't ask me any questions about Jason. I'm on emotional overload, and my adrenaline is fading fast.

"Wanna tell me what that was about? I can't leave you alone for two minutes, can I?" Tanner chuckles.

"Just a bitter ex, and no I don't want to talk about it. Let's go back to having a good time." I reply, hoping it's enough information to keep him happy.

"That sounds like a perfect idea."

We walk up the stairs, his arm around my waist and his hand resting on my hip, letting everyone know I'm with him. The party has picked up on the second floor. He steers me toward a group of guys all hanging out together, and I notice Quinn is already in the midst of the group. Tanner tips his head toward the group as we walk over.

"Well, well, well, who do we have here, Tag?" one of the guys asks.

I take a quick look around at all of them, and good lord, they all look as though they've walked out of *GQ*. This is way too much hotness for one area.

"Tag?" I look at him with a raised eyebrow.

"Just a nickname the guys call me."

"Cute," I smirk at him.

"This is Ashley Mitchell," he tells the blond one who's just spoken. "Ashley, this is my friend, Alex Conway."

"Hello there, Alex. Pleased to meet you." I stick my hand out for him to shake, but instead I'm pulled in for a very friendly hug.

"The pleasure is all mine, gorgeous." Alex flashes a smile before bending over to kiss my cheek, all while looking directly at Tanner.

"Watch it, Conway!" Tanner practically growls, snatching me from Alex's grasp.

"Okay, boys, easy! Quinn, wanna come with me to the ladies' room?" My bravado from earlier is fading fast, and I need to talk to her about my run in with Jason. A Quinn pep talk is definitely in order right now.

"Why on Earth do ladies always need a friend to piss with them? I've never understood why you can't go alone," Alex asks after chugging half his beer.

"Because we can't talk about who we think has the bigger dick in front of you guys. Wouldn't want any bruised egos," Quinn quips back.

"No need to go all the way to the bathroom to discuss that. We can whip out our dicks and show you right now. No need to waste your time debating. I win, hands down. Sorry Tag, but I got this one. Wanna swing your fine ass over this way now, Ashley? No need to spend any more time on Little Dick here."

Damn. I think Quinn may have met her match in this one.

"If you need to announce you have the bigger dick, then you don't. Probably barely six inches. Guys with big dicks never need to advertise. They let their cocks speak for themselves." Quinn smirks at him.

"Ooohhh! Burn!" one of the other guys says.

"Ouch!" another yells.

"Will you marry me?" comes from the back of the crowd.

Tanner and I chuckle as Quinn and Alex stare each other down, and I can't help wondering who'll break first.

Alex laughs. "Damn, woman. I think I just fell in love. Don't you worry. I will *definitely* be proving to you that my cock can speak for himself, and he is absolutely bigger than six inches."

"Yup, sure, that's what they all say, sugar. Let's go, Ash." She grabs my hand and turns to Tanner. "We'll be back, Superstar."

After we're out of earshot, I start talking, "Holy fucking shit, Quinn! I just ran into Jason downstairs. He was in full asshole mode like he was the one who came home and found me banging someone else in our bed. Talking all this shit, telling me how I look slutty tonight, saying I was trying to score free drinks and whatnot. I can't go there tonight. I can't have a walk down memory lane. I can't! I won't let him make me feel like shit." I know I'm only rambling because I'm getting worked up thinking about the effect those assholes from college still have on me.

"Whoa! Chill the fuck out and stay the hell away from that area of the past. Those guys were a bunch of sorry ass losers, just like Jason. Right now, I'm having fun and you're having fun and neither of us needs to deal with the emotional fallout of you bringing up the past. Let's get our drink on and forget about the dickless wonder. I mean, honestly, he isn't worth the amount of energy you're spending on his dumb ass! You have a seriously fuckable Superstar back there who's only looking at you. Why are we even talking about Jason?" This is why I need Quinn. She puts everything into perspective for me.

"You're right as usual," I admit taking a deep breath. "He is pretty damn sexy. Let's go get wasted. For the record, I'm not fucking Tanner tonight. I'm not ready for that. I'm just going to have a great time and see where it goes, but it won't be going in my vagina,"

Chapter Ten

TANNER

I **NOTICE HER** the moment she comes back into view. It's almost impossible not to. She's downright perfection tonight. With the way her dress hugs every magnificent curve of her body, I'm having a real hard time keeping my dick in check. All he wants to do is get closer to her. I can't say I disagree with him, but it's really uncomfortable walking around with a raging hard-on.

So far, the night has been really good, although Alex hasn't shut the fuck up about Ashley or her friend for the last ten minutes. He's captivated by Quinn, and it's fun to watch. I haven't seen anyone ever get to Alex like this.

The bastard better stick to trying to get with Quinn though, because if he touches Ashley again, I can't be held responsible for my actions. I'd really wanted to lay out the douchebag downstairs earlier. I'm almost positive Ashley has no clue how much of their little spat I heard from the way she shut down our conversation when I asked about it. I really want to know what that scene was all about. She looked pretty affected. I couldn't have been happier when she threw her drink on him, but I would've preferred it if she had thrown a fist—my fist—in his face instead. She stood up for herself, and that's enough for me. I'd have been happy to put that asshole in his place, but Ashley had it handled. Plus, I didn't want to charge into the situation not knowing what was really going on. It seems as though Ashley's the type to be guarded, and I think she probably would have closed herself off if she knew how much I really heard. The last thing I want is to push her farther into herself. I want to break her out. It's a compulsion that I have no control over.

I heard the douchebag say something about fucking Ashley not being worth my time. He must have some serious brain damage. Ashley is by far the most beautiful woman in the club tonight. It wouldn't be a hardship at all to sleep with her. Actually, it would be the highlight of my month. She isn't trying to catch my attention like so many of the woman here at the moment. They all think they're slick with their side glances and winks. So not sexy. Desperation is such a turn-off, and these women are throwing it out in spades.

"Hello, beautiful." I smile at her as she approaches.

The smile that lights up her face is bright enough to illuminate the whole floor. God, she's absolutely stunning, and I know she has no clue just how stunning she is, which makes her even more attractive.

"Hey there, handsome. What're you guys up to?" she asks. "I hope we aren't cramping your style tonight. I know you didn't plan on hanging out with us." Her insecurity is cute only because of how oblivious she is to the way every guy is looking at her.

"The minute I spotted you, I had no intention of being with anyone else for the rest of the night. I haven't stopped thinking about you since we had dinner, but everything has been so hectic. That article of yours has done wonders for my image, but not for my spare time." I laugh. "So what were your plans for the evening, baby?" I notice her shiver each time I call her 'baby.' I don't think she's even aware she does it, so she clearly isn't aware of how hard my cock gets when she shudders like that.

I can't remember having this problem before. No one has ever affected me this way. I've never called anyone 'baby', but with Ashley, it rolls off my tongue like second nature. I'm not kidding either, I haven't been able to get her off my mind.

Since I haven't been able to reach out to her, I've been checking out her other articles over the last few weeks, and she's been making nightly visits to my fantasies. It's as though she's inside my mind, taking control of me the instant I'm alone. I wonder what she's doing, if she's happy, how her day has been. Not to mention all the sexual positions I've pictured fucking her in.

She draws me back from thoughts of her ass, perched up in the air in the middle of my king size bed, to the present. "I'm checking this place out for my next review. Basically, my job is to get drunk on their fine martini selection and have a good time. I'm behind schedule, though. I need another drink," she says, holding up her now empty glass.

"Yes," Quinn adds. "You're nowhere near drunk enough. And nowhere near fulfilling my requirements of you this evening!"

Oh man, if looks could kill right now, Quinn might be on her death bed from the glare Ashley is shooting her way.

"And what were your requirements for this evening, Quinn? Maybe I can help Ashley here fulfill them," I offer, curious as to the reason Ashley's glaring daggers at her friend.

"Nothing you need to worry about, Tanner," Ashley answers before Quinn has the chance to respond.

"Umm, yes, he should worry. He can help you with them," Quinn says before turning her attention to me. "I told Ashley here she needs to loosen up, have fun, and find a hot man to help her with her plumbing problem. I still need to find my own bed-warmer for the night."

"Look no further, Angel! I'm right here. I'm already in love with you, so it only makes sense for you to take me home," Alex chimes in. "Let me show you how amazing and large my cock really is."

"Hmm, might take you up on that, sugar. Let's go test out your dance moves, and we'll take it from there. Ashley, we already know this fine-ass man over here can dance. So he can clearly hold a great fucking tempo. Case closed! Go get your vagina in working order again," Quinn calls over her shoulder as she drags Alex, who looks as happy as a pig in shit, toward the dance floor.

Ashley looks mortified, and I almost feel bad for her. "I swear to God some days I really don't know why I remain friends with that girl."

"Come on, let's get you another drink or three so you can lose your inhibitions and tell me more about your mission." I guide her over to the bar to order another scotch for myself and a blueberry martini for Ashley.

"She wasn't talking about anything. Ignore her," Ashley says, taking a sip of her drink.

"Oh yes, she was. Maybe you should explain before you accomplish your goal of getting drunk. That way you'll actually have control of what you tell me. Either way, I'll have my answer, baby." Right on cue, there's that little shiver I love.

"Let's just get drunk and dance. No need to talk now. Drink and dance. That sounds so much better." With that, she downs the rest of her martini.

Okay, we can play 'get Ashley drunk and dance.' Not the fun that I'd been hoping for, but fun nonetheless. I won't sleep with her if she's hell-bent on getting wasted. Not my thing. I never sleep with anyone super drunk, and it's a situation I don't want to find myself in. It hadn't really been my plan to sleep with Ashley tonight in the first place, but I wouldn't have minded if the night had taken a turn in that direction. She does make my dick hard as hell with her sexy little dance moves. I'm more than happy to see that the girls have a good time and make it home safely, though. *What the fuck is wrong with me?* I don't fuck random girls, and I don't play babysitter either.

"Alright, let's get you another drink. Then we can go sweat some of it off." I order another martini for her and then guide her to the dance floor. Ashley is on at least her fourth drink, and with those hot as hell fuck me shoes she's wearing, I'm betting that dancing isn't going to last long. So I take the lead, giving her something to lean on.

Feeling her ass sway against my cock is utterly amazing. I close my eyes and let the music take over, which probably isn't the best idea. Now all I can picture is fucking her, naked except for the heels, to the rhythm of the music. I add the fantasy to my list of things to do with Ashley as soon as I crack her shell.

After a few songs, I lean in and kiss the spot right behind her ear before I ask, "Want to go get another drink and sit, or do you want to keep dancing?" Ashley's become pretty off balance and her glass is empty again. I'm not sure if her martini has disappeared because she drank it or sloshed it all over the floor, but I'm feeling confident that Ashley's at her limit. I'll cut her off after this next one. I don't want her sick, after all, and I want to get her over to a couch before she can't stand anymore. If she falls in that dress, the whole damn club will see her pussy and possibly her tits as well. I can't have that. I'm the only one who's going to get to see any of Ashley's private parts tonight. Besides, her current state of mind is perfect for fishing out some answers.

"We can sit. I think that might be a good idea." She slurs, and I realize she may actually be further gone than I thought.

"Okay, baby, come on." I take her over to some oversized couches set up in the corner of the room and then head to the bar for drinks.

"Can I have another Scotch, a peach martini, and two bottles of water, please?" Ashley certainly needs to get some water in her, and some food. As I walk back toward her, I decide to order some appetizers when I next see a waiter. I'm hoping the water will distract her after she finishes this round because she probably won't like it when I cut her off.

When I get back to the couch, I hand her the bottle of water first. "Here you go. Are you having a good time? Going to give them a good review?" I ask, wanting to get her talking.

"Without a doubt. This place is fantastic. What were you doing here tonight? You never said. I mean, you already know why I'm here. What about you guys? It's so great to see you! And your friends seem really awesome. You didn't really introduce anyone, though. You'll have to tell me their names." Aww, drunk Ashley rambles. I love it. This conversation is going to be fun, and I doubt she'll remember much of it tomorrow.

"Some of the guys and I decided that we wanted to have a laid back night out, and everyone's talking about this place. It was a no brainer to come check it out ourselves."

"Some of the guys, huh? And how do you know the guys?" she asks, sipping on her martini.

"Well, Alex and I have been best buds since high school. He's actually one of the team's trainers. The rest of the guys are my teammates," I say.

"Holy crap! You mean I've been partying it up in the hottest club around with the hottest quarterback around and his whole team as well? No wonder I'm getting death stares from all the chicks around here. Makes much more sense now." She giggles. Great, that last drink has given her the giggles. If she were any other chick, I'd be gone already. I can't stand drunken giggling. My sisters are famous for it.

"Yup, so you want to tell me what Quinn was talking about earlier? Having a plumbing problem?"

"Fuck Quinn and her big mouth. She has no idea what she's talking about. My plumbing's fine. Vaginas don't magically close after seven months without sex. I mean, seriously, where she comes up with her logic is beyond me. It's not my fault I have morals and can't sleep around guilt-free like her." Ah, so there's been no one warming her bed for the last seven months. That knowledge makes my inner primitive caveman extremely happy.

"No, I have to say I agree with you there, I don't think vaginas close up after a few months either. So the dickhead downstairs was an ex?"

"Ugh, please don't bring him up. I have no desire to talk about that fucktard. He's made my life hell since we broke up. I don't want to think about him or his dirty dick." Her face has gone a shade redder, and her eyes have hardened into an angry glare.

Okay, she really doesn't want to talk about him. I need to tread lightly here and change the subject.

"I'm sorry, did you say dirty dick?" I chuckle, hoping to lighten the mood. "How does one get a dirty dick? I'm just curious."

"Well, you get a dirty dick when you start sticking it in places it doesn't belong."

And now the bitterness makes sense... Time for a detour before Ashley gets too caught up in her anger and the night is ruined. "Well, fuck him then. You're on to bigger and better things now."

A big smile spreads across her face.

That's an improvement.

"Bigger and better, huh?" Before I know it, Ashley is backward in my lap, dancing.

"Ashley, baby, what're you doing?"

"What does it look like I'm doing?" she asks over her shoulder. "I want to see this bigger and better that I've moved onto."

"Baby, here isn't the place to test drive." I don't want her to regret making a scene in the club. No one seems to be paying attention to us, but you never know when there might be an unseen cell phone camera rolling.

"Then let's take this some place where I can test drive."

Goddamn, I would love nothing more. "Ashley, you're a bit drunk. No need to wake up with regrets in the morning. But I'll gladly take you home if you're ready to leave."

"No regrets. Take me home." Her ass is still moving against my dick. In a move that I don't think most strippers could pull off, Ashley has turned herself in my lap without standing. Her tits are now close enough for me to pull a nipple into my mouth without lifting a finger.

Fuck, how I wish she weren't drunk and we were in private. "Ash..."

That's all I get out before her mouth is on mine. Her lips are soft and plump and definitely on a mission. They move against mine, and her tongue licks along the seam of my lips, seeking entrance. I open my mouth and take over the kiss. Her mouth is heaven. I can taste the peach from that last martini on her tongue. I push my tongue farther into her mouth, probing, searching for the inner secrets of Ashley.

Her hands come up to my neck. She glides them back and up into my hair, making *me* shiver this time. Running my hands up her exposed back, I savor the feel of her soft skin. I tangle my fingers in her hair and pull her closer to me as I delve a little further into her mouth before pulling away.

"Baby, there's nothing more I'd love to do than continue this, but we need to get out of here before we wind up all over the Internet. I'll call for the car." I say leaning in for a quick, chaste kiss before moving Ashley off my lap and onto the couch so I can grab my phone and call my driver.

"Come on," I say after hanging up. "The car will be here by the time we get downstairs." I pull her up off the couch, and we head to the elevator. "Where's your phone? You should send a text to Quinn to let her know you're leaving. I'm going to have Alex make sure she gets home safe."

"Oh, I'm sure that he'll make sure she gets home all right. I'm sure he'll make sure she gets safely into bed as well. Underneath him." She laughs, her giggles returning. "Damn, that was a lot of *sure*s for one sentence."

"It sure was," I laugh.

When we reach the bottom floor, Reggie is there waiting with the car. I usher Ashley into the back of the limo.

"We heading home, Boss?" Reggie asks, holding the car door open for us.

"Not one hundred percent sure, Reg. Let's head that way, though. Either way, we'll be heading in the same direction. "

"You got it." Reg closes the door.

Ash almost immediately finds the mini bar in the back and grabs a bottle of champagne.

"You think that's a good idea?" I ask.

"Of course. We need to toast."

"What are we toasting?" I take the glass from her hand and let her fill it.

"It's not every night I leave a club with the hottest guy there. I think it's mandatory to have a toast to that, don't you?" Her glass is already half empty.

"Yes, I will absolutely toast to leaving the club with the most beautiful woman there."

Ashley's cheeks flush a pretty shade of pink, and she finishes her drink before setting the glass down on the table at the end of the bench seat. I sip my champagne as I watch Ashley, who seems to be thinking. Suddenly, her eyes set with determination, as though she's made her mind up about something. In the time it takes me to blink, Ashley is on her knees between my legs.

"What are you doing?" I ask.

She doesn't answer me but reaches for my belt to undo it.

"Ashley, baby, what are you doing?"

"Shh, Superstar. So many questions." Her deft fingers pull my belt from its loops and go to work on my zipper. My dick is screaming at me to shut up and enjoy what seems to be coming our way, but my conscience has other ideas.

"You don't need to do that. Why don't you come up here and sit next to me?"

"I'd rather be down here," she smirks. This woman must be a magician because she already has my dick out, stroking me from root to tip with a sure rhythm and the perfect amount of pressure.

"Ahh…" My moan is out before I can stop it.

"Sit back and enjoy. Turn off your pretty little head."

That's it. I'm done for. I have no resolve left to be a gentleman.

Her tiny little hand is wrapped perfectly around my extremely hard cock, still stroking up and down in the same amazing rhythm.

"Yes, sweetheart, just like that. It feels amazing." I've never been one to really get into a hand job, but with Ashley's hand working its magic, it feels fucking fantastic. I lean back and close my eyes. Then I feel it—her hot breath at the tip of my dick. It's physically impossible for me to get any harder without my dick straight up exploding.

I open my eyes just in time to see her little pink tongue circle around the head, her eyes are set on mine, staring at me with a gleam in them. The perfect seductress. I lock eyes with her as she closes her mouth around the tip of my cock and adds a little suction. She swirls her tongue around it a few times before she takes my whole length into her mouth. God damn. I feel her throat contract around me, and I'm lost to the pleasure that courses through me with each bob of her head and swirl of her tongue. I can't fight the need to lean my head back and close my eyes. Ashley licks and sucks as though I'm the best tasting lollipop she's ever had. She uses her other hand to cup and roll my balls.

Holy shit. This is the best blowjob I've ever had. I'm not a small guy in the dick department, but Ashley doesn't seem to be fazed by my size. Jesus, could this woman be any more perfect? She lets me fall from her mouth and uses both hands to continue stroking me, watching me intently, studying each one of my reactions.

Watching me while she strokes my cock is so fucking hot and I feel the ooze of pre-cum. In a truly erotic fashion, Ashley leans over and licks the cum from my dick as though it's a rare delicacy and moans.

"Mmm," she says, and the moment she puts her fabulous mouth back on me, I know I'm a goner.

She pulls me back fully into her mouth and massages my dick with her tongue. "That's it. Fucking Christ, your mouth is amazing."

She moans at my praise, leaving me about to explode.

"Ashley, baby, if you don't want me to come in your mouth, you should stop now because I can't hold on any longer with your tongue working me like that."

The next second, my mind goes blank as she increases her speed on my dick and her hand gives my balls a little squeeze, and I think I nearly black out. My orgasm takes total control of my body. My balls draw up, and my whole body shakes slightly with each eruption of cum from my engorged head.

Ashley swallows every drop and licks my dick completely clean. After she's satisfied with the cleanliness of my cock, she sits back on her legs and smiles at me as she licks her lips clean.

Holy fuck. I've never been more turned on in my life by any woman. Her assertiveness and take charge attitude are hot as hell. I'm usually not a fan of oral sex, but right now, I can barely remember my own name, let alone my usual disdain for blowjobs. She's managed to wipe my mind entirely clean. I hadn't been able to think of anything other than the need to come. *Jesus Christ, what the fuck is going on, and when can I get more of that?* If she can make me lose it like that with some good head, I can only imagine what her pussy squeezing my cock can do.

Chapter Eleven

ASHLEY

I'M **STARTLED AWAKE** from my nightmare by a throbbing headache. My surroundings seem off. The bed is comfortable and warm, but everything feels wrong. I'm wrapped in silk instead of cotton, and the pillow under my head isn't broken in like mine. All I can smell is a delicious scent of male cologne, but it turns my already gurgling stomach.

As I look around, parts of last night come flooding back to me. Dancing at the club, the mystery guy dancing with me turning out to be Tanner, running into Jason, getting totally wasted, making out with Tanner in the VIP section of the club, and then giving him a blowjob in the back of his limo. *Oh my God! What on Earth was I thinking?* I practically threw myself on his dick without giving him a choice. I think I even remember him telling me not to do it. I'm such a slut.

The guilt wells up as I look over at him lying next to me. What's he going to say when he wakes up? How am I going to face him? I haven't been sexually aggressive in a long time—since that stupid frat party in college. You'd think I would've learned my lesson. But no, I'm just stupid and easy, and Tanner probably thinks the same thing.

My mind wanders back to the memory of the night that has fucked with my mind for the past seven years, the same memory I'd been trapped in before I'd woken up to this hangover.

It was my freshman year of college, and I'd decided to do what every other girl was doing—explore my sexuality. One of the fraternities was throwing a costume party. Quinn's master plan had been to go all out getting sexified. She'd picked out our costumes: Wonder Woman for her and Tinker Bell for me.

The frat house had been packed. I danced all night with hot guy after hot guy and was having the time of my life. It was the first time that I'd ever really let myself go. This gorgeous senior named Logan was giving me his undivided attention, and I soaked it up. I hadn't thought twice about heading back up to his room. I refused to give him my name so I could experiment anonymously.

When we got to his room, I hadn't hesitated to take off my clothes. Next thing I knew, Logan had me pinned up against the door, and things had gotten hot and heavy quickly. I'm pretty sure we had sex on every surface of his room. After he'd had me against the door, we'd hit the floor, his desk, and then ended on the bed, trying a new position at every stop. The sex was fantastic, and I was more than satisfied by the time we were done.

When he'd gone to the bathroom to clean up, I'd put my costume back on, fixed my hair and make-up, and run off to find Quinn. Finding her hadn't been as easy as one might have thought. I grabbed a beer and walked around, waiting for her to surface. As I was heading out to the back deck, I rounded the corner only to see Logan there with his friends. A smile spread across my face as I thought about all the dirty things we'd just done not twenty minutes earlier. Then I caught what he was saying.

"Yeah, man, that hot little piece of ass was easier than I thought. She was a dirty little slut too. Man, I fucked her on every part of my room. Door, floor, bed, and desk. I didn't even have to work for it, and she told me exactly what she wanted. Talk about an easy fuck, man. She was gone when I came back from the bathroom. Couldn't have gone any better. I love when these skanks know their place and don't make me kick them

out. If anyone sees a green fairy, chat her up and you might just get laid too," Logan suggested.

I was mortified. That was what guys actually thought of girls who didn't mind getting a little dirty and giving some direction? I didn't think I was a slut, and I was so glad that he had no idea who I really was. That sort of reputation was the last thing I needed. I couldn't believe that was what he was telling people. What an asshole. Suddenly, all I wanted to do was get the hell out of there, wash his scent off my skin, and cry myself to sleep.

As if by pure magic, Quinn appeared out of nowhere right at that moment. "Hey, sweets! Having fun? Isn't this party great?" she asked with way too much enthusiasm for me to deal with in my now shitty mood.

"No, it isn't, and I need to leave now!" Before I ran into Logan or one of his friends.

"Okay, Ash. What the hell happened? Are you alright?"

I pulled Quinn toward the door before she could finish her question. "I need to go home and shower. Until five minutes ago, tonight was great, but now we need to get the fuck out of here. I'll explain everything later."

I'd spent the rest of that night showering and crying, telling Quinn everything that happened. She listened patiently to everything and then wrapped me up in a hug and told me not to believe a word that shithead had said. She insisted that he was just a dumbass trying to make himself look better in front of his friends. I wished it had stopped there. Logan told everyone he could from his frat about our escapades that night. I spent the entire semester thinking people were going to figure out I was the slutty fairy. I wouldn't have been able to handle all of those guys knowing I was the girl they all talked about.

The shame of how I felt that night hasn't dissipated. It still rears its ugly head at times, like right now.

I need to get the hell out of here before Tanner wakes up. The last thing I think I could handle would be seeing him look at me with disgust in his eyes. I shift and scoot slowly until I'm out from under his arm and off the bed. Grabbing my dress and shoes from the floor, I head off to find my purse. I don't remember the layout of his house from last night, but I head down the stairs at the end of the hallway. I find myself standing in what I assume is the foyer. As I stop for a minute and take a look around, noticing how amazing this place is. It's one huge open floor.

The foyer, kitchen, dining room and living room are all one combined space. Two sliders lead out to a large deck area. All the tones are very neutral, not what I would expect for a bachelor's place. Looking out the windows, I'm sure the view must be amazing at night. The kitchen is a dream, all black and white with stainless steel appliances. There's a huge center island on top of which I see my purse sitting. I walk over to it as quietly as possible to grab my phone and call for a cab.

Realizing I don't know the address, I fish through the drawers trying to find a piece of mail or something with the address on it. I'm rifling through the one at the end of the island when Tanner makes an appearance, stretching and yawning.

"Find what you're looking for?" he asks with a smirk on his face.

Christ! Why couldn't he put on a shirt?

He stands there in gray sweatpants that hang low on his hips. His happy trail draws my eyes right down to the impressive bulge just below it. His perfectly chiseled chest and abs don't do anything to help my concentration either. *Great, I'm the slut in his kitchen who can't stop ogling him.*

"Umm... I was just looking for something that had the address on it so I can give it to the cab company." Since he's awake, I guess he can just give it to me instead.

He flashes me a puzzled look before walking over and wrapping his hands around my waist. He pulls me to him, the heat radiating from his chest feels so good, but it makes me uncomfortable. So uncomfortable that I'm stiff as a statue in his arms.

"All right, what in the world is going on in that beautiful head of yours? You sneak out of bed, and then you're on a stealth mission to get out of here before I wake up. You couldn't be tenser if you tried. Care to explain?"

Damn, why does he have to be so perceptive? "I was just trying to save everyone the awkwardness and get out of here before things got weird," I explain honestly since the man seems like a human lie detector.

"Okay, I don't even know where I should start with that nonsense, but it's obvious we need to talk, so sit. I'll make us some coffee."

"No, it's alright. Just call me a cab, and I'll get out of your hair." I don't want to hear him tell me how last night was great and blah, blah, blah. I'd rather leave now. I could kill my drunk self for getting the sober, hung-over me into this mess.

"I see you've put your walls back up. Guess I'll have to knock 'em back down again. Have a seat, Ashley. You're not slipping out of my house first thing in the morning like a one-night stand taking her walk of shame. You aren't leaving before we address last night because God only knows where your mind is right now. But wherever it is, I don't like it. We're going to get things straightened out now. Sit!" Tanner orders.

I'm kind of turned on despite my humiliation at being caught trying to sneak out. Sitting as told, I watch Tanner put one of those little K-Cup pods into the coffee maker. He grabs the cream and sugar and puts them on the counter in front of me before turning back to grab the freshly brewed mug of coffee for me. After he hits the start button to brew a mug for himself, he turns to face me once again.

I put a spoonful of sugar in my coffee and add a little cream. Stirring it, I watch Tanner watching me.

When his coffee has finished brewing, he grabs the cream to add some to his cup. After finally taking a sip of his coffee, he looks at me and says, "Start talking, baby. I don't like all the tension in this room, and none of it's coming from me."

"I don't know what it is that you want to talk about."

"Let's start with why you were trying to sneak out of my house like a thief in the night. That's a good place."

"I wasn't trying to sneak out, just heading home. I don't understand what the big deal is." I don't get why he's harping on my escape attempt when most guys would be happy to avoid dealing with their conquest from the night before.

"It's a big deal because you were planning on leaving without so much as saying a word. You could've easily woken me up and asked for a ride home if that's really what you were worried about. But it's not, so

I want to know what the real problem is. Don't give me some bullshit line either. Don't insult my intelligence, Ashley."

His demanding to know pisses me off. Haven't I been embarrassed enough this morning? Does he really need me to vocalize it? "The real problem? I practically threw myself at you last night while I was wasted. I gave you a blowjob you didn't even want in the back of a car on the way home. I woke up knowing the only reason I was still here was because I'd passed out on the way home, not because you wanted me here. So what was the point of sticking around for this awkward conversation?" I'm angry, but I'm also shocked I just said all that. Talk about diarrhea of the mouth.

"Jesus Christ, woman, I don't even know where to start with that. Come here." He sets his coffee down and pushes off the counter, bringing himself to his full height of six-foot-three.

I continue to sit, staring at him.

"Please don't make me ask you again."

I get off the bar stool and walk over to him. He pulls me to his chest and lifts my chin to make me look at him.

"If I didn't want you here, *you would not be here*. I know where you live. Remember? Even if I had brought you here just to sleep it off, you would've slept in the guest room. Not my bed. Not in my arms. As far as throwing yourself at me, think again. I haven't seen anything hotter than you last night, taking what you wanted when you wanted it. I can't tell you how amazing you made me feel, and the fact that you're sneaking out of here like you have something to be ashamed of really pisses me off. Do you regret last night?" His expression grows serious, almost angry.

What does he have to be angry about? "I... Umm... I don't..." I stutter, not sure what the hell I'm even feeling. I'm pissed, humiliated, and angry, but I'm also turned on by the authority in his voice.

"You don't what?"

"I don't regret last night. I just... I just didn't want you to think that I was that chick, you know?" *Holy hell... Did he pour truth serum in my coffee?*

"Why the hell would I think poorly of you? You didn't do anything that would make me think anything bad of you. If anything, I think you're far more amazing than I did twenty-four hours ago. So help me understand, please."

"I was pretty slutty last night, and I didn't want to wait around in case *you* regretted it. I know you could do better than me, and I just didn't want to be here when you realized what kind of girl you took home." My anger has all faded away, and I hear my voice waver. I feel as though I could cry. I don't know how he's pulling all of this out of me, and I'm even more embarrassed now than I had been when I woke up this morning.

"Oh, baby, there's nothing slutty about you. You're amazing, sexy, and I could never regret a minute that I spent with you. My only regret last night was that you were too drunk for me to get a taste of you. I don't ever want you to feel that way about yourself again, especially not with me. There is nothing sexier than a woman who knows what she wants in the bedroom. Your confidence was such a turn on. It's not that I didn't want what you gave me. I was just trying to be a gentleman. As you can see, I couldn't resist you for more than a minute." He kisses the top of my head and playfully smacks my ass. "Now, let's swing by your place so you can change, and we'll go get breakfast and continue this conversation."

He found me a turn on last night? And he isn't trying to kick me out, but wants to take me to breakfast? I'm so confused that I don't know where to begin. Well, my body knows where it wants to begin, but my brain is a whole other story.

Chapter Twelve

ASHLEY

"**DO YOU HAVE** to be at the office today?" Tanner asks on the drive to my apartment.

"No, I just need to hand in the rough draft of my article about Levitate by three o'clock. You really don't need to take me to breakfast. I'm sure you have plenty to do today." Part of me wants him to drop me off and leave. I'm still overwhelmed by everything that has happened in the last twelve hours, and I need some time to process.

"The only thing I have to do today, besides figuring out what is going on in that busy mind of yours, is check on travel plans for this Sunday's game and swing by my mom's," he says as though he isn't a famous quarterback and has all the time in the world.

"Fine, but can we go somewhere normal like a diner? Not a place like the restaurant you picked for dinner." I'm not a girl who's into places where I have to be dressed up just to order some eggs. Too over-the-top for me.

"You want to go to a diner?" he asks as though I've said something so foreign it might as well not be English.

"Yes. A diner with greasy hangover food where I can go eat in yoga pants and a t-shirt." As if on cue, my stomach growls, making me laugh.

"A diner it is then. You really are something else. I don't think I've ever met another woman as easy as you," he smirks at me.

"I think I proved that last night," I sigh, remembering my unsavory behavior again. *Great first sexual impression on the man, Ashley.*

"That's not how I meant it and you know it. I thought we already discussed this, but I guess we'll have to explore it further," he says as we pull up to my building.

"Do you want to come in or wait in the car?" I really don't want him to come in, but it would be rude of me not to ask him.

"Actually, I'm going to take care of a few calls while you get ready so that I can give you my full attention at breakfast." He smiles his million-dollar smile at me and then adds, "We're going to get this situation between us settled once and for all. You can count on that."

What in the world does that mean? Seriously, Tanner's like a hurricane. He comes in full force, demanding to know all the thoughts in my head. He seems to see right through me, as though I have a dialogue bubble above my head displaying everything I think.

Understandably, I'm nervous about breakfast. He has this unbelievable ability to make me spill all my thoughts without hesitation. I don't want to give him all my inner thoughts and dirty little secrets. I'm not ready to be that exposed to anyone. I have a feeling that he's going to ask about Jason, and I have no idea what I'm going to tell him. He'll know if I'm lying. I don't know how, but he will, so I need to figure out a game plan before I get there. I can tell the truth, I can just tell him that he cheated on me. There's no reason to go into the embarrassing footnotes. Omitting isn't the same as lying.

I take a quick shower, change my clothes, brush my teeth and throw on a minimal amount of makeup. After about ten minutes of rushing to get ready, I head back down to his car. He's already seen me at my worst in the morning light, so I don't have to put in much effort to look better than that. I'm already well aware that I'm nowhere near as beautiful as the woman he's usually seen with. Damn, maybe I should have thought about that before I left the apartment. Now I feel really self-conscious. I'm just a plain Jane, and he's used to Malibu Melissa. Sometimes it's easy to forget who he is because he doesn't act like a famous athlete at all. Even with hours to prepare and the most expensive dresses in Quinn's closet at my disposal, I still wouldn't look nearly as good as the women he's used to. Probably why he enjoyed last night. He didn't even have to work for it. I'm sure that his usual type makes him put in a lot more effort. With looks like theirs, he probably falls at their feet.

"What's with the frown, gorgeous?" he asks after I've hopped in and buckled my seat belt.

"Nothing," I say quietly. I need to leave the pity party home. We're just having breakfast. It's not like we're a couple or anything.

"More bullshit, huh? Is that today's special or something? Because you seem to be serving a lot of it up this morning."

Jesus Christ. Can't I just have a moment to myself to be insecure? "No bullshit. I'm fine," I tell him, sporting a smile.

"The fake smile gives you away even more."

"What the hell? Are you a secret CIA agent trained to spot lies?" I ask annoyed. How the fuck does he read me like that? It's starting to piss me off.

"No, I'm just used to seeing people fake it until they make it, and I can tell the difference when you're lying because your face gives you away. It's completely different from your normal, carefree face that I happen to like much better." He smiles. "So are you going to tell me what's wrong or are we going to sit here all day?"

"Ugh, I hate that you do this to me. I'm fine, okay? I was just thinking that it might have been better to put a little more effort into my appearance considering that you're *you.* I forget sometimes because you don't seem like a famous person."

"Why do you do that to yourself? Have I given you the impression that I'm embarrassed to be seen with you? You were the most beautiful woman at the club last night. You were the most beautiful woman in the restaurant when we went to dinner. You're not only beautiful, but you care, which is hard to find. There's nothing wrong with you. I don't want to hear you say one more negative thing about yourself for the rest of the day, got it?"

I stare out the window, thinking about what he's just said. I don't see it myself, but this isn't the first time he's called me the hottest chick.

"What's so funny?" he asks when I start to chuckle.

"I'm just thinking that maybe you've taken one too many hits to the head during games."

"What did I just get done saying? No more negative shit. I *have not* been sacked enough to have brain damage. One concussion in all my years of football. Nothing wrong with my brain, baby."

"If you say so," I reply with a snarky smile.

We drive to the diner in a comfortable silence, which strikes me as odd because car silence usually isn't comfortable—especially when you're with someone you don't know all that well. I suppose I'll just add it to the list of unexplainable occurrences between Tanner and me.

"So what's up with your friend calling you Tag last night?" I ask as we pull into the diner parking lot.

"Those are my initials. It goes back to high school. The only people who really call me that are Alex and Melissa." He ushers me into the diner, his hand at the small of my back.

Chills run up my spine and down my arms, and I'm not sure if they're because of his hand on my back or the mention of Melissa. I'd completely forgotten about his potential girlfriend. I might as well have just had an ice bucket dumped over my head because the mention of her makes me freeze.

"What is Melissa to you really? I mean, you know what everyone says about you two, and I don't want to be that girl. You know, the one who… umm... messes with another woman's man."

Tanner stops midstride and turns to face me. His face looks drawn, and for a second I'm worried that I've stepped over a line I shouldn't have.

Too bad. I need to know. I know what it's like to have someone else sleep, and lord knows what else, with my boyfriend. I won't be the one to do that to someone else, no matter who the guy in question is.

"No, Melissa is *not* my girlfriend. She's a very good friend, probably the best friend I have after Alex."

"Oh, okay." Hearing him say they're just friends makes me feel slightly better. If they're just friends, we aren't doing anything wrong. I decide to put off thinking about Melissa for now.

"You don't seem convinced. We can discuss my relationship with Melissa at the table."

"No, it's fine. You don't need to explain anything to me." I must sound like a needy little girl. Not the impression I want to give. Although I'm still trying to figure out why I give two shits about what Tanner thinks of me.

"Sweetheart, you are killing me. What happened to that 'take what I want' girl from last night? Hmm?" Tanner asks as we slide into a booth.

Good question. I could use a Quinn pep talk right about now. I try to think of what she would say to me. Thinking of her makes me wonder what ended up happening with her and Alex last night.

"Have you heard from Alex this morning? I wonder if he and Quinn left together last night. They seem like a match made in heaven. I haven't seen anyone get to Quinn like that in... Actually, I don't think I've ever seen anyone get under Quinn's skin like Alex before." I laugh.

"No, I haven't." He laughs too. "But given the way they were behaving last night, I think it might be a while until they crawl out from under each other."

We laugh together as we recount Quinn and Alex's interactions from last night until the waitress comes over.

"Are you ready to order?" she asks.

I'm starving, so I jump at the idea of food. "Yes, I'll have scrambled eggs, bacon, and French toast, please. And a coffee."

Tanner looks at me in disbelief, laughing, but remembers himself after a moment. "I'll have a ham and cheese omelet with toast and an orange juice, please."

"What's so funny?" I ask after the waitress leaves.

"Not many women would order a breakfast that big and do it with so much excitement in their eyes. It's nice to see."

"Well, I don't mess around with breakfast. It's the most important meal of the day." I smile, pleased with myself for not thinking twice about ordering my big meal.

"Yes, it is. An important meal to go along with an important conversation," he adds pointedly, looking me directly in the eye.

I can't hold his stare and suddenly feel nervous. "Umm...what important conversation?"

"I'm going to be very blunt with you. I like you. I've liked you since you walked into that conference room. I like you even more after last night." He smirks. "I want to explore this pull between us and see where it goes. That being said, there seems to be some reluctance from you. Your escape attempt this morning is a huge red flag. I don't think I've done anything to make you feel uncomfortable. If I have, let me know. Otherwise, I think we should just have a nice get to know you conversation. I want to get to know you in many, many ways."

I feel the blush creeping up my neck to my jaw and all the way to my ears. *Holy shit! Tanner Garrison wants to get to know me? Me, Ashley Mitchell!* What the hell am I supposed to do now? No way can I keep this guy's interest if I couldn't even keep dipshit Jason happy. What am I supposed to say to that? My head is spinning. If I don't stop it, I'm afraid it might take flight.

"Okay, whatever you're thinking, *stop*! Start talking out loud so I can help you with whatever you're thinking," Tanner insists, interrupting my runaway thought train.

I snap my head up to stare at him. I feel so lost. What the fuck is wrong with me? I'm a pretty, confident, independent woman. How has this man turned me into a twelve-year-old girl at a Justin Bieber concert?

"What do you mean by 'see where it goes'?"

"I mean I want to hang out, do things together, and have sex..." He smiles deviously, "A lot. And see where this thing between us goes."

"You want to be a couple?" I ask, utterly shocked. A couple. I'd thought for sure he would want a "Wham, bam, thank you, ma'am." With the way I keep repeating his questions, I'm fairly certain he thinks I have some kind of comprehension disorder, but let's face it, I don't understand a goddamn thing that's going on right now.

"I'd like to think it's possible for us to get there. In the meantime, I'd like to spend time together and get to know each other, date and let things develop."

"So you really don't have a girlfriend? Is there honestly nothing going on with you and Melissa? I won't be the other woman."

"There is nothing going on with Melissa. We're not in a romantic relationship. I'll tell you more about her if that makes you feel better," he says with a tone to his voice that sounds like a combination of annoyance and anger, maybe even a little bit of pity. Well, too fucking bad.

"Would you, please?" If he tells me about the relationship they have, then I may feel more comfortable. I need to feel secure in the knowledge he isn't dating Melissa before anything else happens.

"Melissa and I have been friends since college. She's probably my only real friend other than Alex. I don't date. I haven't dated since college. I don't trust very many people, as you already know. Most people just want something from me. I think you're different, which is why I'm not opposed to trying to make us work. Melissa and I have an arrangement, I guess. Yes, we sleep together. I guess 'friends with benefits' would be an appropriate name for it. But we aren't in a relationship per se. She's free to do whatever she pleases, as am I. It's just sex to us. She's usually my plus one when I need a date for events when I don't have a reason to go with someone specific. I guess that's why we've been labeled a couple. Since I don't date, I've stopped trying to correct the press. Besides, they're going to write whatever they want anyway."

Our food arrives just as he finishes up his explanation. He's given me a lot to take in. Even if Tanner and Melissa aren't a couple, they've been having sex for years. I'm sure that means something to her, because it would mean something to me, and that unsettles me.

"Are you sure that it's not a relationship to her? I mean, if I were sleeping with a man for so long, it would be more than sex to me."

"Melissa is one of the coolest girls I've ever met. She's practically one of the guys. She's easy-going and totally knows we aren't in a relationship. I'll introduce the two of you, and you can see for yourself," he says between bites.

"Umm, okay. If you think that's a good idea." I don't know that I think it is.

"I do. Now let's talk about you. What's the deal with the douchebag from last night?" Damn, getting right to the heavy-hitting questions. I guess it's only fair since I started with Melissa and their status is a sore spot for him.

"He's my ex, Jason."

"I'd figured that out before we left the club. Why was he being such an asshole?" He asks sternly.

"Good question. I have no idea why he was being such a dick. He's the one who fucked me over, and yet he's the one acting scorned." I still can't wrap my head around Jason's nasty attitude, but I don't know why I should care either.

"So you found him in bed with someone else?" he asks point blank.

How the fuck did he know that?

He must see the question on my face because he answers it before I can get a chance to voice it. "I overheard. I didn't want your night to be ruined, so I didn't say anything. Although, I really wanted to lay him the fuck out."

"Yes, I found him in bed with someone else." I admit, refusing to give any more details. I'm so embarrassed. Just what you want someone you're about to start something with to know. Yay, me!

I don't want to look up from my food, which I've suddenly lost all interest in eating, to see whatever pity is on his face. He's probably wondering what the hell is wrong with me since I couldn't keep Jason happy. I'm still trying to figure that out myself. I'm tempted to excuse myself from the table right now and go cry in the bathroom.

"Ashley, look at me."

I don't want to. I don't want him to see the shame on my face, but I can't resist his command. My eyes travel up from my plate to meet his, which I find burning with an emotion I can't decipher. *Please don't let that be pity. Please, anything but pity.*

"That says much more about him than it does about you. I'm not going to judge you for something that asshole did. I, of all people, know what it's like to want people to see the real you. Please don't hide from me. Don't hide from this," he says, gesturing between us.

Sighing, I reply, "I'll try, but I need you to give me a little time. This—" I gesture between us as well "—is overwhelming, and now you know that I'm still hurting. I don't mean to hide, but I'm going to need some patience from you. The fact that you're *you* doesn't help my nerves." I smile.

"I'm just me. You see more of me than plenty of people who've known me a lot longer. Now, next important piece of business: Why the hell were you sneaking out this morning? Why would you think that I wouldn't want you around?" He gives me a hard stare.

Should I tell him the truth? It might help in the long run. Maybe I could open up with Tanner and be the real me like he says. I'm tired of being the girl who is scared, and I'm sure he's heard much juicier stories than mine. It probably won't seem all that big to him. But I'm not in the mood to completely strip myself bare at the moment, and I haven't been a great judge of character in the past. I'm not sure I trust myself with him. Maybe I'm just being blinded by his God-like looks.

"That's a can of worms that I'm not ready to open yet," I say, making eye contact to press my point. Since he seems to be so good at reading me, he should know better than to push the topic.

"Why not?" he asks in an irritated tone.

"Because I'm not. Don't you think you've found out enough personal and embarrassing things about me for the time being?" I snap. "Excuse me if I don't feel like spilling all my guts to you right away. You aren't the only one who doesn't trust people."

He steeples his fingers and leans forward to rest his chin on them. With a serious look, he says, "I'm not one for playing games. I've given you no reason to doubt me. I understand you've been hurt, but I won't pay for the sins of another for long. I'm not Jason, and I don't appreciate being placed in the same category as him." The tone of insult rings in his words. That wasn't what I'd intended, but I won't be bullied into baring my soul.

"I'm sorry if you feel I've lumped you together with him. I never meant to imply that you're like him, but you also can't expect me to be a doormat. Obviously, I've been there before and won't ever be again. I'm sure you have reasons as to why you don't date, and I'm not just talking about not wanting to be used. You don't see me pressing you for an autobiography over breakfast, so please extend me the same courtesy. I didn't say that I'd never tell you. I just said not yet. Trust needs to be earned. I'm sure that you can relate to that."

He smirks and replies, "Actually, I can. You make a very good point. And to be honest, your little act of defiance is hot and absolutely refreshing. I don't want a doormat. I want an equal. I can see this thing between us being really good. But I do expect one-hundred percent honesty. It's the only way this will work. We need honesty in every part of this relationship." He winks.

Every part of this relationship? What relationship? This isn't a relationship yet. What the hell does he want to know?

"So what do you think, Ashley? Do you think we can get to know each other and give this a chance? "

"Honestly, I'd like to. Just please be gentle with me. It's going to take me a little bit to open up, but I'll try." *I really will.* Tanner is somehow profoundly different from all the other men I've ever met, but that doesn't mean I won't play this game a little defensively. I won't be completely blindsided again.

Chapter Thirteen

TANNER

I'M NOT ABLE to concentrate during the meeting with the team. I can't stop thinking about breakfast with Ashley this morning. She's such an enigma. She's gorgeous on the outside, and I get the feeling she has a wild sexual streak hidden inside. I wonder if she even knows it. But on the inside, she's a nervous, introverted woman. She can be chatty and outgoing, but when she thinks too hard, she goes back to being a scared little girl. I haven't figured her out just yet, and there's nothing more that I want to do. I know I sound like a total pussy, but I don't give a shit. There's something about this woman that has my whole life turned upside down, and I haven't even fucked her yet.

The minute I'd set eyes on her, the inexplicable connection had taken over. God, I can't get her out of my head. Her beautiful eyes remind me of the ocean in the Caribbean. The color changes along with her emotions. They give away her thoughts if you look closely enough. She has a natural beauty about her that's completely rare. I guess it's only fitting since her character is just as rare. The best part is that she has no idea how absolutely beautiful she really is.

She'd sat at breakfast this morning thinking she couldn't compare to the women I'm usually with, but the truth is that she's far superior to any woman I've ever met. It's obvious that her dipshit ex has fucked her up mentally. I hate that I'm going to be paying the price for his mistakes, but Ashley's right: Trust is earned. I'll just have to show her that she has nothing to worry about with me. I'll break open the shell she's hiding behind. I'll be the one to show her that one shithead doesn't define her worth. The fact that I want to get close to her has me thrown for a loop. I never want to get anywhere near other people emotionally, and I don't trust anyone either. It's been a real head trip for me.

The way Ashley is worried says a lot about her. I know that she's attracted to me, but she wasn't willing to do anything about it—aside from the drunken but ultimately amazing blowjob—until she was sure there was nothing going on with Melissa. Most women would have jumped at the chance to roll around with me whether I was attached or not. Another check in the pro column for her. She does have me thinking about whether or not Melissa considers our arrangement to be more than just sex. It bugs me all through the meeting. I need to talk to Melissa to put my mind, and ultimately Ashley's, at ease. As I'm leaving the meeting to head to Ma's, I dial Melissa. I have a few minutes to kill after all.

"Hey, Tag," she answers on the first ring.

"Hey Melissa, what's going on?"

"Not much. Just working. What about you?"

"So basically you're shopping?" I ask with a chuckle. Melissa's a fashion merchandiser, so working for her means checking out the latest fashion trends. I always tease her about her job not really being work for her.

"Shut up, Tanner! What are you up to?" she yells playfully.

"I'm heading over to Ma's for dinner before we head out for the game tomorrow. Coach wants us in Chicago early tomorrow so we'll be well-rested for Sunday."

"Oh, tell her I said hi. I haven't seen her in a while."

"I will, but I also wanted to talk to you about something." I'm not worried about telling her about Ashley, but Ashley is, which makes this conversation a little more difficult.

"Sure, what's going on?"

"I met someone."

"Umm, okay... Who did you meet? Anyone I know of?" she asks.

"I don't think that you know her, but you do know of her."

"Oh, you mean like you met a girl?" There's shock in her voice.

"Yes. Her name's Ashley Mitchell. She's the reporter that wrote the article about me. I've gotten together with her a few times. I took her to dinner to review the article a while ago, and then I ran into her last night at Levitate. There's this indescribable connection between us. After a little coaxing, she's agreed to give things a try between us." I realize suddenly that I really want Melissa to like her.

"That's great, Tanner. I'm so happy for you. You haven't been interested in anyone in years. She must be really special."

"She is, but she's pretty worried about you. She thought that you and I were a couple and refused to even think about getting involved because she didn't want to step on your turf." I laugh. "After I told her all about you, she still seemed worried. That right there tells you how different she is, doesn't it? How many chicks would have said that, Melissa?"

"You dumbass. Of course, she would be nervous after you've told her I'm your fuck buddy. How would you feel if she had a fuck buddy that everyone thought was her boyfriend? You guys are all such idiots." Melissa laughs. I know I'd be fucking pissed if Ashley told me she had a fuck buddy, so I guess I understand her worry a little bit better now.

"What do you think about meeting her? She definitely wouldn't worry after meeting you. I mean, you're awesome, so she would see that she doesn't have anything to worry about."

"Of course I want to meet your girlfriend, Tanner. I can't wait."

"So no hard feelings if I call off our arrangement?" I need to hear her say it out loud.

"I would only have hard feelings if you asked me to be your side-piece, asshole. I'm not a moron. I do understand that a girlfriend means no more sex for us. I'd hope you wouldn't have had any hard feelings with me if I'd met someone I wanted to start a relationship with."

"See, this is why I love you, Melissa. You're the coolest chick ever. Some douchebag is going to be lucky to score you one of these days," I say. I knew there wouldn't be any issues. Hopefully, telling Ashley about this conversation will ease her worries about Melissa.

"Thanks, Tanner. I've got to run. Let me know when you want to get together so that I can meet Ashley. Talk to you later, babe," she says before hanging up.

I feel so much better having talked to Melissa. Now to tell Ma about Ashley. I know Ma's going to be a different story. She's fantastic, but she can be overbearing at times. She means well, but Ma's one of those ladies who thinks nothing is ever good enough for her kids. I remember the grilling that my sister's boyfriends used to get from her, and I can only imagine what she'll do to Ashley. I haven't brought anyone home in years, so my family's going to have a field day with the news. I'd better remember to warn Ashley well ahead of time.

It's been a few week since I've been home. Ever since Ashley's article first ran, everyone has wanted a piece of me. I've done endless interviews and made countless appearances. On the plus side, my image has practically changed overnight. My game has been awesome lately too. We won our home opener last week, and we're confident we can pull out another win this week in Chicago. It's not a guaranteed win. Chicago has a killer defense who could knock me around pretty good if we aren't all on our top game, but I think we're going to pull this one off. I have a gut feeling that we're in it for the long haul this season. It's going to be a big one. As long as everything stays on track, this could be the year for the ring.

Ma already has the front door open when I pull in—a sign that she's waiting for me. Whenever we have company over, Ma always has the front door open, waiting for them to arrive. It's a sort of welcome sign, she's always said. I haven't even made it up the first step of the stoop before she's opening the screen door.

"Hi, baby boy! It's so good to see you. I haven't seen much of your handsome face in person lately," she says, enfolding me into one of her hugs.

"Hi, Ma. It's good to see you too." I return her hug. "Sorry, but it's been crazy lately. You know if I could get here more often, I'd be here."

"Great game last week, son," my dad calls from behind Ma as I step inside.

"Thanks, Dad. Sorry, I didn't have the chance to get up to see you guys after the game. I had press everywhere." After home games, I usually make my way to the suite, where my parents always watch our home games.

"We didn't expect you to. I know how crazy it's been for you lately. I'm just glad they're finally printing things that are true about you now," my dad says, clapping me on the back.

"Me too, Dad. Me too!"

"Are you hungry, dear? Dinner's ready. When's the last time you ate?" Ma asks, ushering me to the dining room. She's always making sure we've eaten. I'm pretty sure she thinks we're incapable of eating without her cooking for us.

"I had breakfast this morning, Ma, but yes, I'm hungry. I just came from a meeting with the team about our travel plans for tomorrow."

"How are things looking for next week's game?" Dad asks, taking his seat at the table.

"Looking good. I think that we can pull it off. We're rolling on a lot of positive energy lately. I'm hoping that it keeps up."

"That article's done wonders for you, huh?" he asks.

"It sure has, in more ways than one."

"Oh yeah? How's that, baby?" Ma asks, setting the salad on the table.

"Well, the woman who wrote it, Ashley, and I have started seeing each other," I tell her, watching for her reaction.

She pauses mid-step while turning with the lasagna pan in her hand. After a moment, she rushes to the table to put it down before turning all of her attention on me.

"Started seeing each other? What do you mean? What happened to Melissa?" Ma asks as though I've just told her I'm part alien.

"Like dating, Ma. Nothing happened with Melissa. We're friends and nothing more. I've told you this over and over." I'm so tired of everyone thinking that Melissa and I are an item, but I'd never noticed until just now how many people believed the rumors, and I am fed up with it.

"Well, you haven't brought home anyone other than Melissa in years. I just assumed you'd come to realize there was something between the two of you sooner or later," Ma answers sadly. “It’s obvious to me that Melissa’s in love with you, dear.”

"The only thing between Melissa and me is friendship, Ma. I actually was just talking to Melissa about Ashley on the way over here, and she sounded thrilled. She can’t wait to meet her." Melissa’s not in love with me. Ma’s just looking for what she wants to see.

"If you say so. Tell us about Ashley," Ma says, still seeming disappointed. Her voice has none of its usual enthusiasm. She’s usually so excited to hear things about us kids, but right now she doesn’t seem all that interested. Her head rests on her hand as she listens to me tell Dad all about Ashley, but she never chimes in.

I spend the rest of the night talking about Ashley, despite my mother’s disinterest. When Ma heads off to the kitchen to clean up, Dad and I head to the family room with a couple of beers. I tell Dad all about the article and how it had been Ashley's idea to spin the article to show the better, truer side of me and how she makes things feel different.

He seems happy to hear it, telling me that sometimes you know right away about a person, that sometimes things just fall into place. "It only took one look at your mother for me to know that I was sunk. I'm not kidding, Tanner, so if you felt that connection the first time you saw her, it’s the real deal. I know I sound like a crazy old man, but I'm dead serious. You and your sisters are the living proof that I know what I’m talking about. I have a wonderful life with a woman whom I love—more than that wonderful life,” he says, finishing off his beer.

"That's beautiful, Dad.” I love the way my dad has never hesitated to tell us how much he loves our mother. It’s such a great thing to see in a world of people divorcing each other faster than they change their underwear. I hadn’t really thought about how special it was until now, and I hope I can be that happy with someone someday.

"So’s your mother, son. Don’t fuck it up if you feel it too.” My dad hardly ever curses, so I know he’s serious.

"I'll do my best, Dad, but the cards are stacked against me. She’s got some trust and confidence issues." I only mention it because I trust my dad implicitly, and I’m secretly hoping he can help me figure out how to navigate this uncharted territory.

"Do you know why?"

"I know a little, and that's only because I saw her run into her ex last night. Otherwise, I don't think she would have told me anything."

"What happened?"

"She caught her ex cheating."

"Well, that's enough to do any woman in. What did she tell you?"

"Not much. Just basically confirmed what I'd overheard them arguing about. When I asked her to explain some of her actions, she basically told me she didn't feel the need to tell me any more embarrassing things about herself right now. I told her that I get where she's coming from, but I don't want to be punished because her ex is an asshole."

"But, unfortunately, you're going to be. There isn't anything you can do about that but show her you aren't anything like him. She's going to need someone beside her while she works through her insecurities. You need to be that man for her if you think that she's worth it. You should ask your mother or your sisters about how to help, though."

I smile, feeling grateful. I don't know what I would do without my parents. They're always there without judgment and tell me the truth no matter what I want to hear. "You're right, Dad. I do think she's worth it, so I guess I'll have to be the one to show her how a real man acts. I've had a great role model, after all."

"Then be that man, son. You are a Garrison, after all. I know you have it in you." He winks. "Go chat with your mother. You know how much she loves it when you kids need her."

"Thanks, Dad." I lean over to squeeze his shoulder in thanks before heading to the kitchen to find Ma.

When I find her making tea, I walk up behind her, kiss her cheek, and say, "I need some advice, Ma."

"Want some tea, sweetie?" She smiles at me.

"No, thanks." I'm pretty sure Ma thinks tea can solve all the world's problems.

"Okay, let's sit then, and you can tell me what's going on," she says on her way to the kitchen table.

I relay my conversation with Dad to Ma and wait to hear what she has to say.

"Poor girl. That must have been awful. You sure have your work cut out for you," she says, eyeing me over her tea.

"She's worth it, Ma. She's special. I can feel it."

"Well, let me tell you a little about the female mind then, sweetie. She's most likely embarrassed you even know that happened, especially since you two are just starting out. No woman wants anyone to know about something so personal. And she didn't have the chance to tell you herself either. You overheard it."

"But it just shows what an ass her ex is. It says nothing bad about her."

"Maybe not to you, but to her, it's a different story. She most likely sees herself as flawed. So she's probably trying to figure out why he cheated and wondering what's wrong with her that he felt the need to go elsewhere."

"That couldn't be any further from the truth, Ma. She's amazing."

"She may very well be, honey. But I'm a woman too, and I'm sure she isn't seeing it the way you do. Chances are she feels like it's her fault he cheated. Her confidence is probably at an all-time low, and she won't be quick to trust again. Especially if she loved this guy. You need to understand that her scars are hers, and they're not about you. She needs you to show her you think she's amazing and she means the world to you. It's what all women need normally even without being cheated on. So now you need to multiply that need by a hundred."

"Okay, I see what you mean, Ma. Thank you." I get up to hug her.

"Anytime, honey. Good luck. But remember something: You've just started seeing each other. You can't demand everything from her all at once. Especially given her last relationship," she says, hugging me back.

Ma's right. I can show Ashley how amazing she is and slowly break her out of her shell. No problem there. I just have to figure out where to start.

Chapter Fourteen

ASHLEY

TANNER: *FAVORITE PLACE TO go and relax?*

It's an offbeat but intriguing question. Seems like he's angling for info for some reason, but I do my best to play along truthfully. I try to remember a time when I'd been able to think about nothing and just relax. The first place that pops into my head is the Brooklyn Aquarium. I've always loved it there. I like it better during off-season, though, when it's peaceful. The place is a madhouse during the summer. The hustle and bustle take away the serenity of it. Whiny kids, overtired parents, and punk-ass teenagers bored with Coney Island with nowhere better to go. I prefer to stand in silence and watch the beauty of nature's creatures doing nothing except what comes to them naturally. Animals never second guess themselves like humans do. They just do what biology dictates and move on. It must be nice. I take a cue from the sea creatures and answer without overthinking for once in my life.

Me: *Brooklyn Aquarium*
Tanner: *Interesting choice. When would you like to go?*
Me: *Together?*
Tanner: *Yeah, our first official date. When would you like to go to the aquarium?*

Knowing he wants our first date to be in a place I feel comfortable, calms my nerves. My heart beats a little quicker, and my stomach does a few somersaults. I don't remember the last time someone asked me what I wanted to do. I tend to go with the flow. Quinn asks where I want to order food from and what clubs I want to hit, but that's usually because those decisions coincide with my job. Quinn has a more dominant personality than I do, which goes well with my easygoing nature. I think it's the key to the strength of our friendship. I can't recall Jason ever asking how I felt, but then again, I never made any counteroffers to anything he suggested.

Jason would ask, "Hey do you want to go here for dinner?" and I'd agree. Or he'd say, "Let's go watch the baseball game at so-and-so's house" and I'd nod my agreement. When Jason said, "I think this apartment is perfect," my response was to pull out a pen to sign the lease papers. I'd never put up much resistance to anything, and Jason had never bothered asking what my true feelings were.

I shake my head, snapping back to the moment at hand. Tanner isn't Jason. I need to keep reminding myself it isn't fair to Tanner or myself to keep comparing the two. Apples and oranges and all that. Tanner's words have been sitting heavily at the bottom of my stomach since breakfast Saturday morning. I know he shouldn't have to pay for Jason's faults, but he also can't expect me to go into something new with walls down and no defenses. It just wouldn't be smart. My wounds are still open. Even so, Tanner has already managed to put a few cracks in my newly constructed walls.

Me: *You're the one with the busy schedule. Tell me what works for you, and I'll make it work for me.*

Tanner: *Team meetings and game films today. Only light practice tomorrow. Does tomorrow afternoon work for you? We can go for dinner after too.*

Me: *Works perfectly. Can't wait.*

Tanner: *Okay. Where should I pick you up? Home or office?*

Me: *Home.*

Tanner: *Okay, see you tomorrow, gorgeous!*

The plan is actually perfect. It gives me a decent amount of time to get the articles I'm working on completed. Then I'll have nothing else on my mind tomorrow.

Quinn and I haven't had any time to talk about anything that happened after we left Levitate, so we're having dinner and a movie at home tonight to catch up. I haven't got the slightest clue as to what went down with her and Alex, and I'm dying for some details there. They really do seem like a match made in heaven.

I also haven't had a chance to tell her about anything that's happened between Tanner and me. I can already see her eyes bulging out of her head when I tell her about it all. So between Quinn and work, I have enough to keep me from obsessing over tomorrow's date. Even though I can feel the nerves setting in, I force my attention back to my laptop, determined to get my work done.

"FOOD'S HERE, BITCH! Get your hot ass out here. I'm not waiting!" Quinn yells to me from the kitchen where I'm sure the take-out is waiting.

Getting out of the shower, I dry off quickly and throw on some comfy sweats. I know better than to think she's kidding when she says she won't wait. I've never seen anyone with an appetite as big as Quinn's. And her healthy appetite extends to so many things: sex, food, shopping… I grab my hairbrush on the way out of the room, wanting to brush my hair out before it dries. If I keep on it, my hair will dry pin-straight for tomorrow, and that's my favorite way to wear it. I usually don't wear it down and straight; normally putting it up in some way or other for practicality's sake. But I have a feeling Tanner asked me to a place I feel relaxed on purpose, so I've decided to stick with the theme and keep everything relaxed, including my hair. It's just a plus that it also happens to be my favorite style.

By the time I get to the living room, Quinn already has her plate piled sky high with lo mien, fried rice, sweet and sour shrimp, and an egg roll. Her chopsticks are in her hand, ready to dive in.

"Quinn, you do know that gluttony is one of the seven deadly sins, right?" I ask, grabbing a plate from the cabinet.

"So is lust, but you don't see me giving a shit about that one either, do you? Besides, all of that sin stuff is a bunch of contradictory bullshit anyway." She shovels some rice into her mouth.

"Why contradictory? Never heard anyone say that before." Sometimes this girl really baffles me. I've spent days at a time trying to wrap my head around her logic before deciding it's better to pretend that she never shared her fucked-up opinions with me in the first place. Sometimes I think she could give those conspiracy theorists some new ideas.

"Because we're all taught to fear the wrath of God, right? Do right in life, and God will reward you, but do wrong and fear God's punishment in Hell. Wrath is a deadly sin as well, so why is it cool for God to indulge in deadly sins but not a mere mortal? Fuck that! God doesn't get to have all the fun. I don't give a shit what he's done. Can anyone prove it? Nope. Therefore, I will enjoy what time I have on this Earth any which way I see fit. The only one I have to answer to at the end of the day is me. And I fully approve of all my choices." She smiles devilishly.

"Even the choice of dress you wore to the sorority formal junior year?" I ask with a smirk and a raised eyebrow, questioning her assertion.

"All right, so I can't be perfect one hundred percent of the time. You'll have to settle for ninety-nine-point-four-percent. Besides, tulle was in then."

"Yeah, for four-year-old ballerinas." I laugh.

"Whatever. Shut the fuck up and tell me about your time with the hottie quarterback."

"Nuh uh, you first. I want to hear about the hottie best friend who gave you a run for your money. I must say I've never seen anything like that before. Not many people can keep up with you, lady."

"Not only could his mouth keep up with me, but his definitely bigger than six-inch penis had no problem keeping up with me either." She beams while telling me all about her day in bed. I hadn't known it was possible for a woman to orgasm so many times in one day, but according to Quinn, it most definitely is.

I can't help the small bubble of jealousy that rises up when I think about Quinn's ability to own everything she does. I wish it were so easy for me.

"Okay, enough about Alex and his magic penis. I want to hear about Tanner's magic penis. It is magic, right? Please tell me you hit that. I swear to God, if you didn't get a piece of that fine ass this weekend, you need to be worried about my wrath, not the wrath of the man upstairs." She stares at me fiercely.

Thank God I've got something to tell her. If I didn't, I'd be fearful for my life right now.

"Well, I did get a piece, just not with my vagina."

"What the fuck does that mean? Let's go! Out with it! NOW!"

"I kind of gave him a drunken blowjob in the back of his car on the way home before I passed out and had to sleep it off at his place." I spit the words out all in one breath.

"Okay, first of all, never give without receiving when you're not committed to someone. It makes you seem easy and like a pushover. Next time make sure you get yours. Rule number one. But I won't lecture you on that now, because I'm proud you let go for a night. So what happened after?" Quinn asks, getting up to refill our wine glasses.

"He caught me trying to sneak out before he got up the next morning." There's no point in trying to hide my embarrassment from her. She'd see through me, and besides, I want Quinn's advice. I don't want to be a hot mess forever.

"You didn't, Ash," she says, her voice full of exasperation.

"I had the nightmare about the Halloween party, and then I woke up in a strange bedroom not remembering how I got there. What the hell did you think that I was going to try to do? I just wanted to avoid the awkward, 'Thanks for blowing me last night. See you around, slut' conversation," I explain, feeling suddenly annoyed. I have no idea who I am annoyed with—myself… Tanner… Quinn… Jason, for making me more of an insecure mess, or the stupid bastards from college who triggered my neurosis? Why can't I just be normal? I just want a regular sex life so I can do and ask for whatever the hell I want. I'm sick of hesitation and regret and second-guessing. Why is that so fucking hard?

"You know what, sweets? Time to grow the fuck up. I love you, but I seriously can't take this shit anymore. You're an adult, and you can do whatever the fuck you please with whomever you please. Stop letting those dickheads from college rule your life. It was years ago. It's time to let it go. Stop letting that douchebag Jason get to you too. I'm sorry, but he would've cheated on you no matter what. He's a cheater, and that's what cheaters do. Stop blaming everyone else and woman the fuck up. If you want this thing with the football player to go anywhere, you need to own yourself, or it won't work with him or anyone else."

I stare at her, feeling as though my jaw is on the ground. She's never given me so much tough love before, and I'm not sure what to make of it. I don't know if I'm mad at her for being insensitive or glad that she's being brutally honest with me.

"Wow," is all I manage to get out.

"Sorry, sweets, but the truth hurts. It's a dirty job, but someone has to do it. So tell me what happened after he found you sneaking out."

I spend the next half an hour recounting my morning with Tanner, telling her about the conversation at his house, the relationship talk we'd had at the diner, and our aquarium date tomorrow.

"He sounds like a pretty damn great catch to me, but I'm going to give you a few pieces of advice. Do yourself, and him a favor, and go into this with an open mind. I would hate to see this thing go south because you're still doubting everything. Chances are you'll be the one to push him away, and that'll be all on you. Give yourself a break. Be free, have fun, and listen to your gut. He seems like a straightforward guy. Even if it goes nowhere, let him show you something new. Ask for what you want. I swear he won't think less of you. You know I wouldn't lie to you, sweets," Quinn says, hugging me.

God, I have the world's best friend. "I love you, Quinn. I promise that I'll try." I say with a smile.

"Good, now go refill our glasses, slut, and I'll tell you more about all the naughty things I asked Alex to do to me the other night."

THE ANXIETY I'VE had all day leading up to the date turns out to be completely unfounded. I've never felt more comfortable on a date in my life. Tanner's such a great guy, and I feel terrible for having judged him so harshly before meeting him. The aquarium is the perfect spot. We walk around for hours looking at all the different exhibits.

"What's your favorite animal here?" Tanner asked as we entered.

"It's probably a tossup between the sea otters and the penguins."

"Which one would you like to start with?"

"How about we don't start anywhere and just go with the flow?" I suggested.

"That sounds perfect."

That's exactly what we did, no set plan in place other than to enjoy each other's company. I'd taken Quinn's advice to heart last night and have done my best to let everything go today. Our non-plan eventually leads us down to the boardwalk and then to a nearby sushi restaurant.

"This is probably the most contradictory place I could've picked for dinner." I laugh, settling into my chair at our secluded corner table.

"Why's that?"

"You told me to pick a place I felt comfortable, and now I am eating what I find most comforting. I guess the fish wouldn't say they feel the same way about me,"

"Don't be too hard on yourself. I hear this place refuses to make otter or penguin rolls." He smiles, laughing too.

My heart skips a beat, surprised he remembers the answer I gave him earlier. The day has been a great one. It's been a long while since I've felt this happy and free. My cheeks hurt from the amount of laughing I've done.

"Are you up for some heavy talking now?" Tanner asks.

I nod. With the way Tanner always wants to talk I'd had a feeling this was coming. At least this time, I feel more relaxed, and I'm doing my best to not overanalyze anything.

"I know this has been a great day and all, but I need to know the answer to the question I asked you the other morning at the diner. It's really been weighing on me. Did I do something that made you feel like you needed to leave before I woke up?" A look of worry covers his face, and it breaks my heart that he thinks he's done something wrong.

"Oh my goodness, no. No, not at all, Tanner," I reassure him.

"Then why? I don't like feeling as though I made you feel uncomfortable."

"You didn't. Not at all." I feel terrible for making him think he'd done something to make me want to run from his place as if it were on fire.

"It really wasn't anything you did. I woke up that morning after having a bad dream. I was hung-over in an unfamiliar place, and then I started to remember everything that had happened the night before. I mostly remembered being in the limo and you telling me I didn't need to do what I did but I did it anyway. I felt slutty, so I figured if I left before I had to see you, it wouldn't be as bad as facing you." I shrug, trying my best to act as though telling him all that wasn't hard.

"Oh, sweetheart, you couldn't be any further from the truth. I wanted what you gave me that night. I've said it already, but I'll say it again: I only said you didn't have to because you didn't have to, not because I didn't want it, and so I didn't feel like an asshole for letting you do it. Your sweet little mouth wrapped around me was nothing short of heaven. Believe me. And I'm not a fan of oral sex."

"What?!" I cough, choking on my drink. "What guy doesn't like oral sex?" I've never heard of a man with an aversion to blowjobs.

"I wouldn't say that I don't like it, but I've always found it to be the most intimate act, so I've always felt weird about it. But that night, I couldn't think about anything other than your mouth working me perfectly. An interesting aspect of our connection, don't you think?"

"You mean you and Melissa don't have oral sex as a part of your benefits package?"

He laughs. "Benefits package?"

I shrug and give him a smirk before shoving a spicy tuna roll in my mouth.

"Don't get me wrong, we've done it, but it honestly has never felt right, and I don't really care for it. It's something so intimate that it should only be shared with people you truly care about. I know it sounds weird, but there's never been a real connection between Melissa and me. I've never had a real commitment to any woman. Call me crazy, but I don't like the idea of licking a pussy when I don't know exactly where it has been or letting someone suck my cock without knowing where their mouth was last."

I accidently swallow my tuna roll without chewing all the way as I fight to keep from laughing at Tanner's confession. I try to keep from choking as my eyes water from the wasabi.

"Are you okay?" he asks, looking concerned.

"I'm fine. I don't think that I've heard anything that funny in a long time. But after explaining it like that, I can see where you're coming from. No pun intended." I wink.

We finish our dinner with light conversation about the Jet's win last Sunday and their upcoming game against Denver.

"Would you like to come back to my place or go home?" Tanner asks as we get back in the car to head back toward New Jersey.

I get lost in thinking about how to answer his question before I catch myself overanalyzing. Do I want to go Tanner's? Yes. Am I okay with something happening at Tanner's? Yes. So before I can change my mind, I answer, "Your place."

Tanner's face lights up like a Christmas tree, and I'm certain I've made the right choice.

Chapter Fifteen

ASHLEY

"**CAN I GET** you something to drink?" Tanner asks, closing the door to the garage behind him. I've almost forgotten how stunning his home is.

"A glass of wine would be great."

"Sure thing," he says, a wicked smirk on his face.

Bastard. I know exactly what he's thinking, and he's getting nothing from me while in a drunken state tonight. One glass is all I'm having.

Walking into the den off his kitchen, I'm drawn to the window showcasing a beautiful view. It didn't look this gorgeous the other morning, but at this time of day it's captivating. The city is just lit up for the evening, and the sun has almost set. Its light reflects off the river in luminous shades of pink and orange. I don't think that I've seen a sunset so gorgeous before.

Tanner reappears, handing me a glass of wine. He stands behind me at the window, close enough for me to feel the rise and fall of his chest with each breath he takes. He runs his hand up my arm to my shoulder and sweeps my hair off to one side, baring my neck. My whole body breaks out in goosebumps. I feel his breath on my skin before his lips touch my neck. He kisses the spot where my neck and shoulder meet. I can't help but close my eyes and enjoy the feeling of his touch. It's soft and tender but strong at the same time, a touch that I can't deny.

Leaning my head back against his chest, I let out a breathy sigh. Tanner's lighting my body on fire with his simple touches and light kisses. My whole body is attuned to him with seemingly no effort on his part. I'd felt the same way when we were dancing at the club.

He takes the glass of wine from my hand and places it on the end table. He reaches out a hand, grabbing mine, and gives a little pull to spin me around to face him before pulling me to his chest.

He slides both of his hands up my arms, and they come to rest on my shoulders. He gently kneads his way up with his thumbs, tilting my head back with his fingers. I peek at him from beneath my lashes and find him staring at me with a level of desire in his eyes I've never seen before. The unabashed way he's watching me sets my body further ablaze. I've never in my life felt so coveted.

"Ashley, I want nothing more than to spread you wide in front of this window," he whispers between kisses. "The city lights illuminating your body, but only if you want it too," he says, suddenly stopping all his ministrations. I know if I put a stop to this all right now, he'll let me, no questions asked.

I don't want him to stop. I don't want this heady desire to fade out. My whole body is on edge just from the look in his incredible green eyes. I notice the flecks of gold glowing more brightly now than they had been earlier. His breathing has deepened just as mine has. He's as affected as I am at this moment, and there's no way that I'm stopping now.

Instead of telling him with words, I push myself up on my tiptoes and fuse my mouth to his, sliding both of my hands up his chest to the nape of his neck and into his hair. I've been dying to touch his hair ever since our godforsaken interview. I pull away slightly from the kiss, but only enough to open my mouth and trace his lips with my tongue, hoping to gain entrance into what I'm sure will be nothing short of heaven. I know we've kissed before, but I don't remember much of our last encounter.

Tanner's arm snakes around my waist, and his free hand rests in the middle of my back. What little control I may have had in this kiss is now gone. The arm around my waist tightens possessively, and he leans me further against the hand on my back. In my dipped position, Tanner has a better angle to dive into the kiss. His lips are strong against mine, leaving me no choice but to follow his lead. Now it's Tanner who licks across the seam of my lips, and I instinctually part them for him. My body completely softened and molded to his.

My mind has been completely wiped clean of everything other than Tanner's mouth on mine. His tongue explores every area of my mouth it can reach, and I take all he gives. Christ, if he can do this to me with just a kiss, I can't imagine how it'll feel when it's not just his tongue inside me.

Tanner breaks the kiss and slides his hands to my waist. His strong hands grab the hem of my shirt and gradually pulls it up, putting my upper body on display for his viewing. I do nothing to stop him. I'm merely his puppet now. He has me so far under his spell I'll do whatever he wants.

"I need to see this beautiful body of yours. I've thought of nothing but stripping you bare and having you spread out beneath me since I saw you in that dress at the club," he whispers, his lips at my neck. "You have me totally mesmerized. No one has ever turned me this inside out before. My dick is perpetually hard because of you. Please tell me that you want this as much as I do."

"I may want it more." There's nothing I want in this moment than to have him touch me, bend me, stretch me. Any contact will do.

"Hmmm, how badly do you want this, baby? I want it more than anything else. If you want it more than me, then you want it a whole hell of a lot," he says, unbuttoning my jeans. He pushes his hands into my pant legs, rubbing his palms up and down my thighs. Suddenly, my pants are at my ankles, and Tanner is on his knees in front of me. He pulls my ankle boots off, one at a time, then tugs my pants the rest of the way off, leaving me standing there in nothing but my panties and bra. Sitting back on his haunches, Tanner looks me up and down, as though examining a piece of fine art, lust oozing from every pore of his body.

As he stands, Tanner trails his fingers up my thighs, making me shiver in anticipation. It is at this moment I realize Tanner still has on all of his clothing. I want to the see the masterpiece of his body as well, and

I decide to be a little daring. Seeing the longing for me not only in his eyes but in the snugness of his pants as well, I know there's no reason to be shy. I push away from him slightly and circle him. Leaving my fingers on him to trail across his torso, I walk, watching as Tanner's eyes follow my every move. I come to a stop once I'm standing back in front of him.

"You aren't the only one who wants to see a beautiful body, handsome," I say as I slide my hands under his shirt to feel his abs. *Holy hell.* I've never felt anything so hot in my life. Hard planes covered in soft, luscious skin. I stroke the divots in between his muscles back and forth and trace around all eight of his abs, sighing. I need to see this perfection.

I reach for the top button of his shirt and slowly undo each one. When I reach the last one, I guide the button-down over his broad shoulders and down his strong, toned arms. The muscles in his arms feel almost as amazing as his abs, and I have to fight not to get distracted by them, needing to see his still concealed stomach and chest before I explode.

Tanner must be able to sense my eagerness because a slight glimmer of humor glints in his eyes. Grabbing the hem of his white t-shirt, I pull it upward. I have to stand on my tiptoes to pull it over his head, but he leans down a bit to help me pull it from his body.

Good fucking lord. It's even more magnificent than I'd thought it would be. Not only does the man have an eight-pack, his hips slope into that sexy "V" every man should be required to have. I feel my panties dampen at the sight of the glorious body in front of me.

"Like what you see?" he asks with a devious smirk.

I take a step closer and drop to my knees. Leaning my head forward, I kiss the slab of muscle before me. There's no way I can keep my mouth off him.

Sitting back on my heels, I look up to tell him how beautiful he is. "Jesus, Tanner. I don't think that I have ever seen anything this magnificent before."

"You have no idea how happy that makes me," he says, dragging me back up to capture my mouth with his. While distracting me with his mouth, Tanner reaches around my back and unhooks my bra with practiced ease. Clearly, he's had a lot of experience with that. He slips the straps down my arms until my bra falls away from my body.

"Just as perfect as I expected them to be." He bends to take one of my hardened nipples into his mouth.

The sudden warmth of his mouth ignites my body further. My head drops back, and I enjoy the pleasure that spreads through me. Bringing a hand up to my other breast, Tanner rolls my neglected nipple between his thumb and forefinger. The sensation is incredible, and I want nothing more than to discover all the things this man can make me feel.

I reach for the button of his jeans and pop it before pulling down the zipper. The anticipation of reaching what's hidden beneath the denim is worse than waiting for Santa to come as a kid. I may have already had the pleasure of seeing and tasting him, but my memory is a bit fuzzy. Sliding my hand under his boxers, I find a very hard, very large erection waiting for me. I can't hold in the gasp that escapes me. I hadn't remembered his cock being so big. *Holy shit!*

"That's right, baby." Tanner beams. "It's all for you." And with those words, my panties are completely soaked. No one has ever talked so dirty to me, and I couldn't be more turned on. That is until I feel Tanner's hands slip past the edge of my panties. "You like that don't you? You like knowing my cock's hard as hell because of you, and I have no problem letting you know it."

"Yes," I whimper. I'd thought my body had been on fire before, but those flames don't even compare to how I feel now. With each centimeter, his hand slides further into my panties, more nerve endings fire. I almost think I could orgasm from a strong breeze at the moment. Tanner has parts of my body throbbing that I didn't know could throb, and he hasn't even hit the best spot yet.

"Do you think you'll be able to keep yourself from coming once I get my hands on this sweet pussy of yours?" he asks as casually as if we were talking about the fucking weather.

I feel my face heat up at the word 'pussy.'

"No need to blush. I know how turned on you are because I'm just as hot for you. So turned on my dick hurts. I can't wait to feel this beautiful pussy. How wet are you, Ashley?"

I know what he's doing. He's trying to get me to let go and just be free, but I don't know if I can do that just yet.

"Tell me how wet you are? I want to know what I'm going to feel when I finally get my hands on you, my fingers in you."

You can do this, Ashley. You can do this. There is nothing wrong with it. "I'm soaked," I whisper.

The next thing I know, Tanner's fingers are sliding between my lips, and he murmurs in agreement. "You sure are, baby. Is this all for me? Do I make you this wet?" he asks, coaxing me back into his dirty conversation.

"Yes, Tanner, you and only you," I tell him as he circles my clit, 'round and 'round.

"I can't wait another minute to be inside your warm pussy. Please tell me you want it too." He reaches for the end table where my wine glass still sits with his free hand and pulls open the drawer. He pulls out a condom from inside. *Hmm, always prepared. I wonder if he was a Boy Scout.*

"Yes, I do. Please…" I want it with every fiber of my being. I've never needed release this badly before.

"Please what? Tell me what you need. Tell me how to please you," he whispers in my ear. He's pushing me in every way possible, as though he knows I need him to do this, to open me up. Oddly enough, it makes me trust him more. I want to tell him what I want, I just don't know if I can.

"I want…" What the hell am I supposed to say? Am I supposed to try and sound sexy? Make it sound dirty? Or just tell him straight out?

"What, baby? What do you want?" He presses his body against mine once more. I guess he's finished putting the condom on. "Think with this," he says, stroking my pussy again. "Not with this." He kisses my temple.

"I want you to fill me." I'm not ready to say I want him to fuck me. It just doesn't seem to fit this situation. 'Fill me' was the second thought to come into my head.

"That I can most definitely do for you," he says, circling me before sealing his mouth over mine.

Grabbing my hips, Tanner pulls me to his body. He bends his knees slightly and lifts me up. I have no choice but to wrap my legs around his hips.

Pulling back from our kiss, he says, "I've been dreaming about having these exquisite legs wrapped around me for weeks."

He lowers me to the ground and spreads my legs wide, "So fucking beautiful." He stares down at my naked body in reverence. He grabs his now-protected cock and rubs it up and down the length of my pussy, each swipe driving me closer and closer to the edge.

"Ready?" He holds himself poised at my entrance. I nod, giving him the go-ahead to take us both to heaven.

I'm a ball of sensation as he slowly pushes himself forward. *Fuck.* I've never felt this full before and he isn't even fully inside me yet. Each inch of him awakens another place inside me that feels like it's never been touched before. He pauses halfway in, looking down at me. I'm not sure what he's waiting for, but I nod in reassurance. I haven't changed my mind.

With my nod, he thrusts into me. My eyes roll back from the immense amount of pleasure coursing through my body. I feel him hitting something that's never been stimulated before, and I have no idea how to handle a pleasure this intense. I can't help but moan. "Oh my God."

"Feel that, baby?"

"Oh my God, yes," I cry out again.

Tanner lifts himself off of me just enough to fit his hand between us. Before I can figure out what he's doing, I feel his thumb on my clit, and then there's nothing but stars and blackness. My body convulses around his massive cock, even as he continues to thrust through my orgasm. The swirl of his thumb paired with the thrusting of his cock draws out my pleasure until I'm gasping for breath. Tanner pulls his hand out from between us and uses it to stroke my hair.

"You okay, baby?" He slows his tempo to a leisurely pace.

"Yes." I sigh, and a smile spreads across his face.

"Good, because the real fun is about to begin." That's the only warning I get before he pulls out of me completely. He lifts me by my ass and pulls himself up to sit on his knees. He sets my ass between his open thighs and throws my legs over his forearms so that my knees are resting in the crooks of his elbows. He pulls back on my legs and impales me on his cock once again.

"Holy shit," I scream while Tanner hisses out a "fuck yeah."

I can't keep my mouth shut as he drives into me over and over. He hits that same place deep inside me, and those intense feelings from earlier return, causing unintelligible words to spill from my mouth.

"Ah, ah, ah, oh God." I moan again and again, unable to do anything but to lay back and take everything that Tanner dishes out. I've never felt anything like the sensation currently building inside me.

"You feel so amazing. I knew you would, I just didn't realize it would be this great. God, your pussy is incredible." His words ring out in staccato as he thrusts into me, a man on a mission. The mission might be to kill me with pleasure. I can't handle the overwhelming sensation within me. Sex has never felt like this before.

"Tanner, I can't… I've never… Oh my God," I try to tell him that I've never gotten off more than once during sex, that I can't hang on much longer. My body is all out of release, and now it's just torture, teasing me with the possibility of something I know I can't have.

"Yes, you can, baby. Just trust me. Turn off your head. Let go."

I try. I try really hard. I close my eyes and focus on each thrust as it hits that place deep inside me. Whatever it is he's hitting has been dormant my entire life. Each nudge of that spot has me seeing stars.

"It's your G-spot. Just give into it, and I promise your life will never be the same."

I do my best to clear my brain and think only of Tanner: his amazing body, those gorgeous green eyes, how full of lust they were when he looked at me earlier. Realizing that I don't need to imagine him, I open my eyes and look up at him. He stares at me, his eyes fixated on my breasts. I can only imagine how they must look as they bounce up and down. He moves his gaze up and locks his eyes on mine. We simply watch each other, and the emotions running through his eyes are enough to push me over the edge. I feel the pleasure mounting, and it's a force so great that I don't know how to handle it. My body quivers with the promise of release.

"Let go, baby," he says. "I'll catch you."

I'm gone. My entire body shakes from the power of the explosion within. My legs lose feeling for a second and my lips feel fuzzy from the ragged breaths I drag in between each scream I let out. I barely recognize the voice crying out as my own.

"Oh, oh, oh, fuck. Jesus Christ. Tanner!"

My body goes limp, wrung dry of every ounce of pleasure. I feel Tanner tense up, and then his cock pulses inside me. My name is on his lips as his orgasm takes over. I can't explain what it does to a girl when a man like Tanner Garrison says her name as he comes.

My life will never be the same.

Chapter Sixteen

ASHLEY

HOLY SHIT!

Nothing has ever felt so good. I've had some crazy sexcapades in my life, but none have been better than sex with Ashley. I've never felt someone quake in pleasure the way she did. I want to bang my fists on my chest like a caveman knowing I made her experience that sort of high.

And her first release didn't even come close to how it felt when she finally fully let go. Doing that required trust, and it's incredible to know she trusts me enough to give in and relax with me. Even if just in the moment of ecstasy, it's still progress. A small amount of trust is a huge step for someone who's been through what she has. I can't help but smile at the realization.

I lean down to run kisses along Ashley's neck and jawline. She's just starting to come back to herself, a look of pure bliss on her face, as though she doesn't have a care in the world. This woman does wonderful things for my ego.

"You okay, baby?" I whisper in her ear.

"Mmmhmm ..."

"A man could seriously get used to this. You're stuck with me now. No way am I giving you up."

"I don't think you should get too used to it," she says. "I have a feeling it's going to take a while before I can move again. Holy shit, Tanner."

I laugh. "I know what you mean. Why do you think I haven't even bothered trying to pull out of this heaven? My dick is perfectly happy to continue residing here, and I can't argue with him there."

"You're crazy." She turns her face to the side as though she's trying to hide.

No. No way am I letting her climb back into herself now. I need her to break out again, even if it's only for a little bit. "Don't do that. Don't hide from me." I turn her face back toward me. "Please don't. There is no need for you to hide." I reassure her with kisses.

She looks up at me, and I see the self-doubt in her eyes, but I also see that little glimmer of trust. I smile before pulling out and standing up. I offer her a hand, which she takes. As soon as she's on her feet, I waste no time pulling her to me and kissing the hell out of her.

"Thank you," I say after I release her lips, realizing she actually needs to breathe in order for us to get to round two.

A horrified look crosses her face. "Are you thanking me for sex?"

"God, no, although I probably should be thanking you for that." I laugh. "I was thanking you for trusting me. I get that it's hard for you, and I wanted to let you know I appreciate it."

Her face turns a cute shade of pink, and she lets out a little giggle. "Oh…"

Kissing her again, I give her a light smack on the ass. "Come on. Let's go see if there are any more windows you like in the bathroom."

She laughs and sticks her tongue out.

I pick up our clothes and grab her hand to head to the shower. "Careful. There are things I can do with that tongue."

She hurries along behind me, quickly pulling her tongue back into her mouth.

AFTER A SHOWER accompanied by light teasing and a little groping, we head out to the couch to decide on a movie.

"No chick flicks," I say.

"No chick flicks." She laughs. "I was thinking more like a comedy." She scrolls through the On Demand listings. "Oh, how about Pitch Perfect?" she asks, bouncing up and down excitedly.

I don't love the movie, but it isn't horrible. "As long as I don't have to watch the puke scenes. That shit is nasty." A shiver of disgust runs through my body just thinking about them. They make me want to puke myself.

"I promise," Ashley agrees. "I don't really like them either."

After that matter is settled, we cuddle together—and by "cuddle" I mean that Ashley wraps herself around me like a blanket, which makes me very happy—and start the movie. I have more fun watching Ashley laugh at Fat Amy than I do watching the movie. Her laugh is utterly infectious, like a melody to my ears. Seeing her being all smiles and carefree is a beautiful thing. About halfway through the movie, Ashley falls asleep. I can't help watching her instead of the screen, even though it makes me feel like a creeper. She's even more beautiful asleep. There are no walls she's fighting to keep up. No self-doubt. No wondering or questioning. Just Ashley. And just Ashley is perfect.

I slide her head off my lap and stand up. It's time we went to bed. Fitting my arms underneath her, I pick her up and curl her into my chest. She instantly nuzzles her face into my neck, and a smile spreads across her face.

"Where're we going?" she asks in a sultry sleepy voice. The tone of her voice goes straight to my dick. I'm in so much trouble with this one.

"To bed. You're tired." I'd love to go again, but not when she's tired. I don't want to push her.

"What if I'm not that tired?" she asks, her face still buried in my neck, her eyes still closed.

"What do you have in mind?"

"I wouldn't mind another go, but I don't have enough energy for another round like before... Maybe just some lazy, non-acrobatic sex?" She opens one eye to look up at me.

"I'll take any kind of sex you want to give me, baby. Fast, slow, upside down, or hanging from the ceiling. It's all fine by me."

"Ceiling sex?" She snickers. "No, I'm good on the ceiling sex."

"Just saying, baby. Just saying." I smile.

We reach the top of the stairs, and I head toward my bedroom. I've never taken someone to my bedroom for sex. Melissa and I usually use the guest room. It's my private sanctuary, but I don't hesitate for a second to head in that direction with Ash in my arms.

Nudging open the door with my foot, I make my way over to the bed and lay Ashley down in the middle. She's a magnificent sight, laying there all languid and sleepy, but seductive as hell. Not even trying one bit. Damn, this woman is really turning me inside out.

Climbing onto the bed, I straddle her legs and pull her to a sitting position. I pull off the t-shirt I'd given her to wear earlier and lay her back down. I slide down her legs, divesting her of my boxers as I go. I stand after removing all of Ashley's clothes to take off my own, and watch as her eyes follow my every move. They fall on my erection the instant I free it and grow hooded with lust.

"Enjoying the show, baby?" I love coaxing her into talking dirty. It's a major turn-on for me, and I suspect it is for Ashley too, even if she won't admit it yet. That's okay. I'm in no rush for her to admit anything.

Her body's reactions always betray her, as they're doing now. Instinctively, she licks her lips, her breathing becoming shallow, before nodding in agreement.

I climb back onto the bed and place myself between her legs. Starting with one ankle, I kiss my way up her leg and then down the other. Her breaths come more quickly, and I can tell from looking at her pussy how turned on she is.

"Hmm, you like that? I can see your pussy getting wetter with each kiss." Using one finger, I stroke up and down her slit. Her breath hitches in her throat and her back arches. I take the opportunity to lean down and pull one of her pink, pebbled nipples into my mouth. I knead the soft flesh of her breast with my fingers while circling her nipple with my tongue. I give her a good nip, and she lets out a moan that can only be described as irresistible.

"Your breasts are fantastic." I tell her, moving my mouth to her other breast.

She snakes one hand between us and wraps her dainty fingers around my cock. She strokes up and down slowly, and I'm instantly reminded of how well Ash works with her hands.

"Enough of that," I insist. "Much more and I won't make it into your sweet pussy, baby."

"Jesus, Tanner, that mouth."

"It does have many uses." I reach toward the nightstand for a condom.

Sitting back on my feet, I sheath myself and kiss my way back up Ashley's body. A few strategically placed kisses on her inner thighs and hip bones have her primed all over again. I bring my lips to the apex of her thighs and give her one long, slow tongue kiss. I lap her clit a few times before continuing my path upward.

"Now, please," she pleads. "I can't take much more teasing."

"As you wish," I say before burying myself inside her very wet, very ready pussy. It's incredible.

"Oh, yes." She moans, making me want to slam into her over and over like a barbarian.

I have to remind myself to slow down and take it easy. I don't want to scare her. Or break her. "God, baby. You feel so good. I swear this pussy was made perfectly for me. Like it was custom fit just for my cock," I say between long unhurried thrusts. She grows wetter with my words, coating me, which only further fuels my fire. "You love it when I tell you about your amazing pussy, don't you? I can feel you gushing all over me. God, you're making me even harder with that panting. Do you think I can make you scream like before at this pace, Ashley? Because I think I can."

I pull out almost completely with each stroke, slamming back into the hilt again and again. Not with enough force to hurt, but enough to fill her completely. As soon as I find her G-spot again, her moans become higher pitched and much louder.

"Ah, ah, ah. Oh my God, Tanner. Right there."

"Do you want to come, Ash?" A little quicker, a little harder, and a thumb to her clit, and I could have her coming in two minutes.

"Please, please, please," she begs. Fuck, begging is such a turn on.

"Well, I have no choice now that you're begging. I can't deny a woman willing to beg." I place my thumb on her clit, increase my speed, and go to town. The sounds leaving Ashley's mouth should be fucking illegal. They're like sexual crack. God, she really is perfection.

"Tanner! Fuck! OH MY GOD!" Ashley screams before going into full body convulsions. Damn, her orgasm could almost be confused with a seizure it's so strong. And, hell yes, does my head swell knowing that it's me making her shake like that once again.

"Yes, baby, squeeze me! Oh God, Ash!" I come with a final forceful thrust and once again collapse on top of her.

I lie there, waiting for my heart rate to slow back to its normal rhythm, listening to the sound of Ashley's heartbeat. It's pounding a mile a minute, but then again, I'm sure mine is too.

"Damn, I can cut cardio out of my workout with you, baby," I tease her before pulling out.

She laughs and rolls over, curling herself into a post-coital ball.

I remove the condom and get up to toss it into the trash bin. Ashley's already half passed out by the time I get back to the bed, so I shut off the lights and crawl in beside her. I wrap an arm around her waist, pull her close and fall asleep, surrounded by nothing but Ashley.

Chapter Seventeen

ASHLEY

IF QUINN DOESN'T stop with the constant jokes about my 'glow,' I may be forced to kick her ass. Her teasing about how 'a great sex life looks good on me' hasn't stopped since she got home from work Wednesday night. It's been three days of nonstop witticisms from her. When I'd woken up at Tanner's place on Wednesday morning, I'd found a bombardment of text messages from my friend saying she required full explicit details of my Tuesday night exploits.

Unfortunately, I won't see Tanner again until Monday or Tuesday. Images of him in the throes of passion make me horny as hell. Damn, that man knows his way around a female body.

"Stop fantasizing about Tanner's cock and get your mind back here," Quinn bitches, bringing me back to the small bistro where we're having a long-overdue dinner out.

"Don't hate. You wanted me to get laid, and now you're complaining because I can't help but relive one of my best nights ever."

"I'm not hating. I'm fucking jealous. I could definitely use a good ravaging."

"Ravaging? Really? Is this the Eighteenth Century? Call Alex. You couldn't stop telling me all about his, and I quote, 'magic' penis."

"Meh, you know how I feel about repeats. They get attached to the greatness that is my vagina too easily," she explains in all seriousness. Quinn really doesn't like to have sex with the same guy more than once.

"Fuck, Quinn. I don't know whose mouth is worse, yours or Tanner's. I can only imagine how explicit dirty talk between the two of you would be… Actually, on second thought, I don't want to imagine it. My mind might explode."

"Hmm… We'll see how dirty your mouth is after a few more sessions with the sex god," she smiles, munching on a fry.

I can't help but think she might be right. The way that man draws words out of my mouth is uncanny, and the way my body hums from his praises is ridiculous. I think I really do like it, but I don't think I'll admit that to him just yet.

"Ack, that stupid lovesick look on your face really makes me want to punch you. I don't know which Ashley I like better: moping Ashley or I-can't-stop-thinking-about-Tanner Ashley," she growls.

"Oh, shut it, bitch."

THE REST OF the week and into the weekend goes on in much the same way, with me thinking about Tanner and Quinn bitching about me thinking about Tanner. Tanner's schedule keeps conflicting with mine, so we haven't had a chance to see each other since our date. We chat on the phone and text, but that's about it. We've communicated in some form or other every day, so at least I know he hasn't forgotten about me.

This week, I've had three places to review: one new café that opened in Midtown, a small new art gallery that opened last month in Soho, and a boutique that was just remodeled and is having a grand re-opening on the Upper West Side. I had lunch at the café and then checked out the art gallery the same day. They were both quiet and cute, what I would have expected, nothing extraordinary. The boutique wasn't my cup of tea. Definitely more Quinn's style. I'm not into shopping in small, stuffy stores, and I didn't care for the snobby attitude of the workers.

I have to laugh to myself because I know they'll be kicking themselves in the ass when they read my review. The bitch at the counter was so pretentious, acting as though I was an inconvenience to her because I wasn't decked out like the other women in there dropping thousands on the overpriced clothes. I couldn't wait to get the hell out of the store and tell everyone how they treat middle-class patrons. Thankfully, all the articles are done and handed in for editing, so my weekend is totally free.

"Heeey," Quinn says, all smiles as she plops herself down on my bed. "What are your plans for the day? Actually, I don't care what they are, cancel them. We're going shopping." She grins like a Cheshire cat. Never a good sign.

"I don't need to go shopping. You know I hate shopping."

"Well, too fucking bad," she smiles bigger, enjoying my displeasure with her idea of fun. "Make yourself look presentable and get moving."

"Where are we going?" I ask, heading to my closet to get changed. No point in arguing. If Quinn says so, I'm going shopping whether I want to or not.

"I'll tell you when we get there. I don't want to hear all your bitching and moaning on the way. " I'd known that stupid smile meant trouble. "And you *will* have a good time. I mean it," she adds before walking out of my room, presumably to get ready to go out herself.

An hour later, we pull up to Saks Fifth Avenue. *Oh fucking lord. I'm going to kill her.* Not only am I being forced to go shopping, but I've been dragged to a place I don't even care to shop in.

"Quinn, if this is where we were going, why bring me? You know I hate this place," I huff. Everything in there is ridiculously priced, and the sales people are usually just as snotty as that bitch from the boutique I just visited.

"Because you're trying to keep the interest of a very hot quarterback, and it's my job as your best friend to help you do that." She flashes that damn smile again.

"What the fuck does any of that have to do with Saks?" Even as I ask the question, I know the answer and shake my head. "No, Quinn," I tell her. "Not happening."

"Yes, it is, sweets. And before you give me your next excuse, I'm paying, so shut the fuck up and get your ass in there."

Of all the places. Agent Provocateur? Leave it to Quinn to pick a place like this to take me. *Fucking bitch.* "Can't we go to Victoria's Secret instead? I like it there better."

"No, and this isn't our last stop either. Loosen up and have some fun. Christ, it's not going to kill you," she says, a nasty tone sneaking into her voice. "We're going to have fun. Come on." She nudges me out of the car.

"Okay, jeez! Let's go. What's your problem tonight? Need to get laid?" I snicker, proving I can be a bitch too.

"No, I don't, but I want to make sure that you keep getting laid, so we have some work to do."

"Care to explain what the hell that means?" I ask resentfully as I get out of the car, glaring at her. She has a lot of nerve insinuating I need help keeping Tanner interested.

"Care to stop being such an uptight twat?" she shoots back. "We haven't even gone in yet, and you're already being a judgmental bitch. It's fucking lingerie. I can't wait to see what happens when we get to the toy store."

"Toy store?" I gasp, my face turning red at the mere mention of it.

"Yes, toy store. Now stop fucking complaining, and I'll explain. But not until we get inside." With those words, Quinn grabs hold of me and drags me unwillingly into the store.

"Okay, we're inside now. Can you explain?" I ask, suddenly feeling nervous about what she's going to tell me.

"Okay, so I'm saying this out of love. Please remember that." Oh man, she sure as hell isn't about to say something nice. "You're stuck in ordinary, Ashley. A man like Tanner isn't going to be satisfied with ordinary. You need to live a little and open up. You need to own up to your fantasies. You're a hot piece of ass, and it's time you started acting like it."

Wow, I wasn't expecting that. "You think I'm boring?"

"Sorry to say so, but yes, sweets. You're as open-minded as they come, and you don't judge people, but when it comes to you and your wants, you're boring. Men want wild and sexy, and you can be those things if you get out of your own head. Did you or did you not have the best sex of your life with the man?"

"I did." Everything that happened between Tanner and me was absolutely fantastic.

"Because he forced you to get out of your own head. I can tell from what you've told me about him that he's a man who likes power and dominance. Regular missionary sex isn't going to cut it for him for long, honey," she says, looking me in the eye for the first time since starting this awful conversation.

"I don't know what I am supposed to say." Tears pool in my eyes. I know she isn't trying to make me feel bad, but I can't help feeling—well, I don't really know what I'm feeling to be honest. How am I supposed to feel when my best friend tells me I'm too ordinary to keep a man like Tanner interested?

"Sweets, I'm not trying to be mean here. Please understand that." She pulls me into a hug. "I'm trying to help you be the Ashley you want to be instead of the Ashley all the losers in your past have turned you into. You already have everything you could ever need. I'm just trying to show you how to use it to your advantage. I really think Tanner can be the one to bring out that Ashley."

"I know you aren't trying to be mean, but that's basically the same thing that Jason said. I was too boring for him, and now I'm going to be too boring for Tanner too." I sniffle.

"No, you're not. That's why we're here. He obviously isn't too hard to keep happy if he's been banging only Melissa for all these years. Don't worry. We're going to turn you into the sex goddess you were meant to be."

She's right. I need to open up if this thing with Tanner is going to work. It's time to loosen up. "Okay, I'm game. Where do I start?" I muster up a smile.

"Atta girl. We start with the wrapping. Your body is already hot as hell, so let's dress it up and make it irresistible."

An hour later, we're exiting the store, weighed down by bags filled with dozens of matching bra and panty sets in all the colors Quinn considers hot. I also now own two babydoll nighties, four sets of garters and stockings, and a gorgeous shimmery corset that makes my boobs look like a million bucks. I nearly had a heart attack seeing the price when it was rung up—five grand on lingerie. Quinn is insane.

"See, that wasn't bad, was it?" Quinn asks once we're settled back in the car.

"No, I just felt weird when it was time to pay. I felt the lady behind the counter judging me." That snooty bitch behind the counter gave me the stink eye, but I don't know why. What does she expect people to purchase in Agent Provocateur?

"Fuck her. Who cares what people think? It's not like you have to see that lady on a daily basis. And trust me, if she saw who you're going to wear them for, she'd be giving you an even dirtier look. Your man is fucking fine… So who gives a shit what others think? Get out of your head, Ashley."

"He is fucking hot. That bitch has every right to be jealous." I laugh. All in all, the experience really wasn't anywhere nearly as bad as I'd expected.

"Now, let's have some real fun. Time for some sexting, bitch. Give me your phone."

"Do you think that's a good idea?"

"Hell yes, I do. There's no better way to keep his mind on you than sending him a reminder that you're amazing. Sexting can be fucking hot," she says, her tone serious.

I hand Quinn my phone, and she sets the bag up on my lap, making sure the logo is visible. Then she snaps a picture of the bag. She sends the picture along with a text saying "Look at where I spent my afternoon." No taking it back now.

"Now wait until he texts back." I'm not sure he will text back. It's a Saturday, so he's probably getting ready for tomorrow's game. There's also the time difference since he's in Denver and all. Even so, not two minutes later, my phones dings and Tanner's name lights up on the screen. One new message.

"Holy shit! He texted back, Quinn. What do I do?" I fumble with my phone, trying to swipe the screen to open the message.

"Jesus, Ash. Chill the fuck out and read the message," she chides.

Tanner: *Wish I were there. Did you have fun?*

"Give me that." Quinn snatches the phone from me. She types something quickly and hands it back to me.

Me: *I sure did. It was fun trying to decide what would make your jaw hit the floor the fastest.*

"What the fuck, Quinn? Really?"

"Shut up and wait for his response. You'll be thanking me when he fucks you into oblivion next time he sees you."

So I sit there and wait, hoping that letting her send that text wasn't a total mistake.

He texts back almost immediately.

Tanner: *Baby, you in anything from that place would make my jaw hit the floor.*

My cheeks burn as I blush fiercely. It feels like they're on fire. *Thank God he isn't here to see how red my face is.*

"Based on the blushing, I guess he sent you something good. Let me see." She bounces in her seat.

I obediently hand her my phone.

"I told you. Take out that corset and we'll send him a picture of it. That thing is beyond hot, and you could practically lick your own nipples with ease."

I pull it from the bag and lay it out on my lap for Quinn to take a picture. She snaps the picture and sends it. No message.

It takes Tanner less than a minute to respond.

Tanner: *Damn. Can't wait to come home and see that on in person. Thanks for the hard-on, baby.*

Quinn tells me to write back a simple 'anytime,' so I do.

We head from Fifth Avenue in Midtown down to Chelsea where Quinn parks on Twentieth Street.

"Give me your phone again," she demands after we get out of the car. She takes a picture of a storefront, a place called *Purple Pleasure*, and sends it to Tanner as well. "Come on. Let's go check it out." She hands me back the phone and walks toward the entrance of the store.

The place looks intimidating and it makes me a little apprehensive heading in. It's small, but the mannequins in the window are all wearing latex. I can't even imagine what I'll find inside.

"Quinn, are you sure about this place?" I ask, following close behind her.

"Yes," she tells me as we step through the door, but I barely hear her. I can't believe my eyes. Latex everywhere. Whips, chains, costumes, and an assortment of other shit I have no clue about.

"Seriously? What the fuck do you want me to get from in here?"

"Relax, I picked this place on purpose, sweets," she assures me. "I wanted to show you that people have all types of kinks and fetishes and there's nothing wrong with a single one. Some people like to get all dressed up in this shit and then whip and beat the hell out of each other. All for the sake of good sex! So in reality, what you desire is nothing in the grand scheme of kinkiness. So get over yourself."

From the look on her face, you'd think she'd just made the best point in the history of the universe. I guess if I really think about it, she kind of did. If people can own wanting to dress up in all this stuff and not give a shit, I should be able to own wanting to be ordered around and controlled during sex. It's really not that far out there.

"I see some light in those baby blues of yours. Things finally clicking for you?"

"Yes, my super, awesome, amazing friend. I understand what you're saying, and you're right. Time to stop being a baby," I declare confidently.

The ding of my message alert pulls our attention away from the task at hand.

Tanner: *Didn't take you for a full-on submissive, but hey, it's all fine by me. I have no problem looking at you in some serious latex. What are you planning on getting there?*

Me: *I'm not. This place was Quinn's idea.*

Tanner: *Too bad. I love the thought of dominating you.*

"Oh my God! What do I say to that?" I show Quinn the text, feeling conflicted. Here I am, standing in a BDSM sex store, texting Tanner about being dominated, and if I am honest, I'm totally turned on.

"Let me see," she says, considering. "Damn, this man is perfect for you, Ashley. I'm so jealous."

"I'm totally hot and bothered right now," I admit shyly. The thoughts of Tanner running through my mind right now are making me really horny, and I'm so distracted by them that I don't even check Quinn's response to Tanner. I hadn't even realized that she'd taken my phone.

Me: *I didn't say you couldn't. Just don't expect me to be wearing a red leather catsuit while you do it.*

"Dammit, Quinn." I try to grab my phone back. "Give me my phone."

"No. I'm doing you a favor. Chill out."

My phone dings again, and Quinn reads the text to me, still keeping my phone hostage.

Tanner: *Damn, baby. Are you trying to make my dick explode? First images of you in a corset, and now a cat suit? Show a man some mercy. I'm on the other side of the country.*

Me: *It's only fair since thoughts of you owning me are making my panties wet. And I'm surrounded by a bunch of huge vibrating cocks.*

Tanner: *Maybe you should get yourself one of the vibrating cocks for when I'm not around. Because that's the only other cock you'll be getting.*

"This man has it bad, sweets." Quinn beams at me. "See the things that you find out when you grow a pair and voice what you desire? Or at least let me do it for you…"

I grab my phone back at last and stick my tongue out at her before heading over to the vibrator section on the far-left wall. Then I text Tanner back.

Me: *Oh, I think I will. So many to choose from.*
Tanner: *You're in so much trouble when I get back there.*

I smile to myself before grinning at Quinn. "Let's pick out some toys!"

"That's my girl." She high fives me.

Chapter Eighteen

ASHLEY

AFTER MY SHOPPING trip on Saturday, I didn't hear from Tanner again until last night when he texted me to let me know he was heading back to Jersey and he wanted to see me tonight. He also said I'd better be wearing something from my new lingerie collection. I hadn't been expecting him to be in a playful mood considering the Jets lost, but I'm not going to complain.

At the office this morning, I decided to go with the corset set for tonight. I know he likes that one, and it's also my favorite. When I got home, I picked out a black garter and pair of stockings to go with it. Feeling a bit provocative, I choose to wear the garters and corset under the skirt and sweater I'd worn to work, leaving them just slightly visible. I can't wait to see Tanner's reaction. If I'm honest, I'm trying to incite the jealous side I saw come out during our texting on Saturday when he commented that his cock is the only one I'll be getting from now on. Call me crazy, but I like his covetous side.

Tanner had texted me about half an hour ago to say he was on his way to pick me up. Just as I finish retouching my makeup, I hear a knock I'm sure is him. Quinn isn't home to answer, so I hurry to the front door.

I haven't laid eyes on this man in almost a week, so I'm beyond excited to see his handsome face.

I pull open the door, a huge smile on my face. "Hi," I say, raking my eyes up and down his body shamelessly, checking him out. I'd almost swear it has just gotten ten degrees hotter in here.

"Well, hello to you, too." He smirks, knowing full well I'm picturing him naked. He pulls me into his arms, dips me down, and plants his lips on mine. I guess he missed me too.

"Miss me much?" I chuckle when he breaks the kiss and sets me back upright.

"Sure did, especially after you sent those pictures," He smiles and wiggles his eyebrows at me.

"That was all Quinn's idea," I say, suddenly worried that he thinks differently of me after seeing those pictures and texts.

"Remind me to thank her the next time that I see her. Are you ready to go?" He finally takes a minute to look me over.

"Yup," I tell him, purposely popping the 'p.'

"You sure?" A suggestive glint gleams in his eye.

"Absolutely. Come on, I'm starving." I head over to the console table next to our front door, grab my purse, and wait for Tanner to catch up.

"Okay, if this is how you want to play it." He smiles deviously, grabs my hand, and we head to the car.

I can't help but second guess myself now. Was that a good smile or a bad smile? His reaction to my outfit reminds me of Quinn's Cheshire grin from before she took me to the sex store. I have a feeling that smile means trouble.

"What's the matter, baby?" Tanner asks once we're settled in the car. I'm pretty sure he knows what the matter is, but I'm not going to give him the satisfaction of saying it aloud. I've got my big girl panties on—and garters too. If he thinks he can intimidate me, then I'll have to be just as devious.

"Nothing, Tanner." I smile at him, sliding my hand up my left leg as I cross it over my right to give him a glimpse of what's hiding under my skirt. I hear the hiss of his breath catching in his throat, and I'm sure he's noticed my garters. I internally fist pump, ecstatic I can get to him the same way he gets to me.

"Okay then. Tell me about your week."

I oblige, telling him about the places I had to check out this week, even about the bitch from the boutique I didn't like. I recount my weekend adventure with Quinn, but he already knows all about that.

I'm surprised when we pull up to the restaurant Tanner has picked for dinner. I'd been sure that with him picking, it would be some swanky, upscale place. But instead, it's a small, intimate Italian place.

"I do pay attention when you talk, Ashley," Tanner explains. "I know you prefer quiet and laid-back as opposed to expensive and stuffy." He guides me inside with a hand at the small of my back. I have no control over the shiver that runs through my body when Tanner touches me. It happens without fail every damn time.

I catch the hostess checking out Tanner as she takes us to our table. The bitch has balls, I'll give her that. I'm standing right next to him, and we're clearly on a date. We're standing so close to each other you probably couldn't fit a piece of paper between us. Tanner's hand is still on my back, in that spot reserved for lovers and significant others. I want to punch her. She has a stupid, love-struck look in her eyes, and I'm almost positive she's starting to drool. She just stands there as though she's waiting to do something but has totally forgotten what it was.

Even after we sit down, the dumb bitch is still staring at my date, so I decide to make it obvious that she's no longer welcome. I sit back in my chair, square my shoulders, and turn my full attention to her. When she still manages to ignore me, I clear my throat loudly. The moron standing next to our table staring idiotically is finally startled out of her stupor.

"Thank you," I say as she shuffles away, my tone sarcastically sweet.

Tanner chuckles, and I'm sure he knows exactly what that little display was all about. "You're cute when you're jealous."

"I don't know if I would call myself jealous, but I was worried about the safety of the rest of the patrons. They could have slipped and fallen on the drool puddle she was leaving next to our table."

"She can drool all she wants. I couldn't tell you one thing about her because I was too busy staring at my girl, who decided it'd be fun to wear her lingerie to dinner," Tanner reassures me.

I blush a little when he mentions my outfit and wonder if he's trying to subtly tell me he doesn't think it's so cute.

"Are there any more surprises for me somewhere in that outfit?" he asks, using a deep, husky voice I've only heard from him during sex. The voice that makes my panties so fucking wet.

I shake my head no, not wanting to speak right now. I don't want him to hear the longing in it.

A waitress, who thankfully is not mesmerized by Tanner, comes over and takes our order. I decide on the ravioli and a glass of pinot noir and Tanner orders the Marsala and a glass of Chianti. I use the lull in the conversation as an opportunity to take in the restaurant. It's quiet and serene, exactly what I picture when I think of a restaurant I'd find in Italy itself. The tables are each covered with red-and-white checkered tablecloths and set with a single candle in the middle. The candles burn from inside hurricane lamps and give off a soft glow that adds to the ambiance.

I pull my roaming eyes back to our table to look at Tanner. I find him staring at me, and I wonder how long I've been lost in my thoughts of the restaurants of Italy.

"Sorry, I couldn't stop staring. This place is beautiful inside. You're right, it's quiet and peaceful," I say, trying to explain my mental absence.

"It's definitely beautiful in here tonight," he says, his eyes locked on my face.

I feel my cheeks heat up. Thankfully, the waitress comes by with our glasses of wine just then. I pick up my glass, take a sip, and nod to the waitress to let her know it's fine.

"How come you never talk about your family, Ashley?" Tanner asks before sipping his own wine.

I chuckle a little at the randomness of his question but answer truthfully, "We aren't close like you and your family. I'm an only child. My parents and I have never really seen eye to eye. Especially my mother and I. Don't get me wrong, I love my parents, but it's easier not talking to them all that often."

"That sounds sad."

"It can be, especially when I see families like yours. The closeness and understanding. My dad is very reserved, never really caring one way or the other as long as I'm content, but my mother... She's another story. Nothing is ever good enough for her. She doesn't care for my choice in career, didn't care for the college that I chose, has never liked a single boyfriend I've brought home. She's very loving, but also very opinionated. She has no problem telling you when she doesn't like something, and she never likes what I do. So it's easier to not tell her much. Then I don't have to hear her tell me yet again about how I'm messing up my life." I hadn't really planned on telling him all that, but once I'd started, I couldn't stop. Oh well, I'm not the only one in the world who has a mother who doesn't approve of her life.

"I'm sorry your mom doesn't see the amazing person you are. You're an incredible writer. Just look at what you did for me. Sometimes parents can be stubborn when they think they know what's best for us. Trust me, I've been there a time or two." He grins and grabs my hand across the table.

"Thank you. So please don't think that I don't bring them up or around because I don't want them to know about you. It's just easier, you know?" I say before realizing I'd just assumed Tanner would want to meet my parents. Dammit, that was presumptuous of me. We aren't officially boyfriend and girlfriend. We're just dating. I hope he doesn't think I'm making more of our relationship than there is to it.

"What's wrong?"

I feel my face turn red with embarrassment.

"Nothing. Sorry. I didn't mean to assume that you wanted to meet my parents or anything," I say, trying to sound nonchalant.

"Of course I would want to meet your parents. But only if you want me to. My parents are probably dying to meet you."

"Really?" I'm shocked that he's even mentioned me to his parents.

"Yes, I told them all about you."

The only thing I can do is smile back. I'm over the fucking moon that Tanner Garrison has told his parents about me.

"Glad your happy glow is back." Tanner smiles widely at me.

The waitress arrives with our dinner and we chitchat about everyday things over the food. Tanner tells me all about the team's loss yesterday. He's very logical about it though, admitting that it sucks to lose, but you can't win them all. He has a very optimistic attitude about everything, and I'm sure that's a rare quality for a football player to have.

"It's the interviews after a loss that suck. Everyone knows you just lost, so why ask questions like 'How does it feel to get your asses kicked?' or 'How hard was that sack?' The one that always gets me is 'What do you think you could have done differently?' Umm, gee, I don't know, played better and won?" he says sarcastically, shaking his head.

I laugh. When you think about it, they are pretty stupid questions. "Promise you'll tell me if I ask stupid questions when working on a piece?"

"Yes, I'll definitely call you out on stupid questions." He chuckles too.

We finish our dinner and then head back to Tanner's Range Rover. Once we're settled in and buckled, Tanner starts the car. But instead of heading out of the parking lot, he turns to me and slides his hand up my leg and under my skirt.

"Ready to head back to your place and pay for teasing me with all this lingerie at dinner?" he asks, kissing the side of my neck while running his hand up and down the inside of my thigh.

I gulp at his words. *What does he mean by 'pay'?*

"What's the matter? Did you think you'd sit across from me all dinner long wearing that and I wouldn't get retribution? I've had a hard-on all night long, and I had to watch the men in the place staring at you, wishing that they could see what was underneath this. But they can't, can they, baby? Because only I get to see what's hidden in here." He drags a finger along the tops of my pushed-up breasts. If this is how he reacts to a little visible lingerie, I may have to wear a corset every day from now on.

"Do you like the sound of that? Going home and showing me what's hidden underneath this?" He peppers my neck with kisses while the hand beneath my skirt pushes my panties aside.

"Yes," I answer, already a slave to his voice. How does this man do this to me in less than two seconds flat? Every damn time.

"I know. Not only can I feel it, but I can smell just how aroused you are right now."

"Christ, Tanner!" That fucking mouth of his. I've never had a man speak to me like that before.

"I can't wait to get you home and see what you have for me under this skirt," he says, stroking the slit of my pussy with his fingers, dragging my wetness up and around my clit. My whole body shudders. He pulls his hand out from under my skirt and puts the finger that was just playing in my wetness into his mouth, seductively licking my essence off of it.

I'd almost swear that I hear my panties just melt away. Tanner doesn't say another word. After he removes his cleaned finger from his mouth, he puts the car in gear and drives toward my apartment.

I'VE BEEN ON edge since Tanner dropped his comment about retribution. I'm grateful I live less than ten minutes from the restaurant because I'm about to die of anticipation. I have a feeling this is what Tanner had planned all along. He's priming me without even touching me. Slick bastard. I want to tell him I've figured out his game, but I like it, so I'll play along.

He hasn't said a word since we left the parking lot, but I'm sure that's part of the game. The goal seems pretty simple: keep Ashley in a perpetual state of eagerness—eager to know what he meant, eager to hear his next dirty words, eager to feel his hands or any other part of him on my body. Keep me so on edge that I explode. He may get his wish soon.

When we enter the condo, it's straight down to business, and it plays out like every fantasy I've ever had combined into one. Tanner slams me against the door as soon as it's closed. He pushes my arms behind my back until he can grab both wrists in one hand. His free hand shoves my skirt up around my hips, exposing my stockings and garters. I hear Tanner hiss out his approval again.

"Damn, baby. This should be illegal. I can't believe all this was hiding under there," he says, dropping to his knees. He runs his tongue along the garter straps. The heat from his breath being quickly cooled by the air conditioning makes my skin break out in goosebumps. Tanner reaches around to find the zipper of my skirt, unzips it, and pulls it to the ground.

I step out of it and kick it to the side as Tanner sits back and lets his eyes roam my legs. The appreciation in his eyes has me thanking Quinn tenfold.

Tanner releases my hands just long enough to remove my sweater and expose the corset. My sweater hits the floor soundlessly, leaving nothing to distract Tanner from taking in the view of my secret ensemble.

"I don't know if I've ever seen anything hotter than you, baby," Tanner says, circling me. He runs his fingers along the tops of my breasts just like he did in the car. Coming to a stop behind me, he sweeps my hair to the side and kisses my neck in the exact spot that makes my knees buckle. I feel his hands moving at my back, but I can't tell what he's doing through the thick fabric. That is, until my breasts are free and my corset hits the floor. "So beautiful." He cups my breasts, using his thumbs to flick my nipples back and forth in a near perfect rhythm.

"Mmm..." I hum out in gratitude, thankful for the sensations Tanner's sending coursing through my body.

"Like that?" he asks, using the voice that turns my insides into mush. I could probably come from the sound of his voice if I really tried. The deep timbre reverberates through my entire body.

I nod against his chest. I love when we're like this. He makes me feel so small but so safe, which is new for me. I've never felt this sort of contentment before with a man. How does he know how to play my body like a fiddle?

"What did you buy other than lingerie on Saturday?" Tanner slides his hands down my sides and runs them over my hips. His fingers move at an achingly slow pace towards the apex of my thighs.

"What do you mean?" I know exactly what he's talking about, but I don't want to admit what I bought out loud. "I'm talking about the vibrating cock you purchased."

"Maybe I didn't buy one," I say, trying to make him doubt his conviction.

"That's a shame because I've been picturing pleasing you with it all night." He sighs in mock disappointment.

Images of Tanner holding my vibrator are enough to have me dripping. How is it that everything he says makes me hotter and wetter? I'd always thought women who talked about melting for their men were full of shit, but I totally understand now.

"Does the thought of me playing with you with your vibrator turn you on?" he asks, skimming his fingers over the area I want them most. "I think it does. You're soaked, baby. Where is it?" he asks again.

"My nightstand." I give in, needing to see if the reality compares to the fantasy in my head.

Suddenly, I'm scooped up and thrown over Tanner's shoulder. He smacks my ass and heads to the back of my condo. "Where to, Ash?"

"Back and to the right," I tell him, lifting myself up and glancing behind me to make sure he's heading in the right direction.

He opens the door to my room and tosses me onto the bed. "This one?" Tanner asks, pointing to the nightstand on the right side of my bed.

I nod excitedly. I'm glad that I went with a normal vibrator instead of one of the crazy ones Quinn had suggested. I would have been mortified if he pulled out the twelve-inch purple monstrosity Quinn had thought was perfect.

"You've been using it. Haven't you?" Tanner asks with an eyebrow raised.

How would he know that I used it this week? I start to panic, thinking maybe it has dried, crusty remnants on it or something. I always wipe it down, but maybe I hadn't done such a good job last time.

"Relax, Ashley, there's nothing wrong with using it." He must be able to see the doubt and worry on my face.

"How do you know I used it?"

"Well, you just bought it. If you hadn't used it, I'd assume it would still be in the package. Not exactly rocket science to put two and two together, baby." He smirks at me while climbing onto the bed with me. He turns the knob to turn it on, and he brings it down to my legs. He drags the vibrator up and down my legs slowly, one at a time. "Did you like using this?" Tanner asks using his seductive voice again. He seems to have caught on to the fact that he can get me to do just about anything when he talks to me like that.

"It's fast and efficient," I sass him.

"Is it now?" He grins as he drags the vibrator up straight to my clit and holds it there.

"Ahhhh," I moan, my back arching up. Then the vibration disappears.

Tanner brings it back a few seconds later, making me moan once more. Then it's gone again. He continues this for a few minutes until I get fed up.

"Dammit, Tanner," I growl. "Stop teasing me."

"You think this is teasing? I've been thinking about you playing with this since Saturday night. I've had images of you in different getups flashing through my mind for two days. I had to eat across from you wearing that damn corset. So who's been teasing whom?"

I can't find words to answer him since he's now dragging the vibrator up and down my entire slit. All I can think about is the need to come. I want Tanner to fuck me now.

"Please," I whimper.

"Please what, baby? Want me to fuck you with your fake cock or the real one that has been aching for you for days?"

"You. Definitely you."

"That's what I thought. This thing can't compare to me, can it, baby?" he prods.

"Not a chance in hell."

He shows me, twice, exactly why that vibrator can never compare to the sexual force that is Tanner Garrison.

Chapter Nineteen

TANNER

THINGS HAVE BEEN continuing to fall into place. We kicked ass in our game today and won against Miami. It was a close one, tied twenty-one to twenty-one in the fourth quarter, anyone's game. I had just dropped back to pass, but none of my receivers were open. As if the football gods were on my side, a hole opened up that gave me a direct line to rush the ball in myself for a touchdown. There was still four and a half minutes left on the clock, so we decided to go for the two-point conversion, forcing Miami to have to score twice to beat us. Darren was able to get the ball over the plane into the end zone for the two points. Our defense held Miami to a three and out, and the rest is history. I love games that come down to the wire like this one. It makes the win that much sweeter. Afterward, I couldn't wait to get back home tonight. There's only one person I want to share my victory with, and I can't stop thinking about her.

I hadn't been able to spend much time with Ashley this week. She's been a total trooper, though, never complaining, always happy with whatever time I can give her. I can't explain how happy that makes me feel. Christ, if Alex could see inside my head right now, he'd definitely call a meeting to revoke my man card. Even I have to admit I sound like a sappy, pussy-addicted bitch. The funny part is that I haven't even gotten that much pussy, but what I have gotten has been spectacular.

Ashley's finally opening up bit by bit, but I want to open her up more, and soon. Soon, like after this post-game circus soon. I want to really break Ashley out of her shell for good. I can tell there's a real gem hiding behind that insecure exterior. I guess I can't blame her for her insecurities—she did find that douche-nozzle ex of hers fucking someone else. I'd imagine that's enough to make any woman swear off sex. But she hasn't thrown the towel in yet, and she's been willing to try again with me. I can't wait to show her just how much fun we can have, and I plan on showing her tonight. We're almost done here at the stadium, and my plan is to take a detour to Ashley's instead of going home.

Once I get into my car and Reg has sped off, I decide to text Ashley.

Me: *Hey Beautiful, what are you up to?*
Ashley: *Watching the highlights from some hot quarterback's amazing win against Miami today.*

I love that she's keeping up with the team. It gives me hope that I'm not the only one who's almost obsessed here.

Me: *Oh yeah? Are you liking what you see in those highlights?*
Ashley: *Do you mean those tight-as-hell white pants that make your ass look delicious?*

I can't help but laugh at that comment.

Me: *Delicious? I think it's your ass that's delicious. But I'm more than willing to put it to the test to find out who wins. I'm putting my money on yours, though.*
Ashley: *Mmm, I think it's a win-win either way. Don't you?*
Me: *Well, considering one of us has done more tasting than the other, I think it's you who's winning.*
Ashley: *Oh no. We can't have you sporting a sad face after such a big win. What can we do to make it better?*

Ah, the perfect segue for me to break out the big guns.

Me: *Well, since you're not here to make it better yourself, you'll have to give me something else to work with. Tell me what you're wearing.*

It takes a few minutes for her to respond, and I almost think she isn't going to answer me. Then I hear the ding of a text message alert.

Ashley: *The temperature here seems to have risen considerably in the last 20 minutes, so I'm just hanging out in a tiny tank top and boy shorts.*

At this moment, I want to personally thank the person who designed those boy short things because he is my hero. They were clearly created to show the perfect amount of ass with just a hint of the Promised Land hiding underneath.

Me: *I hope that means that sweet ass of yours is watching those highlights at home instead of at a bar.*
Ashley: *And if I am in a bar?*
Me: *Then your fine ass is going to be reddened before I taste it. But I have a feeling you just might like that. Would you, Ashley? Would you like me to spank your ass until your pussy is dripping?*

She doesn't respond right away, but I'm sure that she's feeling shy rather than turned off, so I decide to give her another nudge to see how far I can get her to go.

Me: *Dripping wet, Ashley. I would have you so turned on your panties would be soaked. And since they're so wet, we really have no need for them, so I'd pull them down your legs, making sure my fingertips hit every sensitive spot on the way down. All while kissing your neck and telling you how turned on I am by the fact you're so wet for me.*
Me: *You're aching, aren't you, baby? You want my hands all over that fantastic body of yours don't you?*

Ashley: *God, yes, Tanner! I want you so bad. Please don't stop.*

Holy shit. She must be touching herself. I know she is.

Me: *Ashley, are you touching that pretty pussy of yours? You are, aren't you?*
Ashley: *Yes, Tanner. God, I can't help it. I wish it were you touching me.*
Me: *I will be, baby. Soon enough. Tell me how you feel. Tell me how soft your pussy is. Are you making yourself quiver with pleasure? Because if I were there, you would be quivering. Your pussy would be on pleasure overload.*
Me: *After touching every part of your pussy with my fingers, I would then use my tongue once I was done enjoying the taste of your perfectly erect nipples. Do you like that, Ashley?*
Ashley: *I'm so wet, Tanner. I hate that I have to stop touching myself to answer you back. I love everything you want to do. I wish I was quivering with all the pleasure I could be. It would be so much better if you were here with me.*

I'm about ten minutes from her house. I need to time these texts out perfectly if I want to wind up at her door before she comes. She's not coming without me. I need to be the one her pussy contracts around during the height of pure pleasure. I want my body to bring her there, not her fingers or my words in her head. I need to keep her typing so her hands aren't on her pussy.

"Reg, I'll give you an extra fifty if you can make it there in five minutes," I promise my driver. I don't know if I can last much longer than that. My cock is so hard it fucking hurts. I'm pretty sure I'll have an imprint from my zipper permanently embedded in him before I can get him into Ashley's pussy.

Me: *What would you want me to do, Ashley? Tell me. I need to know how you want me to please you, baby.*

Ashley: *I want it all Tanner. Everything you just said. I want your fingers, your tongue. I want that huge cock of yours that my toy can't even compare to. I want to feel you everywhere. I need it. Oh my God, I need to come so bad.*

Me: *You need to come?*

Ashley: *Yes, Tanner. Please make me come.*

Perfect timing. I'm out of the car and ringing the doorbell about five seconds after receiving her last text. I hope Quinn's not home because that might be awkward, but she won't stop me.

I stand there for a few minutes, hearing scurrying noises from behind the door. Finally, Ashley answers the door looking ready to be fucked and horny as hell.

"You need to come, baby?" I ask, a huge shit-eating grin on my face.

"God, yes!" she answers, flinging the door open and pulling me in by my tie.

"Your wish is my command."

Chapter Twenty

ASHLEY

HOLY FUCK! **I** cannot believe Tanner just showed up. Thank God, though. I'm so horny I think I could die. I want what only Tanner can give me. I'm so wound up I don't have the energy to be even the slightest bit embarrassed about the texts we've been sending back and forth for the last hour.

"How are you doing, Ashley?" Tanner asks with a smug smile.

I glance down at his suit pants before answering, wanting to see if he's as turned on as I am. I'm more than happy to see that his pants seem to be quite snug in the crotch.

"About as good as you are, it seems." I smile, looking down at his erection.

"We're both about to feel really good, baby," he says, closing in on me. "Why don't you show me what you were doing before I rang the doorbell?"

There's no way I can do that in front of him. I don't care how turned on I am. I've never touched myself in front of anyone.

"What's wrong?" He looks very pleased with himself. "Don't you want to continue?"

"I... I... can't... do that... in front of you," I tell him with my head down. Being brave through text messages is one thing, but I don't know if I can pull it off in front of him.

"Do what, baby?" He spins me around to face away from him and brushes the hair off my right shoulder before placing light, sensual kisses up and down my neck. "You can't play with your pussy in front of me?"

I don't answer him because I can't. My eyes keep fluttering closed thanks to the way he's kissing my neck and making every part of my body hum. I can't seem to think about anything other than where he's going to place the next kiss. His hands have joined in the fun and run softly up and down both sides of my body, coming very close to skimming my breasts. Lord, how I would love nothing more than for him to move those hands up and play with my nipples. I feel the hardness of his cock against the small of my back. He's making himself as hot as he's making me. I'm not sure how much more teasing I can handle. I need to be touched, and I mean really touched.

"Don't you want this? I know I want nothing more than to spread you open and devour you."

My insides liquefy at his words. I want that. To be devoured. To be owned. I want him to do every naughty thing he has on his mind to me and more. If Tanner continues to stroke and kiss every part of my body other than my core, it's very possible I'll implode.

"Please," I beg. It's all I can manage to get out at the moment. I've never been this on fire before. I can feel the pull from my pussy. It's begging to be touched, begging for release. I wasn't too far from finishing when he arrived, and now my body wants the pleasure it was promised.

"Please what, Ashley? What do you want?"

"I want you."

"Want me how? Tell me what you want me to do. I don't know exactly what you like yet. I need you to teach me how to please you, baby. If you can't ask for it, then I can't give it."

Oh, fuck. He's determined to draw this out and make me tell him everything I want. I can't do that. Not yet. No way. My mind is spinning with the need for release, but also with fear—fear of embarrassment. I'm way out of my league here.

"You need to relax. Stop thinking. Tell me what you want, what you need. It's just me here. Talk."

"I...I need you to…touch me. Please."

"Touch you where? Here?" He moves his hands up under my shirt to cup my breasts. Each of his hands covers an entire breast. He pushes them together and up and rolls my nipples between his thumbs and index fingers.

I can't hold back the moan building within. It feels so good. My whole body is on fire. "Mmm, yes. There," I say, laying my head back onto his strong chest. I feel nothing but the sensations coursing through my body.

"Is this the only place you want me to touch you? You seem very needy right now. Why don't you tell me what else you need," he croons into my ear while caressing it with the tip of his tongue.

I really want the tip of that tongue somewhere else, but I remember him saying he doesn't care for that. I don't think I can get the words out to ask for it knowing he isn't fond of giving oral. God, I would love nothing more than to have him lick me from top to bottom.

"What are you thinking about? I can feel the change in your body." Tanner continues to tease my ear and neck with kisses and nips.

"I need you to touch my pussy. Please, Tanner."

He places a hand over mine and glides them down my body. As our hands push under the elastic of my boy shorts, Tanner says, "Show me what you want me to do. How do you like your pussy stroked? Hard, soft, fast, slow?" His voice is both commanding and sensual, the tone alone hypnotizing. It takes over my brain and wills me to do as he says.

As though I have no control over my own hand, I slide my fingers down to the top of my pussy and run them gently over my clit. Tanner's hand over mine follows my motions. He urges my hand down to my opening and pushes one of my fingers slowly in, up to the first knuckle. He then adds a finger of his own, circling it around mine. The two different motions have my whole body humming. He pulls his finger back and brings mine with it, easing our fingers back up to my clit and circles it. I follow along, enjoying every single sweet sensation I'm feeling.

"Keep playing with your clit, Ashley," is the only warning I get before Tanner's hand descends back to my slit. He dips a finger in and pulls it back out to spread my wetness around. He strokes and rubs, stimulating me in ways I didn't even know were possible.

"Do you like that? Would you like me to continue petting your pussy or would you like more?"

"Please, more. God, I want more." Who the hell is this wanton creature that has taken over my body? I don't have time to think before my subconscious spits out the answers it knows I'd hesitate to say.

With my consent, Tanner pushes two long, thick fingers into me and starts stroking. He curves them, applying pressure to the just the right spot. My knees buckle, and I let out the breathiest moan I've ever heard myself make.

"Ooh, God, Tanner."

"Not quite baby, but pretty damn close." He chuckles, pumping his fingers, making sure to hit my G-spot over and over. The pleasure is so intense that keeping up the pressure on my clit, standing up, and enjoying what he's doing all at the same time is nearly impossible. His superpower of reading my thoughts must kick in again because the next thing I know, he's pushing me toward the back of the apartment, never missing a beat with the fingers he still has buried in my pussy.

"Open the door," he orders.

"Okay." I push open the door.

I'm pulled into the air and tossed down onto the bed. Tanner grabs both of my ankles and pulls me to the end of the bed before dropping to his knees. He pulls my panties down my legs, making sure his fingers brush every sensual spot on the way down, just the way he promised he would in his text. After dropping my panties on the floor, he slides his hands back up my legs. They settle just under the apex of my thighs, spreading me wide.

I can't take my eyes off of him, this beautiful man on his knees between my legs. I know that he doesn't like to give oral, so I know that I have to say something. I refuse to be like everyone else in his life, taking things from him.

"You don't need to do that," I say, even though I want nothing more than to feel that tongue of his inside every one of my hidden nooks and crannies.

"Do you want me to lick your pussy?"

"Only if you want to."

"I asked if you wanted me to lick your pussy. Answer me."

"Yes, I want nothing more, but I know how you feel about that…" I don't even get to finish my sentence before I feel the warmth of his breath on me and the wetness of his tongue as he laps at my lower lips. I may have just invented a new gymnastics move with the way he's sent my overly sensitized body flying into the air.

"If I didn't want to eat your pussy, I wouldn't. Never hesitate to ask for something you want. What we do in the bedroom is between you and me. If you want something, ask for it. Because I'm going to take every single thing that I want from you," he says before resuming his delicious assault on my pussy.

His tongue circles my clit the same way my fingers just did, except he's using a hand to spread my pussy lips as wide as they will open, making everything taut and the pleasure more intense. He adds his fingers back into the mix, and I know I'm not going to last much longer. The fingers he has in my pussy are magic, caressing all the right spots. My breathing becomes shallower, my hips moving of their own volition, my mouth issuing little indecipherable moans. The walls of my pussy quake, and I feel my orgasm just on the horizon.

"Oh God! Oh God! Oh fuck, Tanner."

"Come. Let go, baby! I want to see you lose it," he says, and it's as though a switch goes off in my brain.

My back arches up off the bed, my legs shake around Tanner's head, and I let out the kind of scream you only hear in porn as my world bursts into flashes of color. Wave after wave of pleasure keeps coming as Tanner continues to stroke me through my orgasm. He lightly caresses my nub with his tongue as he waits for me to come back down.

"So beautiful. I need my cock in you now, Ashley." He reaches into his pocket and pulls out a condom before dropping his pants and pulling off his boxers.

"We don’t have to use that if you don’t want," I tell him. "I’m on birth control. I use the patch." I roll to my side to show him where I have it on my hip. "And I was tested after I caught Jason cheating on me. I'm clean."

He seems lost in thought while he unbuttons his shirt and removes it along with his tie, looking as though he can’t quite believe what I’ve just said.

“I’ve never had sex without a condom,” he tells me. His eyes meet mine before he looks back down at the patch. “Are you sure?”

“Absolutely.”

He doesn’t say anything else for a few minutes, just stands there stroking his shaft up and down. God, he has a gorgeous cock. I’ve never seen anything like it before. Long, hard, and perfect. I practically salivate just looking at it. I'm still a little intimidated by the size, but since I’m already so worked up, I’m not terribly worried.

"I hope you're ready, baby. I wasn’t kidding when I said I’m going to take what I want from you, and what I want is to fuck you like you have never been fucked before. So if you have any objection to that, now is the time to say it. I don’t think I’ll be able to stop once I slide bare into your perfect little pussy."

God damn, if I were still wearing panties, they’d be soaked all over again. My subconscious strikes again, spitting out words before I can put together a complete thought. "Fuck me, Tanner."

With no more hesitation, Tanner climbs onto the bed and kneels between my spread legs. He wraps his hands around my thighs and pulls me down to meet his cock. He slides his hands under my ass, lifting me higher before impaling me on his thick, rigid erection. "Holy Shit," he says at the same time I yell out, "Oh fuck."

I feel so full, so impossibly full. Tanner hits every sensitive spot possible with each thrust, and all I can do is hang on and pray like hell I don’t die of pleasure.

"Eyes on me. I want to see your beautiful face while I fuck this amazing pussy of yours. I’ve never felt anything this like before. You're so tight and hot. You make me feel like a teenager again. I don’t know how long I can last in this heaven before I come harder than I've ever come before."

I snap my eyes to his and take him in. His muscles all bulge; he's wound so tight. Watching the way he slams into me over and over is so fucking hot. I feel myself growing wetter and wetter watching him take what he wants from me. It isn't long before I feel a familiar pressure growing in the pit of my belly, and I decide to ask for what I want.

"Harder, Tanner. Fuck me harder."

And fuck me harder he does. He pulls out and flips me over. He slaps my ass as he tells me what he wants. "Put your gorgeous ass in the air, Ashley. You want harder, you're going to get harder." He pulls me up by my hips and pushes my upper body down to the bed. He wraps his hand in my hair and pulls my head back. Using my hair as leverage, he pulls back and slams his cock back into me repeatedly.

"Ahh, fuck, Tanner. Yes!" Every nerve ending in my body is on fire. My whole body is shaking. I feel the release coming, like a tsunami in the making.

"Are you close, baby? I'm ready to come. I need you to come with me."

"Yes, please. Fuck, I need to come."

The pleasure is so intense that every second it takes me to get closer is pure torture. He keeps up his fast rhythm until I'm in a delirious frenzy. I just need a little push to get me over the edge. Tanner's right hand leaves my hip, and when it returns, it's not where I expect. He's lubed his thumb and now gently massages my back hole.

I tense slightly. This is foreign territory for me. I've never had anything near my ass, and I'm not sure I want to either.

"Relax. Trust me. I won't hurt you," he says, continuing his ministrations. The sensation is odd but enjoyable. He applies a little pressure, rubbing his finger in small circles slowly, and I'm done.

"Yes, Ashley. Fuck yes, baby. Come. Squeeze my dick with your pussy," Tanner yells, thrusting harder, chasing his release while mine is still going. Everything has gone black except for the little stars I see behind my closed eyes.

"Fuck, Ashley," Tanner bellows as he slams into me one final time, pulling me to him.

I feel his hot cum filling me along with every twitch of his cock as it does. *Holy fuck.* I've never felt anything so earth-shattering in my whole life. My world has been rocked.

We stay locked together for a few more minutes, catching our breaths, before Tanner pulls out. He stands over me while I roll over and curl into a ball.

"I'll be right back," he says, lightly smacking my ass before heading to my bathroom. He returns a few minutes later with a wet washcloth in hand. He kneels down next me, says "Open," and pushes my legs apart. He gently wipes away the traces of his essence and my residual wetness before tossing the rag into the hamper.

"Is it okay if I stay?" he asks, looking down at me.

"Of course." I roll to one side of the bed so he can lie down.

He climbs in next to me, wraps his arms around me to pull me to his chest and kisses the top of my head. I smile to myself, laying a hand on his chest. He has no chest hair, and his skin feels incredibly soft. I can't help but pet him.

"What's going on in that pretty head of yours? You okay?" he asks.

I continue to pet his chest while he strokes my back. I'm amazed at how comfortable we are with each other. There's none of that weird "What do I say now?" phase going on.

"Nothing. Just thinking about how comfortable we are right now."

"I want you to always be comfortable with me. There's no reason for you not to be. I find everything about you beautiful and amazing. And what we just did was absolute perfection." He kisses the top of my head again.

"It was, wasn't it?"

"It sure was. I just have one question... What happened to you, baby? Why are you so shy when it comes to sex?"

"Nothing happened. I've just always been afraid to ask for what I want. I feel like saying it will make me seem like a whore," I answer without hesitation. No point in lying if he's going to know anyway.

Besides, I want to be open with him. I feel as though I can really be myself around Tanner.

"Why would that make you a whore? Unless you were asking every guy you met to fuck you… But even then, it's your business and no one else's."

"When I was a freshman in college, I decided to explore my sexuality. I went to a Halloween party, met a hot guy, and we hooked up. Afterward, I was trying to find Quinn, and what I found was the guy I'd just slept with talking shit about me to his friends. He said I was easy and down for anything. He told his friends to go find me since I'd probably be down for more. I was humiliated. People talked about that girl for weeks after, and I was always worried they would find out she was me. It gave me a complex, and since then I've felt that I would be slutty if I took or asked for what I wanted. I always wonder how people would look at me if they knew that I wanted to be owned or manhandled a little. Quinn has been telling me for years that it doesn't make me a slut, but it's hard to move past it. In my mind, I know what I want, but my mouth can't ever seem to get it out." Saying it aloud, I realize how silly it sounds, but no one ever said that insecurities needed to make sense.

"Well, baby, I can tell you one thing: I will own you. I'd love nothing more than to dominate you. I don't think you're a whore or a slut. I think it's a huge turn-on. That said, it's no one else's business what we do. I would love to show you how much fun we can have together if you'll just let me. I just need you to trust me."

"I do," I say, and I know it's true. I can tell he genuinely cares for me.

"Then that's all that matters, baby." He holds me a little tighter and kisses my forehead.

Chapter Twenty One

ASHLEY

THE AMOUNT OF time I've spent at Tanner's this past week has put me behind on my laundry, and I have at least three loads that need to be done this morning. I'd told Tanner as much when he asked why I needed to leave so early on a Friday. I've been spending nights at his place lately to make things easier for him. He spends most of the day working out and practicing with the team, and it's just more convenient for him to be in his own bed at night. I'd never realized how much work a football player does during the season. There are days when Tanner is already sleeping when I get to his house. Those are the times I love the most, when he looks so vulnerable and carefree. He's even more beautiful asleep if that's possible.

When I'd gotten back to my condo that morning, Quinn wasn't home. I've eaten and showered, and now it's time to get to work. I turn on the stereo and get started on the laundry and cleaning. I grab a pile of clothes and toss it into the washer before heading back to my room to pick up all the dirty laundry still littering the floor. I gather all the trash lying around and throw it out while I'm at it.

Looking down at my unmade bed, I can't remember the last time I changed the sheets. I grab the comforter and toss it into the corner next to the laundry basket. I grab some new sheets from the hall closet and come back to pull off the dirty ones. When I bunch up the flat sheet to toss it in the basket, something on the sheet has it sticking to the fitted one still on the bed. *Eww, gross!* It's probably a dried cum stain from Monday night when Tanner was here. I look closer to what has the sheets sticking together. *No fucking way!* I instinctively reach to rub my right hip, not believing my eyes. *This can't be happening.*

My birth control patch is not on my hip, but right in front of me, stuck to my sheets. *No! No! No!* I changed my patch on Monday like I always do, but must not have stuck it on as well as I'd thought. I immediately grab my phone to google what to do, finding one website that says I should put a replacement patch on right away, and as long as it hasn't been more than seven days I should be good. It also says to be safe I should use a backup contraceptive for the next few days just in case. *Well, that won't be a problem.* I won't see Tanner again until at least Monday or Tuesday.

I run to the bathroom and put on a new patch. In all the years I've been using the patch, I've never had one fall off. I blame it on Tanner, and his love of digging his fingers into my hips. Thankfully, it's only been off for just over seventy-two hours. I should be okay.

I FEEL AS though I've totally dodged a bullet with the patch situation. Of course, it had to happen the same week I tell Tanner we don't need to use condoms. My fantastic luck strikes again.

I spend the rest of the afternoon cleaning the condo until Quinn gets home and decides we need a girls' night in, complete with Chinese and wine—her favorites.

"I'll go for the wine, but I don't want Chinese." I'm tired of lo mien and sweet and sour shrimp.

"What do you want then?"

"How about Indian?" I ask, in the mood for something different.

"Not my first choice, but fine," she huffs as though it's the biggest inconvenience in the world. In all honesty, it probably is for her.

"So how was your week with the Superstar?" Quinn asks as soon as I hang up after placing our dinner order.

"Sex-tacular." I laugh at my own stupid joke.

"Really?" Quinn looks at me as though she might disown me, "That was lame even for you, sweets."

"Whatever."

"Well, I guess the sex must be that good if he has you making lame jokes about it. At least there's a plus side."

"It is, and it's an everyday occurrence. But it's not just the sex. I feel like I'm a different person when I'm with him. I feel like he gets me in ways that no one other than you does." It honestly feels as though a great weight has been lifted from my chest, but I can't help feeling anxious too.

"You say that as if it's a problem."

"Do I? I guess I'm afraid to let my guard down. God, my past with men sucks. Who's to say that I won't get burned again?"

"That's a part of life. Things happen, but you can't not live or take chances because of it. You run the risk of missing something great if you do that. But I'm not the person you need to be talking about this with. He is."

"We aren't even really a couple. Why would I tell him all of this? To scare him away? What if he decides that I'm not worth the baggage I bring to the table?" I ask. I don't know why a man like Tanner would want to deal with baggage, and Lord knows I have plenty.

"Well, then you'll know before things get too far, but I don't think that will be an issue, sweets. You're the only one that doesn't see your worth." She smiles at me.

"I'm not the only one. My mother would surely tell you what a disappointment I am." I sigh.

"Fuck your mom. I'd like to slap that woman for adding to all your doubts. I know she's your mother, but don't listen to a word the woman says about you and your worth. She wouldn't know your worth if it bit her in the ass," she says, flailing her arms in frustration.

I can't help but laugh at Quinn's animated spiel. She's never liked my mother.

While I'm still laughing, my phone rings and Tanner's name flashes across the screen. I swear he has ESP that lets him know when I'm talking about him.

"Hello," I say after swiping the screen to answer.

"Hey, baby, I know it's super late notice, but can you be ready in an hour?"

"Ready for what?"

"A fundraising gala this evening," he replies.

"Are you kidding me? There's no way that I can be ready for something like a fundraising gala in an hour. I don't even have a dress to wear to something like that." *Is he serious?*

"Come on, Ashley. I was just asked to go. It won't be for long and it's a good cause. You can even cover it for work," he adds as though he's trying to entice a child into eating her vegetables.

"That's a great idea, but there's still no way I can be ready in an hour," I insist just as Quinn rips the phone out of my hand.

"She'll be ready in an hour, Tanner. I'll make sure of it." She hangs up before I can protest.

"What the fuck?" I yell. "Why would you tell him that? There's no way I can pull that off. I have no dress, and I'd have to do full hair and makeup."

"Will you chill the fuck out and shut up? I have a closet full of dresses, and your hair and makeup won't take that long. Stop your bitching, and let's get to work. You don't turn down a chance for a night out."

I stand there, staring at her in utter disbelief. *She can't be serious.*

"Move your ass, bitch. Time's a' ticking," she calls over her shoulder on her way to her bedroom.

Not even an hour later, I'm standing in front of the full-length mirror checking myself out. I have to say I look damn good. I'd picked a royal blue sequined gown from Quinn's closet, a mutual favorite of ours. It makes my eyes pop. We've paired it with black Louboutin pumps. My hair is down and curled. Quinn has clipped it at the nape of my neck so it hangs, all to one side, down over my shoulder. My eye makeup is very natural, just black eyeliner and mascara with shimmery nude eyeshadow. My red lips pull the whole look together perfectly.

"Never doubt me," Quinn says smugly.

"I don't know about never, but in this case you were correct," I admit defeat.

I'm just finishing my look off with some earrings when the doorbell rings.

"I'll get it," Quinn yells, bounding for the door.

A few moments later, Tanner stands in my doorway, a huge grin on his face.

"I knew you'd be ready," he says, sauntering over to me like the king of the world.

"No, you didn't, and don't think I'm not pissed about this." I smile despite myself.

"Let's see if you're still pissed at the end of the night." He plants a kiss on the curve of my neck.

"Yes, let's see indeed." I step out of his reach. "None of that," I tell him. "We don't have time. I was only given an hour's notice for this evening."

"Yes, and you didn't even need it all. Reggie is waiting for us in the car." He ushers me from the room.

"Here," Quinn says, handing me a black clutch. "I put everything you might need tonight in here already."

"Thanks for all your help, Quinn," Tanner says, smiling at her and leaning over to kiss her cheek for good measure.

"Anytime, Superstar. Have fun!"

"WHAT SHOULD I expect tonight? I've never been to an event like this before," I ask Tanner after we're seated in the town car we're using for the night.

"It's a fundraiser for underprivileged children. Just dinner and dancing and boring speeches, but the cause is more than worth enduring them for."

Now I understand why he accepted at the last minute. He has that soft spot for kids.

"So what's with the last-minute invite?" I ask, curious as to how the event came up out of nowhere.

"The tickets were given to the Jets organization, but whichever big wig was supposed to go couldn't make it and requested me to go in his place since it's for kids and I got all that hype in the press from the Jesse incident."

"Well, that was smart." Good for the team, good for the event. I guess that's why these organizations pay boatloads of money for PR people.

"Sure was. So all we have to do is show up and have a good time." He grabs my hand and brings it to his lips to kiss.

When we reach the gala venue, I stare wide-eyed when I realize where we are: the Grand Prospect Hall. It's a beautiful stone building with that old New York feel to it. The gold accents around the windows give it an antique air. There's a red carpet rolled out leading up to the entrance lined with photographers. Lights flash from every angle as each car lets its occupants out.

"Jesus, Tanner! You didn't tell me it would be like this," I say, feeling panicky. *I don't think I can do this*. Photographers and reporters yell people's name as guests emerge, calling for them to look this way or that way.

"Relax, baby." Tanner rubs my arm. "You're with me, and I'm a pro at this type of thing. Just follow my lead."

Yeah, great. Just follow his lead. My hands are shaking, and I feel sweat forming on my brow.

"You'll be fine," Tanner says in a soothing tone, the one he uses when he's trying to get me to latch on to an idea of his. I've heard that tone a lot in the bedroom. I blush at the thought.

"Okay." I square my shoulders and straighten my spine. *I can do this. I hope.*

"All right, when we pull up to the entrance, I'll get out first. You can follow by grabbing my hand when I offer it to help you out. Just follow me and smile," he instructs.

Reach for his hand. Follow and smile. I think I can manage that. I smile at him and nod.

Then the chaos ensues.

The instant I step out of the car, people are yelling for our attention.

"Tanner, Ashley, this way," someone yells.

"Tanner, where's Melissa?" someone else calls out.

"Ashley, what's your relationship with Tanner?" another voice asks over the roar of the crowd.

What the hell is going on? How do these people know my name? Oh my God, do they think I'm Tanner's new mistress? My thoughts swirl like a twister inside my head. *Just keep smiling.*

Once we're inside the building, I turn to Tanner to ask all the questions that are running through my head. "How did they know my name?" I whisper, doing my best to make sure my smile stays in place.

"I had to give the venue your name for the guest list. I'm assuming that's where they got it."

"You usually bring Melissa to these things, right? Now they probably think that I'm your new side piece," I reason.

"No, they don't."

"How do you know that?"

"Just trust me," he says just as a couple comes up to us to say hello.

"Tanner, so glad you could make it," the man says, offering him a hand. He's much older than Tanner, with gray, thinning hair.

"Thank you, Mr. Simon," Tanner says, shaking the man's hand.

"Who is your lovely date?" Mr. Simon asks.

"This is my girlfriend, Ashley Mitchell," he answers smoothly. I feel my eyes bulge out of my head when I hear Tanner drop the 'girlfriend' bomb.

"Pleasure to meet you, Miss Mitchell."

"You as well, Mr. Simon."

"This is my wife, Patricia," he announces, smiling at the woman beside him.

"Nice to meet you," we both say in unison.

"Mr. Simon is part of the organization's management department," Tanner informs me before the two launch into small talk. My mind won't focus on anything they're saying. All I hear is Tanner's voice on a loop in my head, calling me his girlfriend.

After a few minutes, we leave the Simons and make our way toward our table. We're stopped a few more times, and I'm introduced to more people Tanner already knows, but I'm on autopilot. I smile and nod when necessary, but I lose focus again each time Tanner informs someone else I'm his girlfriend.

"Girlfriend?" I ask when we finally make it to the table and have a minute alone.

"Yes," he replies, smiling as though he's won some kind of lottery. "I think it's time we make that declaration, don't you?"

"Umm … I … uh … yes?" My mind scrambles for any word in the English dictionary.

"Are you okay with that, baby? I think it's the perfect time to tell everyone all about you."

"Is this what you meant when you said that they won't think of me as your side piece?" I ask. I won't agree to be his girlfriend just because the tabloids need a story.

"Well, partly yes, but that isn't the reason I'm saying it." He must be using his mind-reading skills again, either that or my face is giving all my insecurities away.

"You sure about that?"

"Absolutely. I've wanted you to be mine since that stupid interview, even when I wanted to strangle you. I only said we should start off slow because it was only a matter of time until you were mine anyway. And you are mine, Ashley. I can see that you're getting more and more comfortable with the idea of us every day, so it's time everyone else knew you're mine too." The smile on his face could light the whole room up on its own.

"Don't you think you should have asked me first?" I ask, trying to sound angry. It's really hard to act angry when you're ready to burst at the seams with joy.

"Nothing to discuss. You. Are. Mine." The look of possessiveness in his eyes is fucking hot!

"You're smooth, Mr. Garrison, very smooth. I'd be honored to be your girlfriend. I love the way I feel when I'm with you," I say, giving him my most endearing smile.

"Well, then we're most definitely on the same page because I love the way that I feel when I'm with you. I think this calls for a dance."

Tanner leads me onto the dance floor, where we dance until the emcee announces dinner is about to be served. On our way back to the table, Tanner informs me that Mr. and Mrs. Simon are the only guests he knows at our table. I'm not sure why it's important. It's not as if I'll be able to help him figure out who anyone is.

Everyone at the table introduces themselves, but I couldn't tell who was who if asked. All the faces blend together over the casual conversation. I sit listening intently to Tanner chatting it up when Mrs. Simon asks me how Tanner and I met.

"I interviewed him for *The City Press* earlier in the season."

"So you're a reporter?" she asks.

"Not a reporter per se. I am more of a journalist. I was covering the interview for a colleague. I write lifestyle pieces on places, events, and trends— anything of interest in the city."

"How nice. And the two of you fell for each other during this interview?"

I fight to stifle a laugh as I answer. "No, I honestly thought he was a jerk going into that interview, and I'm pretty sure that he wanted to kill me during it."

"Then how did the two of you become an item?"

From the corner of my eye, I notice Tanner watching me in rapt attention, awaiting my answer. I smile at him and then direct my attention back to Mrs. Simon. "I saw through the lies the press was printing and met the real Tanner."

He must like my answer because it earns me a warm smile. He leans over to kiss me on the temple.

The rest of the night is wonderful, and the event raises almost two hundred thousand for the children. I doze off on the ride home, and am shaken awake by Tanner when we get back to my building.

"Baby, you're home," he says, kissing the top of my head.

I'd nestled myself into his chest while sleeping. Even unconscious, I'm still drawn to him.

"Already? Are you coming up?"

"As much as I would love to, I can't. I have game prep tomorrow," he says with a frown.

"That's okay. Thank you for bringing me tonight. I had a great time, boyfriend." I smile up at him.

"You're very welcome, girlfriend. Now get your ass upstairs before I change my mind and end up playing like shit this weekend because of it."

"We can't have that, now can we?" I kiss the hell out of my new boyfriend, testing his resolve to leave.

"Out! Now, baby. I only have so much willpower on a regular day. If I throw you looking this gorgeous into the mix, there's no telling what I'll do."

Chapter Twenty Two

ASHLEY

I **FINALLY UNDERSTAND** why Tanner hates moochers, as he calls them, so much. My phone has been ringing off the hook all week. Practically everyone who has my number has called me this week to ask why they didn't know I was dating the hottest quarterback around. I hadn't realized I was supposed to send out a newsletter announcing Tanner and I as a couple. People I haven't talked to in years have called and emailed me. An old guy friend from college messaged me on Facebook asking if I could hook him up with tickets. When my mother lights up on the screen of my phone, I'm sure her reaction is going to be the greatest.

"Ashley, I can't believe I had to find out in the paper that my daughter is dating some hotshot football player," she says. "Do you know what a terrible mother I looked like when a woman from worked asked if my daughter was dating Tanner Garrison and I said no? Then she showed me your picture in the paper."

Clearly, she doesn't care whether or not I'm dating Tanner. She just cares that not knowing made her look like the disinterested mother she is.

"Why would I bother telling you, Mom?" I huff. "So you could tell me how I'm just going to wind up disappointing him one way or another?"

"Ashley Marie Mitchell, don't you take that tone with me! When have I ever told you that you were a disappointment?" I can't believe my mother is this delusional.

"Gee, Mom, I don't know, every chance you get? You tell me all the time how every single thing I do is wrong or how I can do it better." This conversation is pointless, but I let it happen anyway.

"Please, Ashley, you're so dramatic. You know that's not true." Totally pointless.

"Yup, sure, Mom. Oh, by the way, I'm dating Tanner Garrison, the quarterback for the Jets. Just so you know. Gotta run. Bye." I hang up before she can think of something else to yell at me about.

And so went my life for my first official week as Tanner's girlfriend. All the news outlets that covered the children's benefit ran endless pictures of Tanner and me, complete with fantastic headlines.

Hearts across NYC break as hotshot QB Tanner Garrison steps out with new girlfriend.

Jets Quarterback ditches girlfriend Melissa Finnegan for a new hottie.

Tanner Garrison stolen off the market by mystery brunette.

Some headlines are more ridiculous than others. I've never been happier that my name isn't on the lease to mine and Quinn's condo. I'm sure there would be reporters camping out outside the building if it were.

"It will all die down soon. I promise," Tanner reassured me.

"It's fine, really. No big deal. I'm sure by next week I'll be old news."

And I am. Things quiet down quickly when a big domestic violence scandal breaks out at the start of the week. People forget all about Tanner Garrison's new girlfriend when the league's commissioner is forced to hand out suspensions to a handful of players surrounded by unsavory accusations.

IN AN ATTEMPT to be a good girlfriend, I'm studying the rules of football. Since I'm having a hard time understanding them, Tanner suggests we play video game football to go over the basic concepts.

"Ooh, can I be video game Tanner?" I request, laughing at the realization that my boyfriend has a video game version of himself.

"It's not as good as being the real Tanner, but sure, if you want to."

"Full of yourself much, Superstar?"

"Ugh, are you and Quinn serious with that nickname?" He rolls his eyes.

"I'd have thought you'd like it with that ego of yours."

"Yeah, yeah, whatever. So let's go over the basics. You have four downs to try and get ten yards. You have to pick a play and then push this button to throw the ball to the right receiver or to hand the ball off to the running back. Got it?"

"This is like teaching the alphabet to a ten-year-old for you isn't it?" I ask, still a little confused.

"Kind of." He laughs. "Do you get that part?"

"As much as I'm going to, I guess. Let's just play and see if I can pick it up."

I don't pick it up, and video game Tanner gets his ass beat in Madden football by real-life Tanner.

"It's okay, baby," Tanner says, trying to soothe me. "It's not your fault ten-year-old boys can play this in their sleep and you can't figure it out."

That earns him an elbow to the ribs. "Keep it up and your dick will be seeing about as much action as a ten-year-old boy's."

"Oh really? Please! Like you could resist this." He gestures up and down his body to showcase it.

"I've seen better," I say, pretending he doesn't have the most deliciously-sculpted body I've seen outside the pages of a magazine.

"Oh yeah?" He reaches for the hem of his shirt and pulls it up slowly, exposing his abs two at a time. I have a hard time not licking my lips in appreciation.

"Still think it's easy to resist?"

"Yup," I say casually.

I regret saying it the second he reaches for the button on his jeans and pops it. He folds the flap down to expose his boxer briefs, which cling to him like a second skin. He slowly pushes the jeans down his thighs, uncovering the muscular masterpieces inch by perfect inch. I've never found thighs more attractive. Tanner bends down to remove his jeans, which brings my attention to his bare feet. Even the man's fucking feet are hot, and I hate feet. After ridding himself of his jeans, Tanner stands back up, showing me that I'm not the only one who's been turned on by his little striptease.

"Looks like your plan is backfiring on you there, Superstar," I say smugly, nodding toward his hardening cock.

"Is it? The look in your eye says you want nothing more than to get on your knees and see just how hard I am for yourself."

"Is that right?" I ask even though I know it is. The bits and pieces I do remember from our first night together all center on his cock. I know I made him lose it, but my memories are fuzzy. I sure as hell wouldn't mind another chance to have this man at the mercy of my mouth.

"Mmmhmm, baby. I bet if I reached my hand down your pants right now, I'd find your hot little pussy wet just from the thought of having my cock in some part of you."

I fight to hold back the whimper of anticipation forming in my throat, but I lose the battle.

"Sounds like someone isn't having as easy a time resisting as she thought she would," he whispers in my ear after he sidles up to me and presses his hard, nearly naked body against me.

Taking a step back, Tanner removes his boxer briefs to reveal his magnificent cock. I lick my lips at that sight. I was stupid to think I'd be able to fight my attraction to him.

"Ready to admit that you can't deny me?" he asks with a self-assured smirk on his face as he steps back into my personal space.

I reach for his cock, but he knocks my hand away and shakes his head.

"No, no, no, baby."

"What?" I snap, irritated with being denied my prize. I'm done with games. I just want to play with the beautiful cock in front of me.

"Words, baby. I want to hear the words."

"Fine. You win. I can't resist you, especially on display like this." I reach for his cock again, only to be batted away once more.

"Seriously, Tanner?" Now I'm infuriated. He has wound me all up and won't let me have my way.

"Tell me what you want," he demands. "In detail."

Hmm, okay, two can play this game. He got me all hot and bothered with his striptease, and now it's my turn to get him just as riled up.

I reach my hand out and wrap it around his cock, "I want to put this huge cock, that doesn't compare to anything that I've ever seen before, in my mouth. I want to lick it up and down and swirl my tongue around this broad head," I say, mimicking my words with my hands.

"I want to swallow it down my throat and make you groan in pleasure. I want to lap up your essence as it starts to leak out when you can't control yourself. I want to cradle your balls in my hand and massage them as you throw your head back in pleasure. I want to choke on your cum as it pours down my throat, spurt after spurt."

His cock has grown larger and harder in my hand, and I'm almost positive I could make him come like this, but that isn't what I want. I drop down to my knees and act out my words precisely, taking him into the back of my mouth and out again as I lick his head. Keeping it up, I add a hand to the mix and massaging his balls until I feel them tighten up.

"Oh God, Ashley. Just like that, baby. Fuck! So good." His hips start to pump, and he fucks my mouth with wild abandon. It doesn't take long before I feel jets of hot cum hitting the back of my throat, and Tanner growls out an indecipherable moan. "Fuck baby, you are way too good at that," he says after he comes down from his orgasm.

I give him an impish grin as I lick my lips, catching any residue he may have left behind with my tongue. I add a "Mmmm" for good measure.

"I need to fuck you, Ashley. Please tell me you want me to fuck you," he says, pulling me up and nipping my earlobe. His fingers push past my jeans and panties to delve into my pussy. They stroke up and down along the seam until he thrusts them deep inside me, causing me to cry out in pleasure.

"So wet. Is this all for me? Does my cock down your throat make you this wet?" he goads me while his fingers probe and explore.

Knowing he'll stop if I don't answer, I nod.

"Do you want me to bend you over this couch and ride you?" he asks.

I shake my head.

"No?" he asks, sounding surprised.

"No, I want to ride you."

"Well, by all means, baby."

I don't waste any time pushing him back onto the couch and straddling him as I tear my clothes off as fast as I can. I can't get him inside me quick enough. As soon as my panties are gone, I slide right down onto him, my body inviting him in as though he's an extension of it.

A moan of pleasure fills the air as he hits my sweet spot immediately. I lift myself up and slide back down over and over, watching his eyes roll back into his head each time. Tanner grips my hips hard, the added pressure adding to my high as he helps lift me up and slam me back down onto his length, the force making me cry out.

"Let me hear you," he growls. He moves one hand from my hip to my clit. I feel him adjusting himself, planting his feet on the floor for leverage. Then he thrusts his pelvis upward, bouncing me up and down, all the while still pulling me down onto his cock with one hand and working my clit with the other. He has me flying toward my climax at high speed.

"Oh my God! Oh my God! Yes! Yes!" I scream over and over, until the waves of pleasure subside, and I finally come back to Earth.

"Fuck! I love when your pussy clamps down on my cock like that. You squeeze me just right, baby," he says as he reaches his own release.

I feel the telltale twitching of his cock as his orgasm pulses through him, the gush of warmth as he coats me with his cum. Slumping forward, I rest my head against his shoulder as we both wait for our heart rates to return to normal.

After a few minutes, Tanner stands from the couch, his cock still hard inside me, and lays me down on the couch before pulling out.

"Christ, there is nothing hotter than seeing my cum drip out of your gorgeous pussy and down your leg. I love knowing that when you leave here, you're leaving with a part of me still inside you," he says with a possessive gleam in his emerald eyes.

"Fuck, Tanner, I think I just had another orgasm hearing that mouth of yours."

Chapter Twenty Three

ASHLEY

THINGS HAVE DIED down even more over the last two weeks, and no one seems to be paying attention to Tanner and me anymore. We've laid low since the news of our relationship broke, but it finally seems as though we can venture out in public again without being mobbed. Part of me wishes Tanner wasn't so beloved in the New York area. Then no one would give a shit who he was dating or what we're doing. But then he wouldn't be the Tanner that I fell for either.

The Jets are on a bye week this week, so Tanner and I have plans to spend the weekend out together. He's coming with me this weekend to cover my assignments. I have three places to cover and we're going to two of them tonight, a new Italian restaurant on Staten Island and a Sports Lounge that's been picking up popularity downtown. Who could possibly be better company than Tanner at either? Quinn and Alex are tagging along as well. Tomorrow, we're going to check out a fall festival that's taking place over the next three weekends on Long Island. It'll be an all-day event, and I'm sure there'll be more than enough things to check out and write about at the festival.

I'm currently putting the finishing touches on my makeup for the night while I wait on Tanner and Alex. I'm going casual tonight with dark blue skinny jeans, a cream peasant top, and ballet flats. The weather has been unseasonably warm for the middle of October, one small benefit of the terribly hot summer we had.

I'm overcome with excitement when I hear the doorbell ring. Tanner and I haven't been able to spend a whole weekend together since we met. Not that I'm complaining, but it's a nice change of pace to act like a normal couple on the weekend. *Couple.* I still can't believe I'm half of a couple with this outstanding man. Women all over the country would kill to be me. It's such a foreign idea to process. No one has ever been jealous of me that I know of.

"Hey, beautiful," I hear Tanner say from the doorway of my bedroom. The smile that spreads across my face is involuntary, just like the rest of my body's reactions when Tanner is anywhere in my vicinity.

"Hi, handsome." I turn to face him, walking toward the doorway.

His arms immediately wrap me in the most delicious embrace. I love being in his arms.

"I missed you," he says, burying his face in my hair. "You smell amazing." He inhales deeply. "Always so amazing. I love that your scent lingers on the pillows at my place so I can smell you even when you aren't there."

My heart melts. "You know, I'm pretty much a forgone conclusion. No need to butter me up."

He chuckles. "Nothing wrong with letting my girl know how much I love her scent. Every one of them." His eyes go from sweet to devilish in an instant.

I feel my face heating up, but Quinn and Alex burst into my room before I can respond.

"Cut that shit out, Tag," Alex smirks. "I'm starving, and I don't feel like waiting for you to have a fuck-fest before dinner."

At that comment, my face completely ignites. I could probably give Rudolph some competition I'm blushing so hard.

"Don't embarrass Ashley," Tanner chides him. "Besides, you're just jealous that I have better game *and* stamina than you."

"Doll, please tell Tag here that my stamina shouldn't be questioned," Alex says, turning his attention to Quinn.

"He's right, Tanner. The man's a beast in the best possible way." She smiles deviously and winks at me. She knows exactly what she's doing by riling these men up. We're both in for some great sex tonight if she keeps the ego-stroking up. Quinn is definitely onto something.

"Hmm, I doubt that he can keep up with Tanner, though. The man's a force to be reckoned with," I add.

"We can skip dinner and just have a fucking contest here and now. We'll see who can last longer and fuck better. Hope you girls don't need your voices tomorrow," Alex says, sounding completely serious.

Uh oh, maybe this wasn't the best thing to start.

"You're on," Tanner says without tearing his eyes away from Alex.

They can't be serious right now. No way am I having a fucking contest with my best friend and his best friend. I look to Quinn for support, but she doesn't seem the least bit fazed.

"Umm, I don't think that's a great idea," I say, determined to be the voice of reason here.

"You're right, Ash," Alex concedes. "Forget the contest. Let's just have an orgy, and we can teach them some fun stuff." He waggles his eyebrows at Quinn.

"What?" *An orgy?* Alex is off his fucking rocker.

"Could be fun. You said you wanted to explore new things," Quinn says.

"Are you all fucking nuts?" I ask, incredulous.

Then, absolute hysteria breaks out. All three of them are laughing as though this is the funniest situation ever.

"You should see your face, sweets," Quinn says, trying to catch her breath between laughs.

"That was great," Alex chimes in.

Tanner is still laughing as he pulls me to his chest. "My sweet, innocent little Ashley."

"You guys are mean." I'm honestly pissed that this has somehow turned into a "let's mortify Ashley" party.

"That was priceless. Almost as funny as your face when we got to the sex store and you saw all the latex and dildos," Quinn says, reiterating my humiliation. "You guys should have seen how big her eyes got when she saw all the butt plugs next to the twelve-inch vibrators."

What the fuck is going on right now? Is this make fun of Ashley's sexual inexperience day? And more importantly, why is my best friend facilitating it?

"Aww, never seen a butt plug before, Ash?" Alex asks.

"Umm, no," I say, still trying to figure out why they're all ganging up to make fun of me.

Tanner starts laughing again. "We'll have to get you some then, baby."

"Ooh, get her the ones that have the cute gems on the end," Quinn suggests. "She couldn't stop looking at those."

I want to throttle the bitch right now. Some best friend. All three of them may find this topic hilarious, but to me, it's nothing short of crushing. I can't believe they're all having such a grand ol' time at my expense.

"Your face is priceless right now, Ashley," Alex says, destroying what little of my dignity had been hanging on.

"Okay, enough. Leave my prude little princess alone," Tanner says.

No, he didn't! I pull my head back to stare at him.

Quinn's laughter instantly ceases as she gasps. Alex and Tanner are still chuckling to themselves, clueless as to what they've done. I catch a glimpse of Quinn from the corner of my eye, mouth agape, and eyes as big as saucers. She's looking at me with a mix of worry and sympathy. I stare daggers at her and push myself away from Tanner to storm out of the room. The bathroom is the closest room to mine, so I run for it and slam the door behind me.

How dare he call me prude? Who the fuck does he think he is? I pace around the small room restlessly.

Through the door, I hear Quinn telling them they took it too far, and Tanner couldn't have picked a worse word to call me than prude if he'd tried.

"What are you talking about?" I hear Tanner ask. "What just happened?"

"You basically just set off an emotional nuke in there," Quinn informs him. "I need to do some damage control."

"Let me," he says.

"No, trust me. It's better if I talk to her first. You really have no clue what you just did," she whispers harshly.

"Well, someone tell me what the hell is going on then!" he yells.

I'm tempted to lock the door so none of them can come in, but I know that would be the immature thing to do, even if I don't want to see any of them right now.

"Sweets?" Quinn asks cautiously as she opens the door.

"What?" I snap at her, still pacing. "Is it time for round two of 'Humiliate Ashley'?"

"I'm sorry. That wasn't our intention. We were just joking around. It wasn't planned or anything. We were all ad-libbing, and it went too far."

"Yeah, at my expense." I'm getting dizzy with all the pacing, and it feels as though the walls are closing in on me. My anger and embarrassment are turning into sadness. I'm in yet another situation where the man I'm with thinks I'm a prude. "Maybe I'm just destined to be the shy, boring, prude girl for the rest of my life," I say, launching into my own pity party.

"Oh stop it," Quinn scolds. "He didn't mean anything by it. Tanner had no idea what that word would do to you. There's no way in the world he thinks you're a prude, especially with all the crazy monkey sex you guys have."

"No, I don't think you're anything other than amazing," Tanner says from the doorway, his voice filling the small bathroom.

Damn, I wish I'd locked the door after Quinn came in.

"Fuck you, Tanner." Does he think he can just come in here and say a bunch of bullshit and things will be fine?

"Ashley, please tell me what's going on. I have no idea what just happened."

Quinn heads for the door. My gaze follows her shoes across the small space as she squeezes past Tanner and leaves. I don't want to lift my head and let him see the tears pooling in my eyes. I sit on the edge of the tub, trying to gain some composure. Tanner stands there motionless, I assume waiting for me to say something or at the very least acknowledge him. I don't want to. I get that he had no clue what that word meant to me, but I'm still pissed and hurt.

"You're an insensitive asshole, that's what happened," I say after a long while.

"Ashley, baby, please look at me," he pleads. With that tone in his voice, it's almost impossible to deny him anything.

I angle my head toward him but don't meet his eyes. He closes the distance between us, crouches down, and places his hand on the back of my neck. He slides it down and under my chin to tip my face up, giving me no choice but to look at him.

"Baby, please don't cry. I don't know what I did to upset you, but please help me understand so I can fix it."

I try to take a deep breath, and a sob hitches in my throat, knowing I need to explain my anger to him.

"When I caught Jason fucking that woman, he said that it was my fault, that if I wasn't such a prude, he would've been satisfied and wouldn't have needed to go elsewhere."

His eyes go wide, almost as wide as Quinn's had when Tanner made the unintended comment. His face falls and pales simultaneously. Clearly, that wasn't what he'd expected to hear.

Having to tell him all that brings another round of tears to my eyes. I can't hold these in, and when I blink in an effort to clear them away, they fall down my cheeks.

Bringing his hands up to my face, Tanner brushes away the falling tears with his thumbs and pulls my face to his chest. His chest is strong and warm, and I can't help but settle into it and let everything out. The sobs rack my body, and I have no control any longer.

"Oh, baby, I'm sorry. You're breaking my heart right now," he says, squeezing me more tightly. "I never meant to make you sad. It's killing me that I'm the one who has made you so upset. Please know I don't and never have thought of you as a prude. You're beautiful and vibrant. Sex with you has never been anything short of spectacular. You're amazing." He strokes my hair, uttering reassurances as my sobs start to ebb. He tilts my face up toward his and wipes my face once more with his thumbs. "Do you want to talk about it?"

I shake my head and lower my face again, trying to hide my emotions.

"Oh, sweetheart, I'm so sorry that happened to you, but that was all on him. I've never been more sexually satisfied in my life than I am with you. Don't let that dickhead have this type of power over you. Honestly, I'm kind of glad he didn't know what he had in you because now you're mine." He kisses my temple.

We sit in silence for a few minutes—me curled into Tanner's chest and him stroking my back in a soothing rhythm.

"Do you think that you could forgive me? It was really just a joke… A stupid one, but still a joke."

I look up to take in his face for the first time since he walked into the bathroom, and I can see the distress written all over it. The same distress is also visible in his slumped posture.

"It hurts," I tell him. "To hear you call me the same thing he did pulls me back to the place I've been fighting so hard to break out of." I know he didn't mean anything by it, but it still stings.

"I know, baby, and I can't tell you how awful I feel. I don't ever want to cause you pain. I want to be the reason you smile and thrive," he says with sincerity.

"I know," I whisper, and I do. I know that his words weren't intentional.

"Do you think you could forgive me?" he asks again.

"Yes. I'm sorry that I pushed you."

"That's okay. I deserved it," he says, a renewed lightness in his voice. "Do you still want to go out?"

"Yes, I don't want to let Jason ruin our weekend of fun."

"Okay, come on. Let's go let Quinn and Alex know I've groveled properly and you've forgiven me." He smiles at me, and I can't help but laugh.

AFTER I RECOVER from my breakdown, we all head out to Staten Island for dinner. The restaurant, Vincenzo's, is small and intimate, more elegant than your regular pizza joint but not quite fine dining. It's a comfortable family place with a uniquely Tuscan décor in greens, purples, and blues, not like your run-of-the-mill Italian place. I decide that I like its out-of-the-box feel.

Everyone tries to pretend nothing happened back at the condo, but my mind is still reeling. I try to shut it all out and enjoy myself, but despite my efforts, I'm pretty sure everyone knows I'm still upset.

Quinn and Alex banter back and forth like brother and sister, which is gross since they screwed the hell out of each other once. Well, once as far as I know. I'm so envious of Quinn. She's always completely comfortable in her own skin. You'd think that things would be weird between her and Alex after being each other's booty calls, but it seems like just the opposite. It's as though they've been friends forever. All the awkwardness in the restaurant tonight is coming from me. I can't help it, though. My insecurities have come back in full force.

After dinner, we head to the sports lounge. We sit at a high table in the middle of the hustle and bustle. Apparently, it's playoff time for baseball. The Yankees are playing the Sox, which, of course, has drawn a crowd. From what I've pieced together from the conversations buzzing around us, it's an important game. I think the winner of the series goes onto the next round or to the World Series or some shit I don't really care about. The guys watch the game during the lulls in conversation, which there seem to be a lot of. My mind is elsewhere, and I'm missing all the cues for my part of the conversation.

"Excuse me," I say, standing up to head to the bathroom, anything to break up the discomfort. I feel as if everyone is waiting for me to crumple again, and I think they might be right to. I know I've said that I forgive Tanner, but the truth is, it isn't about forgiveness. Forgiveness doesn't erase the memory of his words. Forgiveness doesn't make them unspoken.

"I need to use the restroom, too," Quinn says, standing to follow me.

"You guys already know who has the bigger dick. I'm sure you've compared notes," Alex says.

"Today, we compare girth," she fires back. I let out a laugh.

"Compare away. I'm sure I'll win that too." Alex flashes a cocky smile.

"No shame, sugar. No shame." Quinn shakes her head.

Being that ninety percent of the bar's patrons are male, there's no line for the ladies room, meaning it takes no time for Quinn to get me inside and corner me for an interrogation.

"How long are you going to let the pity party last?" she asks, leaning toward the mirror to wipe away some smudged eyeliner from under her eyes.

"Bite me, Quinn. I'm in no mood for your comments tonight."

"Wow, bitchy much?"

"Excuse me, I'm sorry. I think I have the right to be bitchy considering my best friend helped the villagers orchestrate my public humiliation tonight."

"Could you be more melodramatic? We were just messing with you, and it went too far. Everyone apologized. Let it go."

"Fuck you. Don't dismiss my feelings just because I didn't find what you guys did funny. You don't see me making fun of your commitment-phobia, do you? I've always had your back, and tonight your fun and games went way beyond cool and straight to degrading. I've never felt worse than tonight. It was one thing to hear it from Jason, but hearing it come from Tanner, joke or not, is on a whole other level, and you helped take it there. So excuse me if 'I'm sorry' doesn't make me feel all warm and fuzzy inside." I turn to the door, leaving a gob-smacked Quinn alone in the bathroom.

I storm down the hall to head back to the table, but stop dead in my tracks when I see what's going on there. A woman stands in my spot, her giant, obviously fake boobs, pressed up against Tanner while he signs the jersey she's wearing—a jersey that is about twelve sizes too small for her. The hand that she's not practically groping my boyfriend with flips her shiny blonde hair over her shoulder as she leans even closer, pressing her boobs further toward his face. He grins devilishly at whatever shit she's saying.

First, he calls me prude and now he's letting some blonde bimbo hang all over him? This has felt like the worst day of my life, and it just won't fucking end. I'm so done!

"Can you get your fake tits out of my boyfriend's face?" I ask the blonde as I bump her out of the way to grab my clutch. "I'm leaving," I announce to the guys, giving them as nasty of a look as I can.

They share an uncertain glance, clearly having no idea what to do. I don't wait for a response and instead head outside to hail a cab. I don't really give a shit how much the fare will be to get home. I just really need to get going. I want this night to be over. Not that it matters now, though. In one night with one comment and one slut, I've already been set back almost two months. It feels as though all the progress I've made with Tanner has been wiped away in an instant.

I hear Tanner's voice cut through the crowd. "Ashley, wait up."

Oddly, my body doesn't respond with its usual softening upon hearing him. Now the sound only fuels the angry fire burning inside me.

"What?" I snap. "Want to insult me some more tonight? Haven't had enough yet?" I know I'm being unfair, but tough shit. My whole life seems to be un-fucking-fair, so why not share the wealth of bad luck I've accumulated?

"No," he answers cautiously. "I just want to make sure you get home safely. I'll drive you."

"I don't need you to get home."

"No, you don't, but too bad."

"You can't tell me what to do." I sound like an immature adolescent, but who the hell does Tanner think he is?

"I just did, now get your fired-up ass in the car. We're going to deal with this. Enough with the attitude. I said I was sorry, and I was totally sincere, but it seems like you need something more than that."

He can go fuck himself.

"I don't give a shit what you think I need. I'm not getting in that car with you," I say, lifting my arm to hail a cab.

"We've been here and done this before, Ashley. You didn't win then either." He pulls my arm down and takes me by the hand, urging me toward where his Range Rover is parked around the corner.

Chapter Twenty Four

TANNER

SO MUCH FOR a relaxing weekend off with my girlfriend. If one more thing goes wrong, I'll have hit the trifecta of shittiness. Of course, Ashley would come back from the bathroom just as that girl was asking for an autograph. Yes, she was flirting, but I wasn't biting. It's not as though I could have said no to an autograph request. I tried to make it as non-suggestive as possible, but the woman had a huge rack and was shamelessly displaying it for me. She was coming on strong, but what was I supposed to do? She'd made a comment about how I looked like I could use some company, to which I'd replied that I had great company in my girlfriend who was just using the restroom. Of course, Ashley hadn't heard that. She'd just taken the scene at face value and gotten pissed off. I can't say I blame her, though. I would have been just as pissed if the situation were reversed

I don't want to argue the entire hour-long ride back to my house, but after nearly a half hour of silence, I can't take it anymore and decide to speak up. Ashley beats me to the punch, though.

"You missed the exit to my house," she snaps.

"We're not going to your place."

"I don't want to go to your house."

"Too bad," I reply.

"You can't force me to come home with you, asshole." Her voice is full of anger.

"I know you're pissed, but you could've at least given me the chance to explain. And yes, you *are* coming home with me. We have things to resolve." Even though she has a right to be pissed about my first slip-up, I should have been given the benefit of the doubt with that chick.

"This whole night has been déjà vu. I think that woman could have been the twin of the slut I found Jason fucking in my bed. You know, the same day he told me I was a prude and had brought it on myself."

Fuck, I think there might be pure venom in her veins right now. There's no way for this to get any worse. I'm back in the same box as the douchebag ex again.

"I'm sorry for what he did to you, Ashley, but I don't think you're being fair. I didn't do anything today to intentionally hurt you. She wanted an autograph. It wasn't an ideal situation. I get that, but what was I supposed to say, 'No, I won't autograph your jersey'?" I reason.

"How about telling her that your girlfriend wouldn't appreciate her shoving her tits in your face?"

"I made sure to mention I was there with my girlfriend. I know you're determined to make me the bad guy here, but at least give me a little fucking credit." *Christ, this isn't going to be easy to fix.* I have zero experience in the damaged girlfriend department, and Ashley's about halfway to Crazy Town right now.

"Hmpf…" She huffs but doesn't say anything else.

"What does that mean?" I ask, no longer in the mood for her bullshit.

"It means you're still an asshole." She is really pushing my buttons.

"I've had just about enough of your shit tonight."

"Well, you should have taken me home then," she says, smirking.

I'm about to strangle this woman. I inhale deeply, keeping my mouth shut, determined to make my point when we get home.

I BARELY HAVE the car pulled into the garage and in park before Ashley's out the door, slamming it behind her, and heading up the stairs that lead inside to the kitchen.

After I unlock the door, she tries to push past me to get inside, but I grab hold of her wrist, effectively stopping her.

"No, no, baby. You aren't going anywhere."

"Tanner, don't you think I've had enough for one day?" she asks, her body slumping as though her adrenaline is finally running out.

"Baby, you're upset, but I think you're being a little unreasonable because this whole thing hits a sore spot for you." My arms encircle her. I hope that she just needs to be reminded of how much I actually crave her and her alone.

"No, I'm upset because the three of you sat there and made fun of me and my boyfriend called me prude for not owning any butt plugs. Then, knowing I was already upset, he still let some bar slut serve her tits up to him on a silver platter using an autograph as an excuse. And finally, said boyfriend forced me to come home with him, as though I would sleep with him when all I want to do is curl up alone at home in my own bed," she spits out.

I guess I had been wrong about her adrenaline fading. Her body is tense and poised for battle, ramrod straight and unmoving. Her teeth are clenched together so hard I'm almost afraid she's going to crack a molar.

"My bed is also your bed, and you will be sleeping with me, baby," I say, setting her straight. I won't let her pull away from me.

"No, I won't. I wouldn't want my prudishness to infect you." Her voice is thick with sarcasm.

I'm at the end of my rope with her, and I can think of only one way to fix this mess.

Pulling her toward me, I slam my lips onto hers. I feel the initial resistance in her body, but she doesn't push me away. I feel the battle waging inside her as she fights against herself, wanting to fight against me. Her mind doesn't want to give in, but her body does. Knowing that even though she is angry, her body can't deny me makes me instantly hard. I push myself against her so she can feel my erection.

"Feel that baby? Feel how hard you make me? Does that feel like a cock that thinks you're a prude?" I ask between kisses.

"I never said your dick thought I was prude, just the dick it's attached to." She sneers.

Fucking Christ, this woman is downright infuriating.

"Enough, Ashley," I say, pulling her head back by her hair, forcing her to look at me. "You have called me so many names in the last hour I've lost count. I made one stupid joke with no intention of insulting you, but you have purposely and repeatedly tried to hurt me since then. That chick at the bar was nothing, and you know it." I grab the hem of her shirt and pull it off over her head hastily, but don't remove it completely. I leave it at her wrists and loop the fabric around them, binding her hands together.

I push her through the kitchen as I kiss her until her ass bumps against the kitchen table. Holding her hands up above her head, I give her an insistent nudge to get her to lie back on the table, and she does. With my free hand, I unbutton her jeans. Releasing my hold on her hands, I pull her jeans down and off her legs. She lies on the table, feet still on the floor, in nothing but her bra and thong. My cock swells even more at the sight of her.

But I see fear in her eyes, and it hurts knowing that she now doubts my feelings for her.

"I don't like the doubt I see in your eyes, Ashley. I promise, after tonight, you'll have no doubt how sexy and free I find you. I could see the inner vixen hiding inside you even before you knew it was there," I tell her, running my finger up and down her torso.

Her skin breaks out in goosebumps, but her face remains defiant.

I slide her thong down her legs. When I reach her ankles, I wrap my fingers around them and use them as leverage to push her farther up onto the table.

"What are you—?" she tries to ask, but I'm no longer in the mood to hear anything come out of her mouth unless she's moaning my name in ecstasy.

"Shut your beautiful mouth, Ashley. I'm really tired of hearing all the bullshit that's been coming out of it tonight. So unless I'm hurting you and you want me to stop, shut the fuck up." I haven't been this forceful with her before, but it's for her own good.

She snaps her mouth shut and stares up at me with wide eyes, nodding slightly.

I pull my shirt over my head and let it drop to the floor before positioning myself between her legs. Wetting one finger, I trail it up and down her pussy. She's more turned on than she lets on. I see her wetness glistening in the low light.

I waste no time going to work on her. I run my nose along the seam of her folds, inhaling the scent of her arousal. I lick her up and down before deciding that I need my point to hit home with her. She needs to remember this night the next time she doubts herself or me.

Grabbing her ankles, I pull her back to the edge of the table. Her eyes are still wide with a mix of trepidation and lust. I have babied her in the bedroom up till now, afraid to push her too far, but now seems like the best time to push her limits.

"Stand up," I tell her, my voice stern.

She hesitates, and it pisses me off.

"*Now*," I demand.

She scrambles off the table and stands as close to it as possible. I read the cocktail of emotions on her face. It's as though she isn't sure how she should feel. I see a slight tinge of fear there, and I don't like it. We'll have to expel that one right now.

"Come here," I order.

She moves toward me, slowly closing the space between us. As soon as she's within reach, I grab her hair once more and turn her face toward mine.

"Have I ever hurt you before, Ashley?" I ask

"No."

"Then tell me why I see fear in your eyes?"

"I don't know. You seem angry," she answers.

"I *am* angry, Ashley. I don't like that after one stupid joke you've retreated back inside yourself. I see the doubt in your eyes right next to the fear, and it pisses me the fuck off."

"Sorry," she mumbles.

"You will be."

I spin her around and push her face down onto the table, then nudge her legs apart with my foot. "Spread them."

She obeys immediately.

"Good girl." I rub her ass cheek, waiting for her to relax against the table. After a minute or so, she finally does, and that's when I strike her. The sound of the slap reverberates off the walls.

"Oww," she yelps.

"That's for doubting yourself, Ashley. Don't ever doubt yourself." I rub my hand gently over the spot I've just slapped, caressing it. The minute she relaxes into my palm, I strike her again in a new spot.

"Fuck."

"That was for doubting me. Don't ever doubt me, and *don't* ever compare me to that shithead of an ex of yours. I never want to be placed in the same box as him again," I tell her, stroking her ass some more.

She doesn't relax this time, having caught on to this little game of mine.

I trail my hand toward her pussy. I'm more than confident she's turned on by this, but I need to make sure. I don't want to ever push her to a place where she doesn't enjoy herself.

"Does this turn you on, baby? Am I going to find this beautiful pussy of yours wet?"

"I don't know… Yes?" she replies, questioning rather than answering.

I move my hand more quickly, needing a real answer before I say anything else. Wet. Not dripping wet, but wet enough to tell me that if she lets go a little she'll get there.

"You're pretty wet. Not as wet as I would like you to be. Why is that?"

"I don't know."

"Am I hurting you?" I ask. If I am, this whole thing could really go south.

"Not really," she says, sounding only slightly steadier.

"Not really? So basically you're stuck in your head. Would a prude woman allow me to stand here, bend her over my kitchen table, spread her, and spank her?" I press.

"N-no."

"No, Ashley, she wouldn't. She would be running for the hills, screaming bloody murder. But not you, right?"

"No," she responds, her tone sounding less guarded. I can almost hear her inner walls crumbling.

"No is right. Because you are *not* a prude. Get the fuck out of your head and let go." I bring my hand back down hardon her ass.

She screams out, not in pain but in what seems to me like relief. I push two of my fingers between her pussy lips and finally find what I'd been hoping for: undeniable wetness. I take the same two fingers and plunge them inside her. I use my other hand to press her into the table as I increase my pace. Her warmth grips my fingers, making my cock swell and press against my zipper.

"Such a greedy little pussy you have here."

I remove my hand from her back to unbutton my jeans and unzip them. They haven't even hit the floor before I've removed my fingers from Ashley's pussy and impaled her on my cock, seating myself as far inside her as I can get.

"Ahh!" she cries out, and I still for the moment to allow her to acclimate.

Gliding my right hand up her back, I grab a chunk of her hair, bury my fingers in it, and pull her head back, forcing her to turn to look at me over her shoulder.

"You will never doubt what we have here again. Should I make another mistake that happens to make your head go somewhere dark, you will tell me. Then I will help you immediately return to the present and get the fuck over it. What we do together is absolute perfection, and I won't have you thinking otherwise. Understand?"

"Yes," she replies.

"Good." I dig my fingers into the place on her hips I love so much and drive my point home. I thrust into her over and over, losing myself between the perfection of her pussy and the symphony of her mews.

"Absolute perfection… Play with your clit, baby," I order, knowing that she won't get off on this alone—not yet at least. I haven't taken her this roughly before, and even though her moaning tells me she's loving it, I know she needs that little extra push. A bit of a caressing touch.

"God, Tanner. Fuck."

"Your pussy is heaven on earth, Ashley. A fucking paradise, baby."

"Ah, Tanner, so close," she says.

I wet my finger with my spit before finding her puckered hole and slowly gliding my finger inside.

"Ah, yes, yes, please… God. Oh God! Oh God…" she screams as her orgasm takes over, causing her to clench down and squeeze the hell out of my cock.

I can't stave off my orgasm any longer, and my mind fades to black.

"Ffffuuuccckkk!" I growl, pounding into her harder, milking the rest of my orgasm for all it's worth. My senses are scattered. My chest heaves as though I've just run the city marathon, and there's a buzzing in my ears. As I regain control of my senses, I hear Ashley crying. *Oh, fuck! I hope I didn't hurt her. God, no, anything but that.* "Baby, are you okay? I didn't hurt you, did I? I'm sorry. I didn't mean to, I swear," I apologize, unsheathing myself. I pick her up, and cradle her in my arms as she sobs. I'd swear I just heard my heart crack. "Baby, please tell me what's wrong? Where did I hurt you?" I ask, trying to think of what I did that could've hurt her. Maybe I pushed my finger into her ass a little too hard? We haven't done much anal play. I know I pounded her pretty hard, but I've taken her roughly before, maybe not as hard as that, but still…

"I'm sorry," she says in between sobs.

She's sorry? "For what, baby? Please tell me if I hurt you."

"No, no, you didn't hurt me."

"Then what? What is it, baby?" I ask, needing some clarity.

"I'm sorry I was such a bitch. I'm sorry I doubted you. You were right."

"But why are you crying?"

"I don't know. My head is all over the place," she explains, her head still buried in the crook of my neck.

"Stop hiding and talk to me. What's going on in your head?"

"That was so… intense."

"And?" I push, sensing she has more to say.

"And I liked it. I loved it. What… what does that say about me?"

Now I get it. She's confused by her body's reaction to being manhandled. Her mind is trying to convince her that it's wrong to enjoy something she views as debasing.

"It says that you're finally letting yourself go and giving in to what you've always needed but been afraid to experience."

"Or it says I'm a dirty whore," she reasons, sobbing again.

"No, it doesn't, baby. You like letting go and giving up control. You told me once that you've always been afraid to give in to your desires, but you just did, and you enjoyed it."

"I…I've never ever come like that before. Your finger…"

"It's okay to like that too. There isn't anything wrong with a little anal stimulation," I insist.

"But, it's so…"

"So what? Hot? Because I happen to like it too."

"You do?" she asks, sounding surprised.

"Yes, I like anal and I like dominating you and I've liked every sexual encounter that we've had. So if there's something wrong with you, then there's something wrong with me. Do you think that there's something wrong with me, Ash?" I know I'm on the cusp of breaking down that last bit of wall still standing.

"No."

"And I see nothing wrong with you. You're perfection, and so is what we do. You're so far from prude you aren't even on the same continent. Come on. Let me take you to bed. You've had a long, emotional day, and you'll have better clarity in the morning," I say, holding her more tightly in my arms and standing to head toward the stairs.

By the time I get to the bedroom, she's nearly passed out. I grab a towel out of the hamper on my way past it. Then I pull back the covers and lay her on the bed. Gently, I wipe her clean and then myself since we're both still a sticky mess. After cleaning us off, I crawl into bed next to her and pull her to my chest. I wrap both arms around her and squeeze.

"Thank you," she whispers.

"For what?" I ask.

"For being you, for being patient, for always knowing just what I need… For making me happy."

"That's all I want to do—make you happy," I say, kissing her forehead.

"Well, you're doing a damn good job." She yawns as sleep takes hold.

Thank God for that. Thank God for bringing me this amazing woman.

Chapter Twenty Five

ASHLEY

I **WAKE WITH** the feeling of being watched. Still cocooned in a warm mass of muscle, I'm very comfortable. I don't want to open my eyes, but curiosity gets the better of me. I find a pair of green eyes staring back at me.

"Hi," Tanner says, sounding awake and alert.

"Hi. How long have you been watching me?" My voice is so gravely I might as well have a mouth full of rocks.

"God, you sound so sexy in the morning." His voice holds no note of irony.

"And you look like a creeper in the morning. Why are you just staring at me? Oh my God, do I have drool on my face or something?" I ask, pulling up my arm to wipe my mouth.

Tanner throws his head back and laughs. "No, you don't have drool on your face."

"Then why are you staring at me in my sleep like that, weirdo?" I draw the sheet up to my mouth to cover my morning breath.

"Honestly?" he asks, his face serious as he props his head on his hand.

"No, tell me a lie instead," I answer sarcastically, rolling my eyes.

"Ha ha ha, smart ass… I was afraid of how you'd react this morning, so I didn't want you to wake up alone." He uses his free hand to brush the hair back from my face.

"How sweet! A thoughtful creeper." I smile broadly.

"How are you feeling this morning?"

"I'm fine," I say, looking away.

"Are you fine? Last night was pretty rough and intense."

"I know it was, but I don't want yesterday to ruin today."

"Baby, I won't let last night ruin today, but that doesn't mean we don't need to talk about it. We have to talk about it. If we sweep shit under the rug, it's going to come back and bite us in the ass later. Good relationships are built on trust and communication. Especially with the doubts you have about yourself."

"So you're a relationship expert now?" I ask, raising an eyebrow.

"I want to be an expert in you… In every way possible. But for that, I need you to talk to me about last night."

"Last night was a fucking roller coaster. If you want honesty, my feelings are probably still a little hurt." He looks as though he's going to interrupt.

"Stop," I say. "I know you didn't mean it, but you wanted to know the truth. It still hurts, but I think that has more to do with me than you. A lot of this is hard for me to say out loud, so you need to just bear with me." He nods for me to continue.

"I don't think I ever really loved Jason. I was madder about the mess he left for me to clean up than I was about actually losing him. A lot of that mess was in my head. I told you about college… There's such a double standard when it comes to sex. You can go out and fuck as many girls as you want, however you want, and you're the man. The guys want to be you, and the girls want to be fucked by you. If I do that, I'm nothing but a slut. The guys all gossip about me, and the girls all tear me down with nasty names.

"Now if you throw in the fact that I want to be fucked hard and rough, it's not easy to admit openly. That's not to say I don't like if soft and sensual, but it's just these fantasies that I've always had in my head. I just wanted to explore those desires, and the one time I did, I got an earful about how dirty and slutty I am. From then on out, I played it safe and went with the flow of whatever other people wanted. And what did that get me? A cheating boyfriend who tells me it's my fault he has his dick in someone else because I'm boring and prude. Do you know what that does to a girl's self-image? I'm damned if I do, and I'm damned if I don't.

"Then you come along and you're the hottest guy on the planet and you show interest in me? Me? I'm nobody, Tanner, and you're *you.*"

"You're somebody to me," he says with sincerity.

"I'm getting that. I really am, but I'm still a work in progress. Then last night, with you all making fun of me because I don't own a butt plug and you telling everyone to leave your prude girlfriend alone. My mind automatically went to that place where I'm a nobody again, worried that you're going to get bored with me like he did. I couldn't keep that loser happy. How the hell am I supposed to keep you happy?" A few tears slide down my cheeks.

"I *am* happy. Happier than I've ever been. I've never had a real relationship before, so you aren't the only one learning things, baby. But I need you to understand that I don't look at you the way you look at yourself. I think you're amazing. I've never had a negative thought about you when it comes to sex, and I'm sure as hell not thinking about fucking anyone else. Christ, I've only slept with Melissa for the past six years. I'm not a man-whore, no matter what you've read.

"But that being said, I also need you to tell me when things go too far." He looks me in the eye to impress the point. "I panicked last night when I saw you crying. I thought I'd hurt you, and God, I can't tell you how horrible I felt for those few minutes. I don't ever want to hurt you. So please tell me you'll never hesitate to say no if you aren't comfortable with something. I like fucking you raw. I like fucking you every which way possible, but I know that you're exploring all these things for the first time, and I need you to know it's okay for you not to like something. I won't think any less of you. The same goes *for* liking something," he says while wiggling his eyebrows.

I let out a laugh and then assault him with kisses. Kissing quickly turns into a whole other activity. An hour later, we're in the shower, cleaning up the mess we've made of each other yet again.

"Stop that, we are supposed to be cleaning up, not getting dirtier," I tell Tanner when he gets preoccupied soaping up certain parts of my body.

"I can't help myself around you." He smiles devilishly.

I push up on my tiptoes to kiss him. "Thank you for being you. I know I said that last night, but you really are amazing. Not many guys would be willing to deal with my baggage, but you not only deal with it, you help me work through it. For a guy with no experience, you're damn good at this boyfriend thing. Is there anything that you don't do well?"

"I'm sure there's plenty. I just haven't found any of it yet." He says with a cocky smile.

AFTER ANOTHER ROUND of sex in the shower, Tanner and I get ready to head out to Jones Beach on Long Island for the fall festival. Quinn and Alex are supposed to meet us there later. If I'd been told last night that I'd have face cramps from smiling so much this morning, I wouldn't have believed it. But here I am with face cramps because I'm on cloud nine, all thanks to my wonderful, passionate boyfriend.

"So, what are we supposed to be doing at this festival?" Tanner asks over breakfast.

"Nothing specific. I just need to explore it and find some noteworthy things to write about. Basically, we just need to have a good afternoon."

The drive to the festival takes nearly two hours, but it's a fun two hours. Tanner and I share stories from our childhoods and laugh at each other a lot. We also fight over the radio and what songs we want to listen to. We decide to go old school and listen to the 90's station. He can't stop laughing as I sing along to the Spice Girls' *Wannabe*. He also finds my rendition of *Baby Got Back* hysterical.

"Oh, shut up, I know you remember all the words too," I tell him whenever he points out how into a song I'm getting. I get my chance to make fun of him when I catch him rapping *Ice Ice Baby*. He never misses a beat. Today definitely beats the last time I was caught in traffic…

When we get to the festival, I'm instantly reminded of a county fair back in Jersey. The parking lot is already full, and Tanner apologizes profusely about having to walk what seems like a mile to the entrance.

"A little walking isn't going to kill us. Or are you that out of shape after one week off, Superstar?" I tease.

"No, I'm not out of shape, smart ass. I was just trying to be a proper a date and not force you to exert yourself."

I laugh. "When have you done anything proper with me or kept me from exerting myself?" I shoot him a suggestive look.

"Keep that up and you'll be exerting yourself all by your lonesome tonight, baby," he says.

"Hmm, I'm sure replacement Tanner misses me anyhow."

"Oh really?"

"Yup," I say, popping the p.

"Okay then, let's see how long you can last without the real Tanner."

"You wouldn't."

"I would," he states matter-of-factly. Then he laughs. "You're right, I probably wouldn't. It's not like I can keep my dick in my pants around you."

"Good to know… Very good to know."

I flash my press badge when we reach the gate, and Tanner and I are waved in. The place is huge. There are a few rides, including a Ferris wheel. There are also plenty of food stands, each one selling a different fall-inspired treat: candy apples, pumpkin pies, pumpkin cheesecake—basically anything pumpkin. A few stands offer assortments of jams and locally grown vegetables. Others have games, like bobbing for apples. One booth even has a face painter, as well as an area for kids to paint pumpkins.

Tanner and I walk around for about an hour, checking out different things, and we don't even make a dent in everything there is to do here. We decide to take a ride on the Ferris wheel while we wait for Quinn and Alex, who've just texted to say they'll be here in about twenty minutes.

"You know we have to kiss when we stop at the top," I tell Tanner.

"You expect me to stop at just a kiss?"

"Well, considering it's broad daylight and there are children present, yes." I smile smugly at him.

"I can't even cop a feel? What a lame Ferris Wheel ride." He pouts.

"You copped plenty of feels this morning, mister. I think you'll survive."

"Barely," he insists.

When the Ferris wheel stops at the top, Tanner remains the consummate gentleman and settles for just a kiss. Quinn and Alex are standing by the ride exit, waiting for us when we get off.

"Hey, guys," we each say, greeting them.

"Hey," they both reply, sounding a little apprehensive, probably due to last night's fiasco.

"Sorry again about yesterday, Ash," Alex says sheepishly.

"No biggie. Let's forget it and move on. We have." I smile at Tanner, who responds by wrapping an arm around me and pulling me close.

"You still mad at me?" Quinn asks with a hint of sadness in her voice.

"No, but next time I'm kicking your scrawny ass." I grin at her.

"Sure, you can try, bitch." She smiles back, and just like that, all is right again between us.

The four of us wander around, taking in all the sights. Tanner and I fill them in on the things we've already seen and done when Quinn gets distracted by a row of booths showcasing this year's hot fall fashions. She drags me over to the different booths while the boys follow along dutifully.

"Okay, what's the deal with you and Alex? Have you guys been together since last night?" I ask Quinn when there is enough distance between the guys and us for them not to overhear.

"Do you mean have we been fucking like rabbits since last night? Then yes."

"You don't do repeats, Quinn. What's up?"

"Nothing. He's not really a *repeat* repeat. It's only the second time we've gotten together," she says evasively.

That's as far as I get with questioning her because suddenly we hear a feminine voice behind us call out, "Tanner! Alex! What are you doing here?"

I turn to see who it is, and when I set eyes on her, I don't have to wonder. There's no way I'd mistake the stunning woman hugging my boyfriend for anyone else. After all, I've seen countless photos of them together spanning the last six years… Melissa.

"Ashley's covering the festival for work, so we decided to make a day of it," Tanner answers.

"How cute. Where is she?" Melissa asks.

"Hi," I say as I approach, my voice sounding meek. *Dammit. I can't let myself seem weak or intimidated by her.*

"Hi," Melissa says enthusiastically. "It's so nice to finally meet you. Tanner has been hogging you all to himself."

"Nice to meet you too, Melissa." I smile at her.

"Hi, I'm Quinn," my best friend says, sticking her hand out to shake Melissa's. No one but me will be able to tell by the tone of her voice that's she isn't happy about Melissa's appearance.

"What am I? Chopped liver?" Alex asks.

"Of course not. Hello, Alex baby," she coos.

"Looking' fine as usual, Melissa," Alex says, hugging her.

"Shut up, asshole," Melissa replies to him with a smile.

"Warm and cuddly as usual too." Alex laughs.

"So what are you doing here?" Tanner asks Melissa, pulling me to him.

She waves absentmindedly at the boutique booths behind us. "Working, of course."

"There's no shopping here," Tanner teases, grinning.

"You know I don't shop for a living, Tag," she says, emphasizing the nickname that only she and Alex use.

"What do you do?" Quinn asks.

"I'm a fashion merchandiser," she answers.

"How cool," I say. "Quinn loves to shop"

"You don't?" Melissa asks in a horrified tone.

"No, not really," I answer quietly, suddenly feeling less womanly for not enjoying shopping. I don't like the way this woman makes me feel as though I'm being scrutinized. Quinn subtly elbows me, and I know exactly why. It's her way of telling me to buck up and not let Melissa make me feel inferior.

"You have to be the first woman I've ever met who doesn't like to shop." Melissa laughs. "I love it so much I've made a living out of fashion. But listen, I have to run. Ashley, it was so great to finally meet you. Enjoy the rest of your day, guys."

"Bye, babe," Alex says with a wave.

"Bye, Melissa," Tanner says, letting go of me to hug her good-bye.

"Bye, nice meeting you too," I say.

Quinn tugs me forward while the guys finish up their good-byes, "Don't trust that bitch, sweets. She's as fake as they come. And don't you ever let her intimidate you again. She may be hot, but you're hotter. Her hot comes from an hour of hair and makeup. Yours comes from waking up in the morning."

That's as far as we get on the subject before the guys come back over and we all decide to get something to eat before heading back to Jersey. I try not to let the encounter bother me, but Melissa rubs me the wrong way. She's nothing like Tanner described. Instead of cool and down to Earth, she seems bitchy and condescending. The fact that he fucked her and only her for six years makes me worry.

The ride home isn't as fun as the ride out to the fair, and I'm sure Tanner senses something's bothering me.

As if on cue he asks, "What's wrong, baby?"

"Nothing, just a little tired. Someone wore me out last night and again this morning," I explain, hoping to distract him from my mood.

"You didn't have any objections." He smiles.

"I never do when it comes to you."

"Did you have a good day?" he asks.

"I did. It was nice to finally meet Melissa. She's much prettier in person."

"She's a very attractive woman, but she's got nothing on you if that's what you're getting at, baby."

Man, he's perceptive.

"Thank you," I say, offering him a smile. "You know, you never told me the reason you ended up only being with her for so long."

"Well, it wasn't always that way," he explains. "I had a lot of fun in college, slept around a lot. You know, normal college guy shit. Up until the draft. As you already know, I was a super high draft pick, and it was an important time in my life. Some chick I'd only slept with once the week before the draft showed up right after the draft claiming I'd knocked her up."

"Oh my God." I gasp. He's never mentioned a kid to me before.

"Relax, baby. I definitely didn't knock her up. She just wanted her fifteen minutes of fame, and it was an eye-opener for me. I was about to go into the NFL. I had made it big, and she wouldn't have been the last if I'd continued to sleep around. I decided that it wasn't worth the risk of some chick ruining my reputation before I even got one. Melissa and I had already slept together, but we'd remained friends. So eventually, one thing led to another and we just ended up in an agreement. She never wanted anything from me. She had her own money. Her parents are well off. She wasn't needy, and she never clung. It just worked well over the years. We both knew what it was, and we weren't tied to each other. She was free to do whatever the hell she wanted, but she was always there for me when I needed a release. She's also into what I'm into, so we're sexually very compatible. I didn't really need more than that. Until you, that is." He smiles at me.

"What do you mean that she's into what you're into? What are you into?" I ask nervously, a thousand thoughts swirling in my head ranging from crazy bondage to threesomes.

"Breathe, baby. I'm not into anything hardcore, but as you've already noticed, I'm into control. Not every woman is okay with that type of sex. Control in that part of my life helps make up for the parts of my life I don't have control over. I can't always control what happens on the field. I definitely have no control over what people write about in the papers, but I can have control in my sex life. The funny thing is, though, I haven't felt the need to fuck out any issues since you came into my life, with the exception of last night."

I cringe thinking of Tanner being with Melissa in the same intense way we were last night, but I get it. I don't have to like it, though.

"I can definitely understand where you're coming from with wanting control. In a way, I want control over my sex life too. Not necessarily control in the bedroom, but control in owning what I want," I confess.

"What is it that you really want?"

"I want to feel comfortable with my desires. I want control over my thoughts and feelings about my desires."

"What are your desires?" he presses for more details.

"I want to be coveted, desired. I want you to lose control with me—not give it up to me, but be so consumed by me that you want to own me." It feels so good to tell him that. "You make me feel like it's okay to want that."

"It is okay to want that. There's nothing wrong with any want or desire as long we're both on the same page and honest about it."

"I've never thought about it that way," I admit, smiling.

"That's because not everyone is as smart as me," he laughs.

Chapter Twenty Six

ASHLEY

WE SPEND THE rest of the weekend relaxing at Tanner's. It feels very domestic, and Tanner and I laugh at our apparent domesticity while cooking dinner together. I hadn't been able to contain my laughter while watching him push the cart through the grocery store, and it was even worse while watching him in the kitchen. It took me twenty minutes to make the salad because I couldn't tear my eyes away from him while he fried chicken cutlets at the stove.

"I could totally kill your whole playboy rep with one tweeted pic, right now," I tease him.

"I'm pretty sure you tweeting a pic of me making you dinner would just make me more irresistible, no? Women around the country would be swooning over the awesome quarterback who cooks for his girlfriend. You'd be doing me a favor, baby." He shoots me a cocky smile.

"Jesus, it's getting a little crowded in here with that giant head of yours."

"Which head are we referring to?" he asks, still smiling.

I snort at his comment. "Could you be any more full of yourself?"

"Maybe, but I know you could definitely be more full of me."

"I've been plenty full of you this weekend, thank you very much. And if you want me full of you anymore this week, I suggest you give my vagina a break. I'm seriously having problems closing my legs and sitting down. I don't give a shit what people say, vaginas are definitely not made for constant plowing," I say with a wince. He has ridden me a lot this weekend.

"My poor baby! Do you need to me to kiss it better?" he asks with feigned concern.

"Couldn't hurt." I shrug. Before I know what's happening, I'm being thrown over Tanner's shoulder, and he's turning off the burner for the stove.

"What are you doing? It's time to eat." I try pushing myself up, using his ass as leverage.

"Oh, don't you worry, I plan on eating." He chuckles, continuing toward the bedroom where he deposits me in the center of the bed.

"Tanner…"

"What?" he asks as he pulls my leggings down. "Mmm, no panties. I like. Thank God I didn't know earlier that you were commando under here. I wouldn't have gotten a damn thing done today."

"Really? Now, Tanner?"

"Yes, now. Apparently, I've been a little rough with this beautiful pussy, and I need to make her all better." He smirks.

"Well, far be it from me to stop you," I say in surrender, lying back and folding my arms behind my head.

"Like you ever would." He blows on my clit and everything else fades away. It drives me crazy when he does that. The contrast of the warmth of his breath followed by the coolness of the air sets my body on fire.

Tanner doesn't waste any time. He places soft sensual kisses up and down my slit before licking softly along the seam. He slides his hands up my inner thighs, causing goosebumps to erupt all over my legs. He stops his ascent when he reaches the juncture of my thighs and uses his thumbs to spread me open, and I start to lose it. The sensation of being so open to him makes me hot.

He flattens his tongue against me and licks up and down, covering every square inch of my pussy before thrusting his tongue inside me and fucking me with it. My back arches up off the bed, and my lower body starts to spasm.

"Mmmm," Tanner says, knowing the vibration of his voice against me will set me off. "That's it, baby. Give it to me."

He thrusts his tongue faster and adds his thumb to my clit. I soar off like a rocket, screaming his name over and over. Tanner continues to kiss me softly as I come down from my orgasmic high.

"Does she feel better now?" Tanner asks.

"Exponentially," I say as I sit up and reach for his belt.

He brushes my hands away, shaking his head. "No, that was just for you."

"What about you?" I ask, nodding toward the bulging erection in his pants.

"It's not always tit for tat, Ash," he says, pulling me up and wrapping me up in my favorite place, against his chest.

TANNER DROPS ME off at home Monday morning on his way to the Jets' training facility. He has team meetings and practices all week, and I have three articles to write. He and the team will be working hard this week to make up for the few days they had off, so he's warned me it might be a few days before we see each other again. I'd laughed at his concern for me and told him I completely understood. His job might seem luxurious, but I know firsthand how hard that man works, and it only makes me respect him more.

Tanner makes sure to call me every night when he gets home and I can hear the exhaustion in his voice. Last night, he'd sounded as though he was barely hanging on to consciousness.

"Superstar, why don't you turn it in for the night?" I'd asked him. "You sound so tired."

"I will soon. I just need to hear your voice right now. Tell me about your day." He'd yawned.

"My day was boring. It'll probably put you to sleep. I wrote my article about Vincenzo's, headed into the office for a few hours to catch up on some things and check in with Dom."

"I wish you were here right now so that I could wrap myself around you and get lost in your heaven."

"But then that marvelous body of yours wouldn't get the rest it needs. I can't have the entire tri-state area trying to lynch me for wearing down their number-one quarterback, can I?"

"You're so good for my ego, baby," he informed me.

"Your ego needs no help, buddy. I think you need to call it a night. Good night, Superstar. Sweet dreams."

"If they're of you, then they'll be dirty instead of sweet." He laughed before hanging up.

I'VE SPENT THIS morning writing my article about Newman's, the sports bar we went to Friday night. It takes me a little while because I have to remember things about the night that didn't involve my arguments with Tanner and Quinn.

When I finish the article, I decide it's time for some lunch. Then I realize there's no food in the fridge. Knowing I could use a break, I decide to head to the store to pick up some basics for the house. Only, when I head out to the garage, my piece-of-shit car won't start again. *Ugh, I guess I'm walking to the corner store instead.*

People always make it look so easy to carry those damn brown bags a few blocks, but it definitely isn't as easy as it looks. On my way back to the condo, I'm trying to juggle two bags when my phone rings. From the ringtone, I know it's Tanner. I attempt to shift both bags to one arm, but I wind up dropping them just as I swipe the phone to answer it.

"Fuck!" I yell as the groceries scatter all over the sidewalk. The milk jug breaks and milk splatters everywhere.

"Ash, baby, you okay?" I hear Tanner ask, but I'm not really paying attention as I try to collect my groceries. "Ash? Are you there?" he asks again, concern in his voice.

"Yeah, hang on, though," I tell him, grabbing for a can of soup that's rolling down the sidewalk. I gather up the rest of the things that haven't gotten away and toss them all into the bag that hasn't ripped open. "Hey, sorry." I turn my attention back to him as I pick up the busted milk jug and toss it into the nearby trashcan. I try to wipe the milk off the bottom of my jeans and fail.

"What's going on? What's wrong?" he asks, sounding a little too concerned for how superficial the situation is.

"I just dropped the bags of groceries I was carrying and they went everywhere. The milk jug broke and splattered all over me, and then I had to chase my soup down the street," I explain in a huff as I hoist the bag higher on my hip.

"Well, why on are Earth are you walking with so many bags? Why didn't you just drive?"

"Because my stupid shitty car won't start again." Tanner hates my car. He's hated it since the day we first met. Every time he brings it up, I just give him a dirty look, and he drops the subject.

"I'm sorry, baby. You should've called me. I would've taken you to the store," he chides.

"It's not that big of a deal. I can walk to the store."

"I know you can, but why do it when I could have taken you?"

"It's fine. What's up? How were your meetings today?" I ask.

He doesn't answer right away, and I wonder if something is now distracting him.

"Tanner?" I ask, trying to get his attention back.

"I'm sorry, baby. They were fine. How was your day so far?"

"Not bad. I finished my article about Newman's. I was about to have lunch, but there was no food in the house, hence my trip to the store," I explain.

"Want to have lunch with me instead?"

"I would love to have any meal with you, Superstar."

"You're spending too much time with Quinn." He laughs. "I'll be there in about twenty minutes."

"See you soon," I say before hanging up.

LUNCH WITH TANNER is great, and things are relaxed as we head out to the car afterward. Everything between us is so easy now, especially after our enlightening weekend. I feel as though we'd needed to have that fight on Friday night. In the long run, it's made things so much better between us. I should have known it would be easy to talk to Tanner about my desires. Talking to him about it is like talking to Quinn. No judgment, just understanding. It's so nice to be free with him. I feel like the luckiest girl in the world. Every girl should have a Tanner, but not my Tanner. I'm not giving him up without a fight. I'm so distracted staring at his profile that I don't realize we aren't heading back to my place.

"Where are we going?" I ask once I notice the strange route we've taken.

"I have a stop to make before I drop you off. Is that okay? I probably should've checked to make sure you didn't have plans first."

"No, it's fine. I don't have any plans other than working on my articles."

"Okay, good," he says with a smirk that confuses me.

About fifteen minutes later, we pull into the lot of a luxury car dealership. I hadn't known Tanner was planning on getting a new car. He loves his car.

"You didn't tell me you were getting rid of the Range Rover," I say. "You love this car."

"I do love this car. I'm not the one getting a new car." His smirk has grown into a mischievous grin.

"Then what are we doing here?" I ask, confused as hell.

"You're getting a new car."

"Umm, no, I'm not. I can't afford a new car, especially not a car from this place." Looking around the lot, I don't see a single make that would sell for under fifty grand.

"It's a gift from me."

"No way in hell. You are *not* buying me a car," I screech. *Is he nuts? Why would he buy me a car?*

"Why not?"

"If you have to ask me that, then you know nothing about me," I say, exasperated.

"Please let me buy you a car. It's not like I can't afford it. I don't like the fact that your shitty car could leave you stranded at any point in time while I might be on the other side of the country. It's really not a big deal," he insists smiling at me. He thinks he's won, knowing I usually can't resist him.

His mind control tricks aren't going to work this time. I won't let him buy me a car.

"It is a big deal! Do you buy all the women in your life cars?" I ask pointedly.

"I have, in fact, bought my mom a car before. Once, for Christmas. It had the red bow on the top and everything," he proclaims proudly.

"Well, that's your mother, Tanner, not just some girl you're dating." I'm getting madder and madder the longer the argument goes on, and I refuse to give in.

"You *are not* just some girl I am seeing, Ashley," he says in a very harsh tone.

"Really? Then what am I?"

"First of all, you're my girlfriend and someone I care deeply about. You also happen to need a reliable car. I can afford to give you that and also give myself peace of mind. It's not just about you, Ashley. I can't be worried about you getting stranded somewhere and me not being able to get to you," he argues.

"I'm not comfortable accepting a car from you."

"Please. Consider it a birthday present," he counters.

"My birthday isn't for another month and a half."

"So? What do I need to do to get you to pick out a car?"

I'm getting the feeling that I'm not leaving here without a car, but maybe I can negotiate.

"You're not buying me a new car. It has to be used and nothing expensive. So basically nothing that's in this place," I insist, hoping he backs down.

"It will be new, and it will be from here, so how about we just go pick one out and you shut up?" He grins at me victoriously. "I'll even let you have your wicked way with me later," he adds.

"Ooh, you spoil me," I laugh. I could use a new car and if Tanner wants to buy me one, so be it. I'm not going to argue about this any longer. It seems to make him happy to do this for me.

Less than an hour later, Tanner is signing papers for my new pearl white BMW. Despite all my initial bitching, I do love it. I can't quite wrap my head around the fact that he's just bought me a fifty-thousand dollar car, though. Of course, he wanted it to have the works. At first, I objected, saying I didn't need all the fancy frills. Then I stopped arguing with him because it wasn't worth the effort. I let him pick out what he wanted, and I'd picked the color. Of course, it was one of the colors they didn't have in stock. I told Tanner I was fine picking another color, but he insisted on getting it in white. Therefore, my new car will be delivered to my condo in a few days.

"Happy, baby?" he asks as we head back to his car, a huge grin on his face.

It's blatantly obvious how happy he is. That's all that matters to me.

"Super happy. Just another perk of having a hot, rich football player for a boyfriend," I say without thinking, giving him a devilish smile.

Tanner's face drops at the comment, and I realize my error.

"I'm sorry, that was a really stupid thing to say. You know I wasn't serious, right? I would never use you for material things, Tanner. I don't need the car, you know. I swear! We could cancel the order, and I would be just as happy," I say honestly, hoping he doesn't freak on me. I'm kicking myself for saying that, knowing how Tanner feels about people using him.

"I know, Ash. I just don't like how those words sound coming out of your mouth, even in joke form." He frowns.

I hate the sad look on his face he gets whenever he talks about people who have used him for things. He'd had this same look on his face when he told me about Carrie. His eyes lose their usual sparkle, and his shoulders slump as though he's holding up the weight of the world with them.

"I'm sorry," I apologize again, wrapping my arms around his torso and pulling him close to me. "I really do appreciate the car. No one has ever bought me anything like that before. Thank you."

"You're welcome, baby," he says with a small smile.

"I believe there was a part two to that gift, though. Do I get to have my wicked way with you now or do I have to wait until they deliver the car and have my way with you in the back seat?" I ask, wiggling my eyebrows suggestively.

"Who says it has to be either or?" His smile broadens, a bit of sparkle returning to those gorgeous emerald eyes of his.

"Good point, Mr. Garrison." I lean in to kiss him in the middle of the dealership parking lot, showing him just how much I appreciate all his gifts.

Chapter Twenty Seven

ASHLEY

BY THE TIME my car is delivered Friday morning, Tanner has already left for this weekend's game in San Diego, so he isn't here to share in my excitement. I do text him when it arrives, telling him how excited I am to take her for a spin tonight. Quinn and I decide to go out for dinner instead of ordering in like we usually do just so I can drive her. We also take a bunch of pictures in it, including one of me on top of it to send to Tanner.

"Pose all sexy like those bitches do at the car shows," Quinn instructs, laughing as she demonstrates a pose that makes it look as though she's humping my car's hood.

Shaking my head, I tell her, "You'll have to settle for just a big smile. I'm not putting on a skimpy outfit. It's only a few days before Halloween for Christ's sake. It's not *that* warm." Sometimes I really do question her sanity.

Friday night is the only night I leave my house during the weekend, deciding that it's the perfect opportunity to relax and do absolutely nothing. I've been exhausted, and I have no idea why. I sleep in on Saturday morning and I'm in bed by ten Saturday night, which is unusual for me, but I chalk it up to sympathy fatigue for Tanner.

Sunday isn't much different from Saturday, except that I manage to shower and get out of my pajamas. I put on my Garrison jersey and send Tanner a picture of me with it on to wish him good luck. It's become a sort of ritual for us. The first time I'd worn it, he'd said his number had never looked better and that seeing me in it stirred up something crazy inside him.

Quinn agrees to veg out and watch the game with me until she gets bored, which doesn't take long at all. "Damn, these pants really are a perk to watching football," she admits sometime during the second quarter.

"I know. Have you seen Tanner's ass in them?" I ask, keeping my eyes glued to the television screen.

"Does Alex have a pair of those pants? If he doesn't, maybe Superstar will let him borrow them for a night," she muses, a wistful yet devious smile on her face.

"What's the deal with you two? You've been spending a lot of nights together." It's not like Quinn to get attached, and Alex is the male version of her, so I'm a little concerned, to say the least.

"Nothing really. We get together every now and again and have a good time," is her answer.

"And?" I press for more details.

"And what?"

"Come on, Quinn. You act like I can't tell when something's up with you. Spill."

"Nothing is up with me. He's cool to hang out with, and he gets the deal. Plus, he's not around enough to get attached," she explains, rolling her eyes and giving herself away. Eye rolling is Quinn's signature deflection move when she doesn't want to talk about something. I think she might actually like Alex.

"Okay, if you say so," I say, pretending I believe her. I'm going to get to the bottom of this thing going on between them, though.

"So what are you and Superstar doing for Halloween?" Quinn asks, clearly attempting to turn the conversation away from her non-thing with Alex.

"I don't know. We haven't talked about it. Are you planning on doing something with Alex?"

"Levitate is having a Halloween party. We all had such a great night last time we went that I thought maybe it would be fun. It's a costume party," she explains, looking genuinely excited.

"When is it? You know the guys can't go if it's a Saturday night."

"I'm not an idiot, Ash. It's on Halloween night, which is Friday this year."

"I'm down, and I don't think Tanner will have a problem going. Don't expect us to be out late, though. Tanner has been pretty drained lately," I say, partly as a reminder to myself. I've spent all weekend doing nothing and still can't seem to escape the exhaustion I'm fighting. I can't imagine how he does it. Just during today's game, I've watched him take a whole bunch of hits that looked like they hurt, and he's done a shitload of running too.

"Aren't you a cute little football wife now?" Quinn snickers.

"Blow me, bitch. Someone needs to take care of that man, and that someone is me."

"Whatever! So what are you thinking for costumes?" Quinn asks before shoving a salsa-covered chip into her mouth.

"No clue. What about you?" I steal the bag of chips from her.

"I'm thinking Cleopatra and Mark Antony. I wouldn't mind looking at Alex half-naked in a toga for the night," she says, getting up to refill our wine glasses.

"Woohoo!" I scream, momentarily forgetting our conversation because Tanner just threw for a touchdown.

"What the fuck are you yelling about?" Quinn asks, returning with two full glasses of wine.

"Tanner just threw for a touchdown." I tap out a congratulatory text message to Tanner.

"Oh…" She sits down, seeming completely disinterested. "So you need to think about costumes."

"I will when Tanner gets home. We'll talk about it."

"Ugh, you're like a boring married couple," she says, rolling her eyes and making a face.

AFTER THE GAME, Tanner calls me to thank me for all my game-time texts. "I have a surprise for you for next weekend," he says, his voice full of excitement.

"Well, I got a car this weekend, so that's going to be hard to top."

"How about coming to see me play live in one of the suites?"

"Really?" I squeal like a little girl. "I've been wondering if you were ever going to invite me to a game. I was starting to think you were embarrassed to be seen with me," I tease, careful to keep my voice light so he knows I'm only kidding. I still feel bad about that stupid perk comment I made at the car dealership, so I'm erring on the side of caution.

"Honestly, I didn't think that you wanted to come. You've never mentioned it before. My parents keep asking when they will get to meet you, though, so I figure this might be a nice way to ease you into the experience that is my mother. You can bring Quinn too."

"I don't know if that's a good idea. She barely makes it through the games on TV, but I'll ask her. I'm sure she'd come just to see Alex." I tell him, before filling him in of my suspicions about the two of them.

"They're two peas in a pod, Ash," he says. "Let's just leave them be. We don't want to spook them by pointing out they're dangerously close to being a couple."

"Quinn wants us to come with them to a Halloween costume party at Levitate on Friday. I told her I'd have to check with you. I wasn't sure if you'd be up to it."

"Sure, that's fine. I can't pull a super late night, but I don't mind. But I gotta run for now, baby. We're about to board the plane. I'll text you when I get home. Sweet dreams."

TRUE TO HIS word, I have a text from him when I wake up the next morning telling me he made it home safely. He says he misses me but will see me later tonight.

The drive to Tanner's house flies by in my new car, and I smell food the minute I open the front door.

"You sure know how to spoil a girl," I say as I make my way to the kitchen and find him cooking me dinner again. "I could really get used to this treatment, Superstar."

"You should get used to it, baby." He flashes me a smile that lights up the room before kissing me as though I'm the very air he breathes. Sometimes I forget that kissing is one of this man's fortes. His lips are warm and soft, with a strong yet tender force behind them. He wipes my mind clean with his kisses.

"Mmm, what did I do to deserve that?" I ask after gathering my wits.

"Nothing but being yourself. I missed you."

"I missed you too, but I got to see those awesome pants on you again, so that helped hold me over."

"And I got those pictures of your beautiful face while you enjoyed your new car," he reasons, smiling.

We decide to keep the rest of the weekend as low key as I'd started it off. I tell Tanner all about my sympathy exhaustion for him, and he laughs at me.

"We'll just relax and watch some TV for the night then," he says, soothing me.

And that's what we do. We lie in bed, and I attach myself to him with every limb possible. My head rests on his chest, my legs are entwined with his, and my arm drapes over his beautiful midsection.

"I think this is by far my favorite place to be in the entire world." I sigh into the crook of his neck.

"Yeah? That's good because I really enjoy that you fit me perfectly." He grins before planting another passionate kiss on me.

One kiss turns into another, and before I know it, Tanner is sliding into me as though he belongs no place else. He never takes his eyes off mine. Thrust after thrust, he stares into my eyes with an adoration I've never seen before. I feel as though he's trying to convey something important to me, but no words are spoken. He's speaking with every kiss, with every touch, with every moan of ecstasy that leaves his mouth.

Slow and sensual isn't our usual style, but I have to say it's just as amazing. I feel the reverence he has for my body in every caress, and his worship takes me to new heights. I feel my orgasm beginning to build all the way down in my toes before it rises up through my entire body. My skin tingles and my body shakes until I have no control over anything.

Tanner never misses a beat. He continues to pull himself out almost completely and push his whole length back inside me with each thrust, igniting every molecule in me as he does, over and over, until I can't take any more. The dam holding everything in breaks, and the waves of pleasure come crashing down one after the other. My orgasm seems to go on forever. Just as it starts to ebb, I feel Tanner reach his release, and it sparks mine back to life as though it had never ended.

"Wow," I say between the gulps of air I'm trying to drag into my lungs.

"You're amazing," he says with the same look of adoration in his eyes. He kisses from my forehead down the bridge of my nose and stops at my lips before he unsheathes himself and heads to the bathroom to clean up.

He comes back from the bathroom with a washcloth for me, just as he always does. After I clean myself up, he takes the washcloth and tosses it in the hamper. I can't help but stare at his beautiful naked form. This magnificent man is mine.

Tanner switches off the lamp on the nightstand before climbing back into bed and pulling me back to my favorite spot in the world. We don't speak. No words needed at the moment.

"Good night, Ashley," he whispers in my ear and then kisses the crown of my head.

"Sweet dreams, Tanner."

"They always are with you, baby."

THE WEEK FLIES by, mainly due to my anticipation of the game this weekend. I'm more than excited to see Tanner play in person, to get to see him right after the game instead of hours or days later. Yesterday was Halloween, and I had the task of running all of Tanner's last-minute errands. He didn't have any candy to give out, and when I asked why I couldn't just run to the local *Walgreen's* to grab some bags of candy, he said, "I can't give out the crappy candy." Mr. Superstar needed whole bars of candy and told me to go to *Costco* so I wouldn't clean out *Walgreen's.* He's lucky he's hot, otherwise he would've been getting his own damn candy.

I considered my costume choices as payback, though. When I'd asked Tanner if he had a preference for costumes, he'd said no. His only requirement had been that they needed to be appropriate to hand out candy and take some pictures in.

"When I'm home, I love giving out the candy. A lot of times, kids who watch football, or even parents, will ask to take pictures. You know me. I never say no," he explained, looking like a big kid himself.

So I found Fred and Daphne costumes from *Scooby Doo*. I got to wear a short purple skirt and go-go boots. Tanner got to wear an ascot.

"Really?" he'd asked, looking unenthused when I showed him the costumes.

"What?" I asked, feigning innocence.

"You couldn't have picked a more… umm… manly costume?" He eyed the costume as though it might come to life and slap him for insulting it.

"What's wrong with Fred? He's a crime fighter. Plus, ascots are hot." I smirked, waggling my eyebrows.

"Never again will I leave you in charge of important decisions," he swore, chuckling and shaking his head at me as he snatched his costume from my hand. "We're not putting these on until after the trick-or-treaters are gone, though!"

We had a great time handing out candy, and Tanner had really seemed to enjoy himself. Just as he'd said, kids and parents alike asked for pictures.

"You really like doing this type of thing, don't you?" I asked once the last trick-or-treater had left with his candy bar and a picture with Tanner.

"I do. Kids are great. And Halloween is all about the kids. Which is why you can't give out crappy candy," he said with a stern look. "I remember going out with my parents and sisters and having so much fun. Every year, we'd pick some theme and all have a costume from that. We did the *Wizard of Oz* one year. I was the scarecrow. I can't wait to do that with my kids one day."

"Such a sentimental sap, Superstar," I told him, smiling as I pictured Tanner with a gaggle of kids in costumes.

"Yeah, yeah, go get your ass into that skirt and those boots." He smacked my ass and pushed me toward the stairs.

We ended up meeting Quinn and Alex at Levitate, but none of us stayed all that long. It was overcrowded and crazy enough without adding the costumes. I'd been prepared to take down a slutty angel or butterfly or anything else with wings if I got smacked by one more set of them. The crowd had been pretty young too. It seemed as though everyone who had just turned twenty-one had packed themselves in there, meaning lots of immaturity to go around. After only an hour or so, I asked Tanner if he was ready to head out.

"Thank God! I thought you'd never ask," he said, leaning down to speak into my ear so I could hear him over the din. "Hell yeah. I've been ready for the last hour,"

"We've only been here an hour."

"I know, and I've been staring at your ass cheeks peeking out from under that skirt the whole time. And I'm not the only one." He nodded toward the crowd with a murderous look in his eyes.

"Ooh, you're hot when you're jealous. Come on. Let's get out of here and you'll get a full view of what's peeking out from under this skirt," I teased while fingering his ascot.

A huge grin had spread across his face, and he whispered in my ear, "Let's go!"

I spent Saturday working on some last minutes touches for this week's assignments, waiting for Tanner to call me to tell me he was on his way home. We decided that I would stay the night at his house.

We're heading to the stadium together this morning, just as soon as Tanner's ready. I don't think excited is the best word for how I feel about today. I can't wait, but I'm nervous too. It's the first time I'll be meeting Tanner's family. I have to hand it to Tanner, though. It's a great setting. We'll all have something else to focus on during the lulls in the conversation—or in case they hate me.

Quinn did agree to come, but of course, she's heading to the stadium with Alex. Someone needs to get those two to admit that they're in a relationship. I think they spend more time together than Tanner and I do.

"You ready, baby?" Tanner asks, emerging from his closet ready to go. He looks downright edible in that dark gray suit, and the hunter green shirt makes his eyes shine like a beacon.

"Is that how you go to every game?" I ask, trying to put my tongue back in my mouth.

"Yes?"

"It should be illegal for you to be in public dressed like that. I don't know which is hotter: you in that suit or you in your tight-ass football pants." I shake my head. "I'm going to have to beat some skank's ass today, aren't I?"

"Oh please," he says, rolling his eyes. "But you're looking mighty fine in my jersey, as usual."

I do a little spin for him before I smack him on the ass. "Let's go. You have a game to win."

Tanner spends the ride to the stadium telling me all about his parents. Margaret and Andrew Garrison. They've been married for thirty-five years and can be nauseatingly romantic sometimes, so I shouldn't be alarmed by any public displays of affection. It's possible that his sisters may make an appearance, but he says you never know with them. I get a rundown of the suite. There's anything and everything I could possibly want in there, and he tells me I shouldn't hesitate to ask for a damn thing. Tanner walks me up to the suite before heading to the locker room.

"No one will be here for a little bit, so you can have some time alone to get settled. I gotta go get ready, but remember, don't hesitate to ask for anything. I'll be right up after all the post-game stuff finishes. Just stay with my parents. They know the drill." He kisses me good-bye.

"Have a great game. Make me proud to wear this jersey." I smile with pride. My boyfriend's about to take the field, and I get to watch from up here like football royalty. *Damn, I'm lucky.*

I stand at the front of the suite, against the glass, and watch as the stadium comes to life. The fans trickle in, and the players trickle out. The sideline crews are setting up all the things they need to ensure the game runs smoothly. I spot Tanner the second he comes out, and I catch him looking up toward the suite. I do my duty as his girlfriend, blowing him a kiss and waving. I think I see him wave back, but I don't know if he can even see me up here. I watch him warm up, tossing the ball to the receivers, setting up with the line to run some mock plays, practicing handoffs with the backs. All that Madden playing combined with Tanner's detailed explanations has paid off. I almost completely understand what's happening on the field right now. The way his body moves is so graceful for such a big guy. I'm in total awe of him.

I'm so lost in my thoughts I don't even notice that I'm not alone anymore until I hear someone speak behind me,

"It's amazing, isn't it?" a woman who I can only assume is Tanner's mother asks. She stands there in a jersey similar to mine next to a man who looks a lot like Tanner wearing the same jersey. The smile on her face is full of pride.

"It certainly is," I reply, reflecting a pride-filled smile of my own. "I'm Ashley Mitchell. It's such a pleasure to finally meet you," I introduce myself, offering a hand to them each in turn. "Tanner has told me so much about you."

"Same here, dear." Mrs. Garrison shakes my hand. "It's nice to finally meet the woman who has stolen my son's heart."

"I don't know about that," I say shyly, doing my best to keep my face from turning red.

"Oh, I do, dear." She smiles again.

The three of us chat idly for about twenty minutes before Quinn comes bouncing into the suite, a ball of irrepressible energy.

"Hey, Bitch," she says, kissing me on the cheek. She turns to Mr. and Mrs. Garrison, saying, "Alex said that you'd better not skip out before he gets up here to say hello. He said he missed you last game and he hasn't seen you in a while."

Tanner's parents clearly have no idea what to make of Quinn's brusqueness, and it's amusing.

"This is Quinn, my best friend," I explain. "She also happens to have gotten pretty close to Alex, as you can tell."

"Oh, well nice to meet you, dear," Mrs. Garrison answers. "Thank you for relaying Alex's message. It has been a while since we've seen him." Her smile is almost as proud when she talks about Alex as it had been when she was talking about Tanner, which reminds me of how long they've been friends. Alex must be very close to Tanner's parents too.

We all order drinks and some snacks while we wait for the game to start. Tanner's dad tells us some football stories from Tanner's youth and has us nearly in tears with laughter.

"Thank God for those stories," I say, still laughing after one particularly amusing story about a terrible play of Tanner's. "I was starting to think that he was born perfect."

"I tried, but yes, he does have some flaws," Mrs. Garrison agrees just as the door to the suite opens and Melissa breezes in as though she owns the world.

"Melissa," Mrs. Garrison exclaims. "So good to see you again." She gets up to wrap Melissa in a huge hug, seeming as happy to see her as if the bitch had hung the fucking moon or something.

"Hello, Margaret. Hi, Andrew. It's great to see you guys again too. Sorry I missed you at the last game, but I just couldn't get here. I felt so bad, but Tanner said he understood, so I felt less guilty," she explains.

It's news to me. I hadn't known Melissa came to the games most of the time or that she and Tanner still talked on a regular basis. I'd figured that had ended when their fuck-buddy arrangement did.

"What the fuck is she talking about?" Quinn whispers as she walks over to me.

"I have no clue," I tell her, trying to contain the surprise that's quickly morphing into anger.

"Hey, Melissa," Quinn greets her. "I didn't know that we would get to see you again today. The boys never mentioned anything," Quinn's comment and tone seem innocent enough, but I know that's her way of letting Melissa know the guys haven't mentioned her to us because she isn't important. Watching Quinn get jealous over Alex would be amusing if I weren't just as annoyed about Melissa.

"Oh, I never miss a game. Well, I try not to anyway. Sometimes work gets in the way, like the last home game. I couldn't get here, but that's the first one I've missed in a while. Tanner's been getting me season tickets for years," she says with a very smug smile.

"How nice of him. It's awesome he has such a big cheering section now," I say, attempting to stake my claim as the official head of said cheering section. Tanner is my boyfriend, and she was never anything more than his fuck buddy. I just need to keep repeating that in my head.

Melissa offers a half-hearted smile before heading back over to where Tanner's parents now sit and striking up a conversation.

"I'd really like to fuck that bitch up," Quinn says point blank. "I don't like how she thinks she has some claim over the guys."

"Do you know if Alex ever slept with her?" I ask but immediately regret it, realizing it's probably not the best idea to put in Quinn's head.

"No clue, but I don't care. No way could that bitch ever compete with you or me. Just watch your back around her. I definitely don't trust that twat." She sneers.

I laugh at her brutal honesty. "You have such a way with words, my dear."

The game flies by. The Jets kick some ass, and Tanner has a great game. It's much more fun to watch it happen in person. Apparently, today's game was not only a divisional one but rivalry as well. The Jets and Patriots have quite a bit of animosity between them. I feed off the energy that's rolling off of Tanner, even across all the distance between us. It feels as though I've thrown the touchdown each time he does, and I jump up and down and yell like a crazy lunatic. After each touchdown, Tanner looks toward the suite and blows me a kiss. I'm pretty sure they even show me on TV a few times. Take that, Melissa.

"It's so nice to see him so happy and in love," Mr. Garrison says to me as we wait in the suite for Tanner to finish his post-game duties.

"Well, thank you, Mr. Garrison. I don't think I would say love just yet, but we definitely care deeply for each other," I reply, feeling a little embarrassed. I'm not sure if it's because I'm telling him I don't love his son or because I'm telling him his son doesn't love me. I don't think Tanner loves me, but do I love him? I'd never really given it any thought until now. And that's all the thought I give it for the moment because I'm suddenly swept up into an enormous hug by the man in question himself.

"What'd you think, baby?" he asks, setting me back down on my feet.

"I think you were fantastic as always," I answer before giving him a kiss that probably isn't suitable for an audience, but Melissa's still here, so I have a point to make.

"You might not say so, but I do. And please call me Andrew," Mr. Garrison whispers to me before congratulating Tanner.

"What was that about?" Tanner asks.

"Nothing. How about we go home and celebrate your performance on the field with an equally stellar performance off the field?"

"I say, what're we waiting for?"

I consider asking him why he's never mentioned that Melissa comes to his games, but the fact that he didn't acknowledge her or even say good-bye puts things in perspective for me and seems to explain why he'd never said anything. She isn't even a thought in his mind and knowing that makes me extremely happy.

Chapter Twenty Eight

ASHLEY

THE LAST TWO weeks have been a whirlwind. Tanner and I have grown closer, my insecurities seem to have disappeared, and I've never felt more secure in myself or in anything else. He does that for me. He lifts me up and makes me better. Tanner and I have something special, and I've been living in a perpetual state of happiness lately. Both of us have been busy since his last home game. Tanner had to head back out of town the night after. The team had a Thursday night game, so they had to head to Arizona Monday night. So we haven't seen each other all week, but we have made sure to speak to each other whenever possible. It sucks being apart, but I understand. It's part of his job, and he loves his job. It's only for a few months a year.

Tanner and I spend the weekend after he gets back from Arizona and Monday night together, doing nothing but hanging out. Tanner and the team have been working pretty hard. Their record of eight and two is amazing, and they're leading their division. Tanner has explained to me that the coach has a philosophy about there always being room for improvement and if there is ever a time to not slack off, it's now.

So when I come down with the stomach flu in the middle of the week, I make up excuses as to why I'm too busy to see Tanner. I think he starts to catch on by the end of the week, but then he has to leave again on Friday before he can confront me. Since then, I've been biding my time, hoping to be better by the time he gets back tonight. I feel bad for lying to him, but there's no way I'm having him come here and get sick. Not a chance in fucking hell. I can see the headlines now: *Star quarterback Tanner Garrison catches stomach flu from girlfriend and can't play this week.*

"Okay, if I didn't know any better, I'd swear you were pregnant," Quinn says, wetting another washcloth to wipe the back of my neck as I sit by the toilet.

I hadn't been kidding when I said that Tanner *could not* afford to catch this. I've been hovering over the toilet on and off for the last week, puking my guts up. There isn't anything left in my body to vomit up but internal organs. I've barely eaten in days because I can't keep anything down, and I'm exhausted. I can't remember ever feeling this tired in my life. Honestly, I think I might be dying.

"No, I'm not Quinn. I just have a stomach virus or something. Can you help me back to bed? I don't think I can make it on my own." I'm not even sure I can hold my own weight at the moment.

"Are you sure you're done for now? I'm going get you some crackers and ginger ale and put them in your room. Then I'll come back and help you. I don't feel like cleaning up any more of your vomit this week, so let's make sure that you're good for right now. I also need to change the garbage can in your room. You seriously owe me for this when you're better, by the way," Quinn says on her way out of the bathroom.

The next thing I know, I hear hushed murmuring at the door. I realize I must have nodded off on the floor of the bathroom. My head isn't even resting on the toilet seat anymore. I'm just lying down next to it.

"She's going to be mad if you see her like this, Tanner," I hear Quinn say.

"I don't give a shit. How long has she been sick? And why didn't she tell me?" he growls at her.

"Don't get pissy with me! She's been sick most of the week. You know she doesn't like to ask for help from anyone, and she doesn't want anyone else to catch this shit, especially you. If I didn't live with her, I probably wouldn't know she was sick either."

"Okay, well, let's get her into bed, and I'll stay with her until morning. I don't have anywhere to be until ten o'clock tomorrow," he says as he pushes open the bathroom door.

"Go away, Tanner. I'm fine. I don't need you to get sick too!" I tell him from the floor.

"Jesus, Ash. You're not fine. Far from it. You look like shit, and I think you've lost about ten pounds since last weekend. Why didn't you tell me you were sick, baby?" he asks, bending down to scoop me up off the floor.

"I'd be careful with the sudden movements if I were you," Quinn warns him. "She pukes really easily, and I'm tired of cleaning it up."

"'I'll get someone to clean the place for you. I don't care if she pukes on me. She needs to be in bed."

I must fall asleep again because that's the last thing that I remember of their conversation. I'm woken up some time later by the need to vomit again. I groan and roll over to get out of bed only to hit a hard wall of muscle. I can't hold back the dry heaving, and Tanner stirs beside me.

"Hey, baby. Here," he says, picking up the trash can and holding it for me.

"You should go. You can't catch this," I insist. "I didn't tell you for a reason."

"Shhh, baby. I know. I know. But you need help. You're super dehydrated and you look like death. Let me help you. I'll only be able to see you a few days this week, and I want to spend as much time as I can with you. Even if that just means holding your hair back while you hang your head over the toilet." He smoothes my hair back from my forehead.

"Why don't you take a sip of this ginger ale and lay back down. Try to sleep. I'll stay with you tonight, but you really need to sleep." He kisses the top of my head and reaches for the cup of soda Quinn left on my nightstand.

I take a sip and then lay my head down on his chest to drift back off to sleep. When I wake again, it's to a kiss on my cheek and the sound of Tanner whispering good-bye and promising to check on me later.

I say, “Okay," and go back to sleep.

I wake up once again a few hours later with an awful feeling in my stomach that has nothing to do with the virus I have. Something that Quinn said to me yesterday flashes suddenly into my mind.

"Quiiiiin!" I scream.

She comes into the room huffing. "I swear to God I'm not cleaning up any more messes you’ve made. I was sure your boyfriend would handle that for you this morning," she says. "Well, you look a little better at least this morning, sweets. What’s up?”

"I need you to go to the drug store for me, please. Right now," I say, panicking slightly.

"Why, what do you need?"

"A pregnancy test or three, just in case. Oh my God, I can’t believe that I forgot." I know I'm getting myself all worked up, but I don’t care. *No way, this can’t be happening. Why didn’t I notice earlier?*

"What? Are you kidding? I was only joking yesterday. You’ve been on the patch for years. Calm down," Quinn says, trying to calm me down.

"About two months ago, I was changing the sheets on my bed and found a patch stuck to it. It had only been off for like three days, and I put another one on immediately after I found it. Google said I’d be fine as long as I used condoms for the next few days. But that was the weekend of the gala, and I didn’t have sex the days following, so I never thought anything of it again. But I don’t think I have had a period since then. I’d just thought it was because my cycle got all screwed up with switching the patch days and whatnot. I never thought I could be pregnant. No way, Quinn. My luck can’t possibily be that awful. No fucking way," I explain, rambling. I ramble when I freak out.

"Okay, okay! Calm down! I’m going now. Be back in a few minutes. Stay in bed until I get back. I don’t need you passing out or anything."

I down almost the entire bottle of ginger ale after she rushes out, hoping to be hydrated enough to pee by the time she gets back.

In reality, Quinn is only gone for about ten minutes, but it feels like three hours by the time she gets home. She comes barreling into my bedroom and dumps a bag of pregnancy tests on my bed.

"Here, I got one of each brand they had at the corner store. Go pee, now!"

I grab a box and head into the bathroom. Ripping the box open, I pull out the test and instructions to read to make sure that I do this right. I'm hit by a wave of nausea, but I do my best to ignore it. I have to figure out what the hell is going on. Thanks to my dehydration when I sit down to pee, I barely manage to cover the entire end of the stick like the directions said. I place the cap on the test and wait. It says it takes three minutes for results. So I wash my hands and stare at the test, waiting for the results to pop up in the little window.

Quinn comes into the bathroom and picks up the stick, asking, "What are we looking for?"

"It will say either pregnant or not pregnant. I can't look any longer. Let me know when it says something." I pace back and forth, waiting for Quinn to speak.

"Okay, want me to show you or tell you?"

I stop pacing and turn around. "Show me," I say.

My world falls apart as Quinn spins the test around and I read the single word in the little window: pregnant.

"Oh my God, Quinn!" I sob. "What the hell am I going to do?"

"It'll be okay. It's not like either one of you didn't want kids, even if it's not how you expected."

"Do you really believe that?" A thousand thoughts swirl around in my head, but none of them are 'everything will be okay'.

"I do, and you should too," she says, hugging me.

God, I hope she's right.

Chapter Twenty Nine

TANNER

I **CAN'T WAIT** for the meeting to be over so I can get back to Ashley. She really did look like death last night, and I'm still upset she didn't want me to take care of her. She can be so stubborn sometimes.

Coach is prattling on, saying that just because we're having a great season so far doesn't mean we're guaranteed a playoff spot.

"A good season means shit if you don't make the playoffs. So let's make sure we don't get ahead of ourselves. We have five more regular season games ahead of us, so let's not fuck it up. Nine and two is good, don't get me wrong, but there's always room for improvement. I want everyone here at ten sharp tomorrow morning for game film." With those parting words, everyone is dismissed.

Coach glances around the room and then heads straight toward me. "Garrison, your game yesterday was phenomenal. Probably one of your best ever. You finished with five hundred twelve passing yards and four passing TD's. Not to mention your rushing TD at the end of the third. Wherever your head has been at lately, it seems to be doing wonders for your game. That said, let's not let your ego get in the way. See you tomorrow, son." He claps me on the back and heads out with the rest of the coaching staff.

"Me? Ego? I have no idea what you mean, Coach," I call after him.

He turns and gives me a weary smile, shaking his head.

I laugh to myself. Come on, we're athletes. We're born with egos. Mine's nowhere near the same size as those of some of the assholes in this league.

As for where my head is at, it's been with an incredible brunette who's currently sick at home. My attitude has been pretty carefree ever since Ashley and I got together. It's weird how little it's taken for me to let my guard down around her. She isn't like any of the girls I've run into over the years. She doesn't want anything from me but me, my time and my attention. But she never complains when she can't get it. She doesn't like asking me for anything, even just taking care of her while she's sick. I know so many girls who would have used that as a way to keep me at their beck and call. Not Ash. She'd rather suffer in silence. Ever since she wrote that article about me, she hasn't asked me for one thing—except down and dirty sex, and I had to pry that request from her in the beginning. It didn't take too much force, though. Now that she's comfortable, she doesn't even hesitate to ask.

I can't help but think about the last time we had sex, which was nearly a week ago. She was hot as fuck, provoking the hell out of me, purposely being defiant.

"Are you going to be a good girl or do I have to restrain you?" I had asked her.

Her response had been to wiggle her fine, naked ass against my cock.

I grabbed a handful of her hair and pulled so she had to turn to look at me over her shoulder. "I think you want me to tie you down and smack that ass. Is that what you want?"

"God, yes. Please tie me down, spank me, and fuck me," she'd practically purred out.

She gets so turned on by being dominated. Fuck, if I don't get rock hard just thinking about her… I love that she got off on everything we did together. I love sex with her, and each time is better than the last. There is definitely something to be said about sex with someone you actually care about emotionally. I've been thinking lately that I may even love her, but I'm not ready to admit that.

I chuckle, remembering how embarrassed she'd been at first about wanting to be pushed, to be controlled, to be taken. As though I could ever think of her as the whore she'd thought it'd make her. Seriously, what kind of assholes had she been running with before? I can't seem to wipe the smile off my face whenever I think of her.

I'm eager to get back to Ashley's place. I hate that she's sick, but this seems worse than a regular stomach virus. I'm taking her to the doctor when I get home if she doesn't seem any better, whether she wants me to or not.

Quinn answers the door when I ring the bell.

"She's in her room," she tells me before heading to her room and closing the door behind her.

I knock on Ashley's door and walk in.

She's curled up in the middle of the bed in the fetal position, her knees tucked under her chin with her arms wrapped around them. Her face is blotchy and red, her eyes bloodshot and teary. She looks terrible. *Yup, I'm definitely taking her to the doctor.*

I sit down next to her and run my hand through her hair, brushing strands out of her face.

"Baby, you need to see a doctor. I'm not taking no for an answer. I'll take you," I insist, continuing to run my fingers through her limp locks.

"I don't need a doctor, Tanner. I know what's wrong with me," she tells me with tears in her eyes. She won't look me in the eye.

"Ashley, this can't be a simple stomach virus. You look worse today than yesterday. I'm worried about you. Please let me take you to a doctor," I ask as nicely as I can while still trying to sound stern.

"I don't need to see a doctor. I already figured out it's not a stomach virus, but I don't need a doctor to tell me what I already know," she says, her voice deadpan.

Huh? Now I'm confused. She sounds delirious and isn't making any sense.

"Do you have a fever? You're not making any sense." I put my hand on her forehead, but it's not hot.

"No, I'm not delirious, Tanner. I'm pregnant," she whispers.

What? No, she's not. She can't be. She has to be kidding just to get out of going to the doctor.

"Yeah, okay, Ashley. Like I'd believe that. Come on, to the doctor," I say, trying to make her sit.

"I'm not kidding, Tanner." She grabs a plastic stick that looks suspiciously like a pregnancy test from the nightstand and hands it to me. From a little window, the word 'pregnant' stares mockingly out at me.

"That's not possible, Ash. You're on birth control. What the fuck is going on?"

Suddenly, all the amazing things I'd been thinking of her on the car ride over don't seem nearly as true, even though I want them to be.

"About two months ago, I was changing the sheets, and I found one of my patches stuck to it. It was only off for a couple days. I googled what to do, and the website just said to put on a new one immediately. As long as it wasn't off for more than seven days, I was supposed to be okay. I thought I was fine because I found it on Friday and you had a game that weekend, so I wouldn't be seeing you anyway. And then we had the gala, and I totally forgot about it. I honestly never thought that being sick was related to that. I didn't even realize that I haven't had a period since then until this morning when I woke up."

"I'm sorry, did you say you googled it?" I ask, utterly shocked.

"Yes."

"And what did your doctor say when you called him?" I ask. *She can't be this dumb.*

"Nothing. I didn't call him. I just put on the new patch and started another round of birth control."

"So you found your patch stuck to the sheets, where it had been there for a few days, and you immediately googled it? Why didn't you call a fucking doctor, Ashley? Why didn't you ask if there was anything else you should be doing? Like, gee I don't know, maybe the morning after pill or something? You google it and decide that whatever some random website says is better than calling an actual doctor?"

I have a feeling I know exactly what she was thinking, but I want to see what she has to say for herself. I can't believe she's just the same as every other bitch out there.

"I figured the information was fine. It... it never said anything about calling the doctor," she says, stumbling over her words.

"Want to know what I think?" I ask.

She nods, and there's a hopeful look in her eyes. It won't be there for long, though. She's not going to fool me twice.

"I think you saw the perfect opportunity to get something from me. That's what I think. Another perk of a rich hot boyfriend, as you said. Any normal person would have called her doctor and asked an actual medical professional what to do. A normal person would have told her boyfriend about said incident so they could discuss what had happened like mature adults. Gold digging whores, like Carrie and you, keep shit like this a secret," I spit out. "You expect me to believe that you didn't plan this whole thing out? You had fooled me into thinking you were different by pretending not to want anything but me, but you aren't going to trick me with that lame story that you just gave me. Don't insult my intelligence. I may be a jock, but I'm no fool."

I'd have to be a complete schmuck to think that this was anything other than a trap.

"That isn't what happened. And I didn't try and trap you. I didn't want this sort of bombshell any more than you do. How can you even think that?" She cries, but the crocodile tears aren't going to sway me. Been there before, and that bitch was a liar too.

"How can I think that? What am I supposed to think? You aren't seventeen. Any grown woman should know better than to rely on Google for a medical decision. You've known about this all week, haven't you? This is why you didn't want me to know you were sick, isn't it?"

"No, no, that's not true," she says, shaking her head.

"You thought I would fall for your act just like that, huh? I might have if I'd known about the situation when it happened two months ago. I would've if you included me in this little dilemma and I'd known you'd tried everything you could. I could have accepted it then, and I'd be here for you. But you lied, and you're using this as a way to play me. I won't be played. You should know that about me. Thanks for taking everything I ever told you about me and using it against me. Hope you're happy because I'm done. And if you're actually pregnant, I expect a paternity test. Apparently you like to keep secrets. Who knows what else you're hiding?" I turn on my heel and I walk out without giving her the chance to say another word. I don't want to hear it. I can't believe a word she says.

I don't know what to think anymore. How could I have missed the signs? I can usually spot them a mile away, like radar or something for users. I felt something different with her from the beginning. This is why I've always stuck to Melissa. I never had to worry about this crap with her. Granted, I've never had real feelings for her either, but at least I knew that this wasn't going to happen. Fuck this shit. I need alcohol.

I dial Alex's number, and he picks up on the second ring. "Yo, Tag, what's up? Come up for air? Ashley let you out of bed?"

"Meet me at my house and stop at the liquor store on your way here. I don't have enough alcohol there to make myself forget." Alcohol is the only thing that'll make my mind shut the hell up right now. I can't believe I've been so stupid.

"DUDE, DON'T YOU think that you've had enough?" Alex asks. Or at least I think that's what he asks. Things are little hard to follow after a bottle of Jack.

"Did that bitch still betray me?" I ask before slamming back another shot. I've been at this for about two hours now. "Then no, I haven't had enough yet."

"Man, you're my best friend, but you're being a real asshole right now. I think you should just stop and think about the situation before you do something you'll regret."

"What the fuck are you talking about? Have you been fucking listening? I already did something I regret. You'd think I would've learned from the past. Bitches always wait until you've hit it big to try and trap you into something. In Ashley's case, she waited until I was falling in love with her. I can't believe I fell for her shit. Shit, I probably gave her the idea when I told her all about what Carrie did," I honestly can't believe this is happening to me again. Who knows if that kid is mine? I can't trust a thing that she's ever told me.

"Don't you think that you're reaching, man? Ashley doesn't seem the type to do something like this. There's a reason we all like her. There's a reason you pursued her relentlessly. Come on, man. Pull your head out of the bottle and think for a minute. I mean, really think logically," my supposed best friend says in a huff.

Whose side is this asshole on? "Think about what? That I should have just kept up what I had with Melissa and left well enough alone? If it ain't broke don't fix it, right? I had to go messing with things when they were working just fine." I can't sit here anymore. This dickhead has me pissed off. Why can't he see this for what it is? "I'm such an asshole. Kid probably isn't mine anyway. We'll see soon enough, I guess. That bitch isn't getting a dime from me until she proves it's mine. Does she think I'm stupid?" I ask as I pace back and forth in front of him.

"I think you're stupid. At this point, I hope the kid isn't yours. I wouldn't want you as my dad with the way you're acting."

Why did I call him? All he's doing is making me angrier. "I'm like three seconds away from planting my fist in your fucking face, asshole. Seriously, what part of her story sounds legit to you? What sane person uses google instead of calling a doctor? Why didn't she tell me about this? It all seems fishy to me. I. Don't. Trust. Her," I say through gritted teeth, clenching my teeth so hard it fucking hurts, even drunk.

"First of all, people use google for shit like that all the time. I'm in the medical field, Tag. Trust me, I know. Do you know how many people ask me shit like 'Hey, I read on google that I should do this or that, should I?' And as someone with decent medical knowledge, I'm going to tell you that it most likely wouldn't have mattered either. If she found the thing a few days later, the damage was most likely already done. I get you're mad at her for not telling you sooner, and I completely agree with you there, but all this other shit is bogus. I'm telling you, friend: you're going to regret this. She made a mistake, but you're making a bigger one." Alex stands, getting in my face.

Whatever. He doesn't know what the fuck he is talking about. I don't give a shit if he is a physical therapist. "Fuck you!" I yell. "The only thing I'm regretting at the moment, other than Ashley, is calling you up, asshole. Doesn't matter anyway. I told her to hit the road. I'm sure I'll hear from her if the kid is mine, but until then, fuck her. I'm not going to be responsible for some other dick's kid. If you're going to continue to nag, you can get the fuck out. But if you decide to put your balls back where your vagina is currently sitting and stop annoying the fuck out of me, you can stay. I'm done talking about this shit. I'm going to finish my Jack and then hit the sack and pray that when I wake up this shit will all have been just a dream."

If only I could be so lucky. I wish I could sleep off this betrayal. It feels like someone stabbed a knife into my back. I really had thought that Ashley was different. How could I have been so wrong? Everything feels so out of control, and there's this horrible churning in the pit of my stomach. I hope like hell it only has to do with the amount of alcohol currently residing in it.

Chapter Thirty

ASHLEY

BROKEN.

That's the only word I can think of to describe myself right now. I don't know how long I lie in bed crying. I only know that I need to get up and shower and return to the land of the living, but I can't wrap my head around everything that's happened.

How the hell could Tanner think this was a trap? How could he think I'm like all the other people in his life? Haven't I proven that I just want him for him over the last few months? Granted, the situation isn't ideal, but was his reaction really necessary? Is this how he treats the people who love him when he doesn't like something they've done? I didn't do anything wrong. Maybe calling a doctor would have been a better option than consulting Google, but I honestly hadn't thought that anything would come of a silly lost patch. I've been on birth control for ten years, I never thought I'd actually end up pregnant after one slip up.

Do I love Tanner? This morning, I would have said yes with no hesitation, but now I don't know. I guess it doesn't really matter either way. We're done. He's made that very clear. I don't know if I would want to be him with anymore after this. I still don't get it. How have I ever given him the impression that I'm like the rest? I've never asked him for anything. I declined most things that he tried to do for me. I treated him like a regular guy. The more I think about his outburst, the angrier I get. He obviously doesn't know me at all. Or maybe I never knew the real him…

I feel a new wave of tears coming. No matter which way I spin it, it still hurts, and it hurts because I did actually love him.

I let myself cry for a few more minutes and then give myself a mental pep talk. Does this situation suck? Yes. Did I ask for this situation? No. Is there a way to change it at the moment? No. Then it's time for me to put on my big girl panties and deal. It isn't just me I have to worry about anymore. I may not be all that thrilled about the pregnancy, but I know I have to do right by this baby. He or she needs one parent on their side. That parent is going to be me.

I drag my ass out of bed and into the shower. All my emotions have been blocked out by nausea, so I'm able to actually function at the moment. The shower feels amazing after so long in bed and does more for my mental state than I'd anticipated. Nothing like a hot shower to pull you out of a downward spiral.

Quinn is waiting for me on my bed when I come out of the bathroom.

"So, how did it go?" she asks. "I heard enough to know that it went pretty bad, but I thought I'd ask for the whole story before I pass judgment on the douche."

"It went pretty bad. It's over. He told me I'm just like everyone else who wants a piece of him. He's convinced himself that I want to trap him." I shrug. For the last few hours, I've been thinking about nothing but him and the situation, but I can't anymore. I need to get moving.

"Wow, what an asshole thing to do."

"Yeah, but what can I do? It is what it is. I can't dwell. I need to focus on what's next, not what happened last. This baby needs someone in its corner. That'll be me. Even if I'm standing in it alone," I say with more conviction than I'd realized I had, and I can't help but smile.

Fuck him. I don't need him, and neither does my baby. It finally sinks in for me: I'm going to have a baby.

"If this is what you want to do, you will never stand in that corner alone, sweets. Awesome Aunt Quinn will be right by your side all the way. You don't need a man to have a baby. He already did his part. I'm your partner from here on out," she says, getting up to hug me.

"It's the only thing I can do." I smile. "I love you, Quinn."

"I love you more, Ash. So what's next?"

"Maybe we should google it," I suggest, laughing. What else can I do but laugh at this point? I refuse to roll over and play dead. "I need to call my gyno and make an appointment. It's only three o'clock, they should still be open."

"Okay, so make an appointment to check on my niece," Quinn says as she bounces over to get my phone.

"Or nephew." I take my phone from her and catch myself looking down at the screen in the hopes that I have a missed call or text from him. There's nothing waiting for me. I feel the moisture building in my eyes, but I hold it back. I pick up my head and look at Quinn. "I wish I could turn off my feelings as quickly as he did. Even after all the shitty things he said to me, I still love him. How fucked up am I?"

"You're not fucked up. You love him. That isn't going to just stop because he went bat-shit crazy on you. Especially with all those hormones you've got going on now. Don't beat yourself up for still caring. That's what makes *you* you, Ash. You have an unbelievably huge heart, and I couldn't be more proud to call you my best friend. Now make that phone call so we can figure out what the fuck is going on in your uterus."

"And that right there is why I am proud to call you my best friend, Quinn."

SINCE I DON'T know exactly how far along I am, the receptionist tells me it's better to come in sooner rather than later. I have an appointment this morning at ten. Quinn offered to come with me, so we spent last night making a list of questions for the doctor.

I've told Dom I'm going to be late today and I'll need to have a meeting with him when I get in. I'd laid out a game plan with Quinn last night. The next year of my life is going to be one fucked up rollercoaster ride, but it doesn't hurt to try to head it off. I'll have only me to rely on, but that's how I want it. I'll have no choice but to ask for help when I need it, but I want to make sure I do as much as I can on my own. Quinn isn't the least bit surprised to hear this is how I want to do things, but she doesn't agree entirely.

"I'm going to tell the doctor you're planning on working two jobs while you're pregnant. I want to see what his take on it is. As long as he feels like it's no big deal, I'll stand behind you," she tells me while we sit in the waiting room.

"If that'll make you feel better, then by all means. But you should know that I'll be working two jobs as long as I can either way. I need to save as much money as I can before this baby comes. After she decides to make her appearance, I can't work crazy hours. I'm hoping Dom will be okay with me doing most of my work from home once the baby does come."

"Don't forget the money you'll be getting from Tanner," Quinn says, turning her stern gaze toward me. "I'm sure that will be more than enough for you to be okay for a while after this little beauty makes her entrance into the world."

"There will be no money from Tanner."

"What the hell are you talking about? That asshole better take responsibility for this baby. You didn't get yourself pregnant all alone."

"It's either all or nothing. She will either have her father or she won't. I won't put the baby through an emotional rollercoaster. How would you feel if your father threw money at you but never invested any time in you? My baby deserves better than that. My baby, Quinn. This is my baby, not his. He wants no part, he gets no part. I want nothing from him. Let's pretend that I'm one of those asexual creatures that can reproduce all by itself."

"You want to pretend you're an amoeba?" she asks, clearly amused by my line of thinking.

"Yes, I'm an amoeba."

"Okay then, Ash." She chuckles.

"Miss Mitchell," the nurse calls from the hallway.

"Coming." I stand, square my shoulders, and take a deep breath. Time to face the full reality of the situation.

Quinn and I follow the nurse, who introduces herself as Lacey, as she leads us into an examination room. She takes my temperature, blood pressure, and weight. Then she hands me a paper cup and tells me that they need a urine sample.

"When you're all done in the bathroom, change into that gown, and have a seat on the table," she instructs. "Dr. Marcus will be in shortly." She smiles at me and leaves the room.

I head to the restroom to pee in the cup, leave it on the counter, and change into the pink paper gown Lacey had indicated back in the exam room. I have a seat on the table and look at Quinn. She's been quiet since we got back here.

"I'm just taking it all in, sweets. Don't worry. I'm still here."

I smile and grab her hand, feeling reassured.

There's a light tap on the door and Dr. Marcus walks in. He's a fairly young doctor, in his late thirties, but I've been seeing him for years. I imagine he was quite the hottie when he was younger. You never see good-looking gynecologists, but I imagine that's because all the good-looking guys don't need to be doctors to look at vaginas. I chuckle to myself considering that.

"Well, good morning, Miss Mitchell. You seem to be in a good mood," he says, shaking my hand.

"Well, I woke up this morning. Isn't that a good enough reason to be happy, Doctor?"

"I guess it is, Miss Mitchell. So tell me what brings you in here to see me today."

"A positive pregnancy test," I inform him.

"Okay, when was your last period, Ashley?" he asks, looking at my chart.

"Umm, I'm not really sure. Two to three months ago, I think."

"You think?"

"Well, I don't really remember, but it was about two months ago. My patch fell off for a few days, and I'm guessing that's when this whole mess started," I explain honestly.

"How did that happen, and what did you do when you realized?" he asks as he makes notes on my chart.

"I found it when I was changing the sheets. I googled what to do. I put on a new patch immediately, and since my boyfriend was out of town for the weekend and I knew I wouldn't be having sex for a few days, I figured I was good. I just kept with the new cycle."

"Okay, next time that happens, please call the office. But you did what I likely would have told you to anyway. But I would have also informed you that there was a good chance that you could become pregnant if you'd had sex during days that you weren't wearing the patch. Now, I'm going to do an ultrasound to see if we can narrow down a due date and see how this little peanut is doing. Have you been wearing the patch regularly since the episode?" Dr. Marcus asks.

"Oh my God! Yes. Is that bad for the baby? I hadn't even thought about that. I'm still wearing it now," I tell him and scramble to pull it off.

"Relax, Ashley. At this point, it won't harm the baby, but I like to know these things just in case. Nothing is one hundred percent. I'll need to do a transvaginal ultrasound. That will be the best way to get a good look at the baby." He grabs a long probe and holds it for me to see. "We'll insert this into the vagina and adjust it slightly until we get the best picture. It might be a little uncomfortable, but it doesn't hurt. I promise"

My breathing picks up, and my eyes go wide. That thing looks like an alien life form.

"Everything will be fine. Just lie back and put your head on the pillow. Scoot all the way to the end of the table and put your feet in the stirrups."

I do as he says.

"Great, now just let your knees fall open, and we'll start."

He grabs a condom and rolls it onto the probe and then squirts some jelly onto it. "This may feel a little cold," is the only warning I get before he starts the ultrasound. When I feel the coldness, I turn my head toward the monitor to see what's going on.

"See that white area in the middle of all the black? The thing that looks like a gummy bear?" Dr. Marcus asks.

I nod because it's all that I can manage. I'm awed by what I see on the screen. That little white blob is my baby. I fall instantly in love with that little gummy bear. I'd never believed in love at first sight before, but I sure as hell do now. I grab Quinn's hand, needing someone to experience this with me.

"That's your baby," he says, pressing a few buttons and clicking the mouse a few times. "Based on the measurements, the computer is putting you around eleven weeks."

"Eleven weeks? What does that mean?" I ask. I don't know much about pregnancy. I'd always figured that I'd do my research when I was ready to start a family.

"It means that next week, you'll hit the three month mark and be out of the first trimester. That's a good sign. Most miscarriages happen in the first trimester. We need to start you on prenatal vitamins. They are very important to the baby's development. Because you are already almost three months along, you need to make sure to take them daily. There will be some samples in the prenatal packet we give to first time moms. Please read the pamphlets in it. There's a lot of information in there. Also, we need to draw some blood today. All routine stuff. Do you have any questions?"

"I do," Quinn pipes up. "She's been really sick for the last week or so. All she does is throw up. Is that normal?"

Dr. Marcus turns to me. "Morning sickness can last for a few days or the entire pregnancy. Most women find that it eases up after the first trimester. If it is really bad, we can give you an anti-nausea medication that's safe for the baby."

"Okay, that would help. Thanks."

"And, she wants to get a second job. Is it okay for her to work two jobs while pregnant?" Quinn asks, throwing me under the bus.

"Well, I suppose as long as you are taking good care of yourself, it shouldn't be a problem. But I don't recommend doing it for too long. Your body is going to go through some pretty drastic changes, and you need to get a decent amount of rest," he says, giving a disapproving look.

"I'll make sure that I take very good care of myself. Hopefully, I won't need the job for long. I do have one question. My boyfriend mentioned the morning after pill. Would taking that have made a difference?" I need to know if Tanner had a legitimate point, if calling a doctor could have meant a different outcome.

"It couldn't have hurt, but I don't have a definite yes or no for you. Typically, one dose is enough to protect you from one act of unprotected sex. Several days is a different story. It wouldn't have been effective at all if conception had already taken place," he explains.

"Thank you." I nod.

"Okay, I'll see you in four weeks then. Please see Lacey on your way out for your packet. Also, please schedule your twelve week scan at the front desk. Here, these photos are for you," he says handing me the ultrasound printouts. "Baby's first pictures. Take care, Ashley," Dr. Marcus says on his way out the door.

I stare down at the black and white photos in my hand. My baby. My little gummy bear. My little peanut. I feel the tears growing in my eyes. "Don't worry, little one. I'll love you enough for everyone that doesn't." And I mean it. My baby will be more loved than is possible. I won't settle for less because she doesn't deserve anything less. The two of us are going to have an amazing life together.

Chapter Thirty One

TANNER

I **WAKE UP** in a pool of liquor-scented sweat. I reach across the bed looking for Ashley but find only cold empty space. That's when everything comes rushing back to me: betrayal, anger, hurt. Everything from the day before surrounds me, reminding me why I shouldn't be reaching across the bed searching her out, but my instincts don't seem to be agreeing with my head. Everything she did should have me hating her guts, but all I feel right now is empty longing.

Chapter Thirty Two

ASHLEY

WHAT AM I going to do? I can pretend to be strong, convincing everyone around me that I can do this, but what happens if I can't convince myself?

Tanner and Ashley's story continues in...

Unrestricted

Now Available

Acknowledgements

This whole idea of writing a book was a vague abstract notion in my head that I'd shared with a friend. "You can do it," she'd told me, and I'd laughed, but she was serious and told me I could definitely do it and I should. So I did, I wrote a few chapters and sent them over to her. Her response was overwhelming. She told me that it was far better than she'd imagined and I should continue, so that's what I did. So for that initial push and every single one of the four hundred that came after, I thank you from the very bottom of heart, Isabelle Richards. Without you, Tanner would have never been born. You have been the absolute best mentor a girl could ask for and an even better friend.

To Kathleen and Stacie, thank you for being my test readers and giving me your honest opinions. It means more than you'll ever know.

To my husband, thank you for your support and listening to me babbler on and on about this book. I know that you really weren't that interested. :)

And thank you to my son, Christopher, who has been pimping out my book at school. I'm sure I'm bound to get a few calls from the school at some point. Thank you to everyone who took your precious time to read my creation. I hope that you loved it as much as I do.

About The Author

Kimberly is a stay at home mom to four beautiful, crazy children by day and a steaming hot novelist by night. She's a Jersey girl at heart and that's where she currently calls home with her amazing husband and children.

Her debut release Inhibitions and the subsequent Uninhibited Series as well as the spin-off Apprehensive Duet both show her love of all things football. But not to worry, she'll still bring you plenty of steam!

When not writing she can be found curled up with a good book or watching her beloved New York Jets. Lover all things romance, including a little M/M action as well as the dark and twisted. She enjoys video chats with her best friends and always loves to hear from her fans on social media.

Connect with Kimberly
Website: www.KimberlyBracco.com
Facebook: www.facebook.com/authorkimberlybracco
Facebook Fan Group: Kimberly's Knockout Fangirls
Twitter: @AuthorKBracco
Instagram: @AuthorKimberlyBracco

47858649R00146

Made in the USA
Middletown, DE
04 September 2017